*For Marlene,
for friendship
and for wonder*
*and beauty of this crazy old life
we all live, however we may live it.
With love, Kath*

BEFORE IT WAS EASY

KATH CURRAN

Copyright © 2015 Kath Curran

All rights reserved. The use of any part of this publication, reproduced, transmitted in any form or by any means electronic, mechanical, photocopying, recording or otherwise, or stored in a retrieval system without the prior written consent of the publisher – or in the case of photocopying or other reprographic copying, license from the Canadian Copyright Licensing agency – is an infringement of the copyright law. This edition first published in Canada by Kath Curran.

Library and Archives Canada Cataloguing in Publication

Curran, Kath, 1951-, author
Before it was easy / Kath Curran.

Issued in print and electronic formats.
ISBN 978-0-9940707-0-8 (pbk.).--ISBN 978-0-9940707-1-5 (kindle)

I. Title.

PS8605.U755B44 2015   C813'.6   C2015-903282-2
               C2015-903283-0

Book design by CCS-Crystal Clear Solutions.
Images licensed from Shutterstock.com.

*With gratitude
for my mother,
then and always.*

Anyone could see she was a little bit of trouble...

– 1 –
HEATHER

I was fourteen, staring out the window, watching snowflakes under the light of the streetlamp, their spin and flutter a dance of such aching beauty, each crystal flake a reminder of all that was lost. Dad gone three years to the day, Claire banished from home until well after the birth of her baby. Would I even know when her child was born? How could Mom have become so heartless?

Promise me we'll always spend the 14th of January together as a family she'd said on the first anniversary of Dad's death. Well of course we'd promised, but here it was only two years later and already down to just Mom, Bobby and me. All because Mom cared more about what the neighbours might say than she did about us as a family.

Making things even sadder, Mom kept playing one mournful hymn over and over, and there was nothing I could do or say because the record had been a gift from Dad the Christmas before he died. That was two years after the ending of the War, a time when everything seemed possible. We'd woken up Christmas morning and there, next to the tree, was our very first phonograph, the cabinet almost as tall as me. Dad handed Mom one present to open and me another; Mom's was a record that had just two songs, that hymn she was playing tonight, and on the flip side, *The Bluebird of Happiness*. The present I opened was a whole album, Bing Crosby's *Merry Christmas*. Claire let out a shriek of delight and begged Dad to let her be the first to crank up the phonograph. I was surprised she knew exactly what to do, though I shouldn't have been; of course Claire would know about something as fun as operating a phonograph.

It's strange to feel like you're having your best Christmas ever without knowing what that's really going to mean. You don't know that by the next Christmas your dad will be gone. Or that three years later on the anniversary of his death in January you'll have come to hate one of those records.

That's not precisely true, I only hated the side with the hymn. I loved *The Bluebird of Happiness*, but Mom wasn't interested in happiness that night. Each time her hymn ended she'd sigh, get up from her chair, slowly cross the room, crank the handle, and then lift the needle back to the beginning of the record. How many more times would she make us listen to that awful, gloomy hymn?

Of course Bobby *wasn't* listening; he was snoring on the chesterfield and that wasn't fair either; when I'd wanted to go to my room Mom had gotten all upset. Was it really too much to ask that the family gather together on one night of the year to remember our father, the man who had given us all so much love? I'd wanted to challenge her, demand why then had she forbidden Claire to be with us, but of course I wouldn't have dared talk back to Mother. In those days children didn't. So instead I knelt on Dad's chair, watching the falling snow under the light of the streetlamp, wishing my sister could somehow magically appear and make it all better.

And that's exactly what happened! Claire stepped into that cone of light with snowflakes swirling all around her! She was seven months pregnant but she walked so tall and proud she looked like Scarlett O'Hara in *Gone With The Wind*. I couldn't hear, but I just knew she'd be humming. Claire was always humming.

I leapt from my chair and flung open the door; she was already at the foot of the sidewalk. She was drenched and you could tell she had to be freezing. Her white summer loafers were soaked through and she was wearing the same thin coat she'd worn when she left for her honeymoon three months earlier. Auntie Etta had sewn Claire's going-away coat—light beige wool with mother of pearl buttons and a silk orchid stitched to the yoke. At the wedding no one could have guessed that my sister was pregnant; now her belly was too big to fasten the coat's buttons, the orchid was sodden and straggly, and in each hand she gripped a sopping bulging pillowcase. She should have looked destitute, but she didn't. At least not to me. She was as beautiful as Cinderella entering the ball.

'I was just staring at the streetlamp wishing you were here,' I cried.

I ran down the snow-packed stairs in my stocking feet and Claire wrapped her arms around me, pillowcases and all.

'My magic little princess,' she laughed. 'Wish upon a streetlamp and I appear. Home again, home again. Jiggedy Jig.'

I'd seen Claire only one other time since her wedding. In September she'd announced that she had to get married right away; the urgency, she'd claimed, was out of a concern for Earl. He was *fragile*. That sounded odd to me, I'd never heard a woman talk about a man being fragile.

They'd met when Claire was a candy striper at Shaughnessy Military Hospital. Earl was a World War II veteran, although he didn't have any missing limbs or scars that you could see; he didn't even limp. Bobby asked Claire if by fragile she meant mentally unstable; he wasn't going to allow her to marry a nut case. Claire informed Bobby there was nothing wrong with Earl's brain, too bad she couldn't say the same about Bobby himself.

Bobby was only two years older than Claire and she didn't much care what he thought. Earl was fragile when it came to love, Claire said. Afraid if he loved someone they'd leave. His mother had died in childbirth and his father couldn't bear to be anywhere near the child who had cost him his wife, so he'd handed the infant over to be raised by a maternal aunt. Aunt Nora loved Earl as though he were her own, but she died when Earl was only twelve and after that, according to Claire, Earl had been afraid to love. In fact he'd sworn he'd never let himself fall in love, but then he saw Claire and he couldn't help himself, she reminded him so much of his dear Aunt Nora. Still, he was terrified that Claire too would leave him, and so she needed to prove to him that she was serious. His heart was too fragile for a lengthy engagement.

The wedding was on the 6th of October. The next time we saw Claire was when she and Earl came for Christmas dinner; by then there was no hiding why the wedding had been rushed. Anyone with eyes could see that Claire was *expecting*—decent people didn't use the word *pregnant*. And anyone with fingers to count on could see that she was expecting way too soon.

Mom was furious. Had Claire even stopped to think about anyone besides herself? Did she have any idea what it would be like for Mom if people saw her daughter in that condition? The humiliation! Mom floundered, not quite sure how to capture the enormity of the injustice done to her. The *humiliation* ... she began again, before finding her momentum. She thanked the Lord our poor father had been spared seeing his family come to this.

And so Claire was exiled until such time that Mom could look the neighbours in the eye and say that the baby had been born premature. Even if idle minds thought otherwise, there would be no proof. But now, here was Claire, scarcely three weeks banished, and we were hugging on the stairs in full view of anyone who might be peering from behind a curtain. Mom, come to see the cause of the ruckus, was standing in the doorway.

Claire beamed up at our mother as if Mom would be overjoyed to see her. She called up to her: 'Mom, I've left Earl.'

For one thrilling, terrifying moment I wondered if now I'd be banished too, if Claire and I would have to find our own apartment, if I'd have to quit school and stay at home to look after Claire's baby while she went to work to support us, but the fact is, my own life was never meant to be as dramatic as my sister's. Mom said, 'Well for Heaven's sake come in out of the weather, we don't need the whole neighbourhood gawking,' and just like that Claire was home again and I knew that everything was going to be all right.

As we climbed the stairs to the front door Claire was already explaining how she'd told Earl she had to be with her family on the 14th of January and then he'd said unkind things about Mom.

Said Claire would never get beyond the front porch.

'I told Earl nothing could keep our family apart on the 14th of January,' said Claire, 'and he told me if I loved you all so much, why didn't I just move back home.'

Bobby, wakened by the commotion, had roused himself from the chesterfield as we stepped inside the room. 'Aren't you a sorry sight?' he said, crossing his arms over his chest and leaning as he always did against the nearest doorframe. The way he was standing there it looked like he might be intending to bar Claire from coming any further inside.

Claire looked him steadily in the eye, then carefully placed the soggy pillowcases on the hallway mat before responding. I so admired my sister, the way she glared back at Bobby, not the least bit intimidated. 'You wouldn't be looking so smug and warm if you'd just walked all the way from downtown,' she said. 'In case you hadn't noticed, it's snowing out there and the roads are covered in slush. It took me an hour to get here.'

Bobby asked if she'd never heard of streetcars. Claire didn't have the money. She'd run out of groceries too; all she'd had to eat for the last week was the layer of her wedding cake that you were supposed to save for your first anniversary. Bobby said it seemed to him she might be exaggerating just a little; she looked like a drowned rat, not a starving one. Claire snapped right back that wedding cake was made of fruit and molasses, so really it was pretty nutritious.

Mom was just standing there, watching, seeming not to know what to do or say now that she'd allowed Claire to come inside. I wanted to ask Claire where was Earl while she was going hungry but my brother didn't like being interrupted. What's more, when Claire and Bobby got started, I could never tell if they were teasing or really arguing; Bobby always had such a loud voice, and Claire was so quick with her comebacks. Normally Mom would have put an end to the squabbling, telling Claire to show some respect for her older brother, but tonight was different. Mom was still standing there as if struck dumb by the sight of her prodigal daughter. Tonight it was Claire who of her own accord turned from Bobby to address Mom directly.

'I almost turned back before I got here,' she said. 'I was so cold and wet and I started thinking maybe Earl was right; maybe you wouldn't let me in. But Mom, at the very moment I was about to give up, I suddenly felt Dad right there beside me. I swear I could hear him whistling. It was *The Bluebird of Happiness,* Mom. Dad was leading me home.'

What could Mom do then? *Let me be kind in word and deed, just for today:* it was a line from the hymn she'd been listening to all evening. It was as though Dad were in the living room too, counselling forgiveness.

That's Claire: my sister was always getting into trouble, but she was smart too, always knowing just what to say.

I thought I saw a tear in Mom's eye as she turned away. 'Stay right where you are,' she said, disappearing into her bedroom. A moment later she was back, carrying one of her nighties. She told Claire she'd best go and get out of her wet clothes. 'And you go in the kitchen and cook up an egg and some toast for your sister,' she told Bobby. 'And put on the kettle for tea while you're at it.'

It's odd, I remember perfectly what Claire looked like that night, how tall she stood, her dark wet hair, her shining eyes, but when I remember Bobby I don't see him how he was then, I see him much older. The beer belly, the quivering jowls. That night Bobby would have been just entering his twenties, a slim, good-looking guy. If only he hadn't always been making fun, making me anxious about what he'd say next.

On a normal night Mom would never have told Bobby to do anything—now that Dad was gone, Bobby was the man of the house—but the night Claire came home everything seemed special. Bobby just turned, walked into the kitchen and did as he'd been told.

Mom went to the phonograph, cranked the handle to wind up the mechanism, and turned the record over.

And it was just like the song said, life wasn't an abyss. Not if you had a sister like mine, my very own bluebird of happiness. Claire waltzed back into our home and the music came alive.

I reached for Mom's hand and we stood there silently, holding hands, feeling every word. Claire tiptoed back into the living room wearing one of Mom's nighties. She took my other hand and drew us gently into a circle, reaching for Mom's free hand as she did so. Did Mom hesitate for a fraction of a second before taking Claire's hand in hers? The three of us stood there holding hands until the final notes faded. The four of us, really, counting baby Nora who would be arriving sooner than later. Each of us alone in our thoughts, bound together in reverent silence, until the muffled clatter of Bobby's efforts in the kitchen brought us back into the present.

'Heather,' said Mom softly, 'why don't you put on Bing Crosby now? Your father would like that.'

Surely there was no other night of the year when Claire could so easily have made her way back home. She moved into the bedroom that we had shared ever since I was seven; in March, when Nora was born, she moved into the bedroom too. No doubt the neighbours were talking, but on the night of the 14th of January, Dad had sent a message of forgiveness. 'Let the neighbours talk,' Mom said.

With Claire at home everything was almost perfect again, right up until just before little Nora's first birthday, when Earl came knocking at our door. Word had gotten around that the baby was named after his aunt; when Earl heard that, he said, he realized what he'd done. He didn't want his daughter growing up like he had. Without a father.

* * *

And now, more than half a century later, here we are. Another January, and me wishing again that things could be different. So many things have happened to my sister, so many terrible things. But this is 2008, not 1951, and this afternoon when I look outside the hospital window I see rain, not snow, and I know in my heart that the only home Claire will ever return to this time is her heavenly home. Mom and Bobby are already up there with Dad.

I see my sister rising up to the pearly gates: strong, proud and beautiful as the day she strode through the slush and the snow to tell us she'd come home to stay. 'Here I am,' she'll cry out, bold as brass. 'Let the party begin!'

And Bobby, teasing: 'What took you so long? Lost your money for the streetcar?'

- 2 -
CLAIRE

They think I can't hear. They think I'm already as good as gone just because I can't seem to get my words out. Oh, they tell each other, talk to her, it will help calm her, but none of them really believes I understand what they're saying. Earl. Good Lord! Heather would never have dared breathe Earl's name aloud if she truly thought I could hear. Why would she even think of the man?

Well, I suppose that's what happens when people decide you're dying; they start trying to puzzle out the meaning of your life, try to stick all the broken, scattered pieces back together. *Humpty Dumpty sat on a wall . . .* That's a good one. Suddenly everything's so important? Just because you're dying?

Nonsense. Heather going on about the night I left Earl, how it was such a big deal, when the truth is I can hardly remember that night. Even so, when she said the only good that ever came from my meeting Earl was Nora, Lord help me if the memories didn't start pouring in. Suddenly I remembered the perfume. I tried to tell Heather that no one had ever given me perfume before, but she couldn't seem to understand a thing I was saying.

Of course these days wearing perfume is damn near a criminal offence. Everyone's so "sensitive". Insensitive would be more accurate. Like the woman ahead of me at the checkout in Safeway who said, 'Would you mind using another checkout, I'm allergic to your perfume.' Well, you don't always hear correctly when you're not expecting someone to talk to you. 'White Shoulders,' I said. Tickled she'd noticed. Clearly, I shouldn't have been.

Or the day I showed up to volunteer at the Margaret Fulton Senior's Centre, hadn't even got my coat off before Sharon got herself all in a tizzy: 'Oh my dear, you can't wear perfume here. Some of our guests might be allergic.'

Can't? I wanted to say. Of course I *can* wear perfume; I *am* wearing perfume.

I was the one with the brain injury, but at least *I* still understood the difference between *can* and *may*. I wanted to turn on my heel right then and there and never return, but I couldn't, could I? I was perfectly capable of putting on my own perfume *and* correcting her grammar, but I wasn't yet able to find my own way home.

Good Lord, has it really been twenty-five years?

Those early days after my aneurysm were not easy. My poor old brain wasn't working well at all and I hadn't gotten used to the loss of most of my vision. I wanted to tell Sharon just what she could do with her pathetic little volunteer position; I wanted to tell her I couldn't find my way home but I *could* stand outside and wait the two hours for my son to pick me up. God forbid her precious "guests" should get a whiff of fine perfume. That's what I wanted to tell her, but I didn't.

Before my aneurysm I never would have put up with such nonsense, but that was *before* and if there's one thing I've learned in life, there's no going back. If I wanted to "work" I wouldn't be wearing perfume.

Well, I couldn't admit it at the time, but I'll admit now that it's a good thing I bit my tongue. Sharon was here the other day bringing me grapes and a gigantic get-well card signed by everyone at the Centre. Get well, fat chance of that. I heard the doctor tell Nora I could have anything I wanted to eat or drink—the "palliative care diet." If she wants a gin and tonic, he said, give her a gin and tonic; it won't make any difference. Of course it won't. Why else would I have signed the DNR? I'm not an idiot; I know what Do Not Resuscitate means. Nora would bring me a gin and tonic if I asked her, but now I don't *want* a gin and tonic. The grapes Sharon brought me were just the ticket. My mouth gets so dry.

Well, if I'd told Sharon what I thought when she said I couldn't wear perfume, I'd have missed out on all those years of friendship, and not just with Sharon, with everyone who came to the Centre every Tuesday and Thursday wanting *me* for their bridge partner, wanting *me* to cheer them up, wanting *me* to confide in. What a hoot, right back where I started. Volunteer card player. As if the whole middle part of my life, the part where I had a career and a family and a brain, all added up to nothing. Good Lord, there I was, starting all over again. The oldest candy striper in the world.

Humpty Dumpty, now I'm doing it too, trying to put all the pieces back together. March 1947. Shaughnessy Hospital. The

Red Cross Lodge. *Make yourself available to talk or play cards. Be respectful.* My first day as a candy striper those were my instructions.

And that man who asked me to be his bridge partner. He was older than most of the other men. Forty, I'd guess. Or maybe only thirty. When you're still a girl in high school any man over twenty is old. I was careful not to stare at the empty place where his leg should have been. I told him I'd be happy to be his partner, only I'd never played bridge before. He asked did I play any other card games. 'Sure,' I said.

I wouldn't have volunteered to play cards if I didn't know how. That's what I'd have said if I'd been talking to my brother Bobby, but I didn't want to sound disrespectful to a man who had been a soldier and was recovering from the war. I told the man I played hearts and gin rummy and whist and I could have added more but that might have seemed like showing off. If you can play whist, he said, you can play bridge. He sat me down and explained how they were different and then we played, and the whole time we played, everything I said was wrong and all afternoon he just glared at me until finally the game was over. And then Mr.—

Damn, I can't remember that man's name. Mr. . . . Hell, what does it matter? Mr. X. That'll do. Mr. X came over to my side of the table. 'Well, Little Miss Candy Striper, can I buy you a coke?'

I wanted to get away, but my time wasn't up, so we sat in silence and drank our cokes. I wanted to ask about his leg, but I was afraid of him, and I couldn't think of anything else to talk about. The next week he spotted me and motioned for me to come over and be his partner again and this time he was so furious at everything I did he wouldn't even look at me. Then he bought me a coke. That's how it was, week after week, and so I learned to play bridge. Who'd have guessed that thirty-six years later that's why they'd want me at Margaret Fulton?

Good Lord, all the years I was in the insurance business, every step up the ladder was because someone begged me to work for them, but to spend volunteer time chatting with seniors at a day care centre, I had to be interviewed. Twice.

Why do you think you'd be a good fit for Margaret Fulton?

I said I could do their bond underwriting. I smiled to show that I was joking, but it went right over that woman's head. The Centre wasn't looking for insurance experts, she said. They were looking for people who could play the piano or get a sing-a-long going or join in on a game of cards.

I told her I played the piano; I supposed I knew most of the old songs and it just so happened I had experience as a volunteer bridge partner.

Oh dear, but you won't be able to play bridge now, will you?
Why ever not?
Well, because you're blind.

I hadn't seen that coming. I'd thought the woman was referring to my brain injury, that she'd decided I wouldn't be smart enough, but she was looking at my white cane. I'd lost ninety per cent of my vision, including all my peripheral vision, I still got lost easily and wasn't comfortable walking anywhere alone, but I could see whatever I was looking at directly, so I could see a hand of cards. It's surprising how quickly you get used to a new way of seeing. You forget that other people aren't seeing things the same way as you.

So there you are—the job I held the longest in my life was volunteering every Tuesday and Thursday at the Margaret Fulton Centre. And they hired me because I knew how to play bridge.

I never played bridge with Earl. Back in those days at Shaughnessy I'd always see him playing cards with a group of men that kept to themselves. But I could feel him watching me. I'd turn around and he'd have this little smile on his face and I'd blush and have to turn away. He was so good-looking. That thick dark hair and swarthy complexion. I didn't know why he was in the hospital, he seemed perfect, except sometimes when he was outside smoking with his back to me I'd sneak a look and I'd see his hands shaking. I wanted to ask one of the nurses if she knew what was wrong with him, but we weren't supposed to talk about the patients. Besides, I wouldn't have been able to ask her without blushing.

That's exactly the sort of story Nora's always wanted me to tell her: how I met Earl, what he was like. But I simply couldn't. When she wanted to find her father I told her Buddy was her father in every way that mattered. She said I didn't understand.

I didn't understand? Good grief. I understood perfectly well. I'd lived with the man. I told her the last time I'd heard about Earl he'd stabbed someone on skid row. You be grateful you have Buddy, I said. But of course she wasn't.

And now, what does it matter? Buddy's gone and no doubt

Earl's dead too. What harm could it do to tell Nora when she comes to visit that I've remembered how Earl and I met? My daughter sets such store by memories.

It was the day Gracie Fields came to the hospital. One of the finest entertainers of our time and Nora won't even know who she is. Gracie Fields, the first performer to entertain our troops behind enemy lines. Smack in the middle of Berlin.

If my mind serves me ... Now there's a good one! If my mind serves me? Well, it has let me down a few times, but it *is* better than most people realize. Still, it's curious how things from so long ago can be so much clearer than who was here to see me today.

Now what was it I wanted to remember to tell Nora about Gracie? Some award she got for being such a good person ... An Academy Award? No, that doesn't sound right. Oh dear ... but it doesn't matter.

The important thing is Gracie was visiting Shaughnessy Hospital and she didn't meet just with the regular staff and patients; she insisted on meeting the volunteers too. That's why I was waiting in line when Earl Ryan came up behind me and whispered in my ear, so low that only I could hear him singing Gracie's song. *You Belong To My Heart.* Well didn't I just! I could feel his breath on my neck and I was done for. I didn't even remember to get Gracie's autograph. The next time I came to the hospital Earl gave me perfume. *Chantilly.*

Good God, I haven't thought of that day in years and here I am in this silly hospital bed and that old shiver just went right down my spine. Like I was sweet sixteen all over again, and the world was my bucket of stars.

What a way for a man to say hello.

- 3 -
NORA

Just days before my grandmother Agnes died I was sitting at her bedside when she confided that I should know something about "mistakes of birth." We were alone in her house where she'd been confined to bed for the last three years, and we were bonding over a teaspoon of brandy. Agnes had never been a drinker, not even a politely social sipper at Christmas, but recently her doctor had suggested that a touch of brandy now and then would do no harm and might help to ease the pain of her final illness.

Elsie, the woman with whom Agnes had shared her home for the last twenty-odd years, begged to differ. A slippery slope, that's what Elsie had to say about brandy. Agnes's son Bob might still be alive if he hadn't destroyed his liver with beer; and Claire, surely Elsie didn't have to tell Agnes about her daughter's problem with alcohol. It stood to reason, said Elsie, that the weakness was in the blood: first Agnes's father, then two of her children. Well, if Agnes was determined to become an alcoholic at the age of eighty, Elsie washed her hands of the whole wretched business.

Elsie had no authority to forbid my grandmother anything—they were housemates, not a married couple, they weren't even related—but with all her huffing and puffing Elsie could make life unpleasant. What's more, not only would Elsie refuse to bring my grandmother a teaspoonful of brandy, but should Agnes manage to rise and serve herself, Elsie would leave the house. The doctor had left strict orders that Agnes was never to be left alone, but, said Elsie, he was also the fool who had condoned brandy in the first place.

On the day I'm remembering I'd come to sit with my grandmother, a visit for the two of us and an opportunity for Elsie to get out of the house, something that might do both her and Agnes some good. Elsie had left me with firm instructions not to allow Agnes any brandy. 'She's becoming dependent,' she grumbled. 'She'll say she only wants a half teaspoon, but we all know where that leads.'

I was thirty-two years old, a graduate student and in the midst of planning for my second marriage; it was rare that I found myself spending time alone with my grandmother and I'd never felt any great warmth nor obligation towards Elsie, who, luckily, hadn't thought it necessary to extract a promise from me. Scarcely had we heard the car backing out to the alley when Agnes asked if I'd mind bringing her a little teaspoon of brandy.

'All that blather about alcohol in the family blood,' Agnes said when she'd had her sip and I'd settled in a chair by her bed. 'Your Uncle Bob was no alcoholic; he liked a beer now and then, but Elsie knows perfectly well it was a heart attack that killed him. If there's a flaw in the family bloodline, it's not the liver. It's the heart.'

Magnus and Uncle Bob had both succumbed to heart attacks and the doctors had told Agnes that her heart was swollen four times its normal size. My white-haired grandmother wrapped her pink shawl more snuggly around her shoulders and smiled coyly. "I guess I'm just too big-hearted for this world."

I'd never thought of Agnes as "big-hearted." She was my grandmother and I loved her, but I'd always found her a little *hard-hearted*, at least when it came to her daughters. How she'd responded to their births was family lore.

Claire, my mother, was Agnes's second child. As the story goes, when a nurse tried to lay the newborn baby on her breast, Agnes pushed it away. 'That's not mine,' she said. The baby had dark hair and the wrong-coloured eyes. 'That's some squaw's baby.'

My grandmother knew what a child of hers should look like: blond hair and blue eyes, which is to say, like Bobby, the perfect child she already had.

'Of course she's our daughter,' said my grandfather. They'd already chosen a name: *Maggie Jean*. In *Maggie* my grandparents, Agnes and Magnus, would have their names forever joined; *Jean* was for Agnes's mother.

'That's not Maggie,' said Agnes.

Magnus said in that case they'd name her Claire. My mother was baptized *Claire Jean Sinclair*—Claire, a diminutive of the family name, Claire echoing my grandfather's certitude.

Six years later, when Agnes discovered she was expecting again, she declared it couldn't be true: she already had her family—one boy, one girl. I'll never know if that meant that at some level she had accepted Claire as her real daughter or if it was simply an acknowledgement that there was already one girl in the family, however that had come to be.

The third child, however, looked like she belonged: blond hair, blue eyes. Agnes said if Magnus had a mind to do so, they could call this one Maggie, but my grandfather was a fair man: the name Maggie had been withheld from their first daughter, they wouldn't be giving it to another child. Suit yourself, said Agnes, leaving it once again to her husband to name their offspring. My aunt was baptized *Heather Anne Sinclair*—*Heather* evoking the wildflower of Magnus's Shetland birthplace; *Anne*, the name of his only sister. I've never known what happened to the original Anne; aside from her name being given to my aunt, she'd somehow disappeared from the family history. But I guess that makes a sad kind of sense; she was, after all, a girl.

Aunt Heather has often told me how Agnes would introduce her family: 'This is my son Robert,' she'd say proudly. Adding, after a revealing pause, 'And these are the girls.'

Robert, from its German roots: *He of Shining Fame*. The Uncle Bob I grew up knowing was a loud beer-drinking longshoreman who teased me unmercifully and died in Seattle in the hotel room of a younger man whose name we never knew. Bob spent his adult life boarding with relatives, including the half-dozen years he stayed with us before Claire finally said it was time for him to move on. None of that ever mattered to Agnes: Bobby was forever her blond-haired, blue-eyed little boy. Her little Robert, named after the man she claimed for her "true" father: Robert Alexander Baxter. *That* was the mistake of birth Agnes was so anxious to talk about the day we bonded over a teaspoon of brandy.

Biologically, my grandmother's father was Bill Baxter and she made no attempt to deny that fact of nature, but as far as she was concerned it was, nevertheless, a dismal cosmic mistake. The man who *should* have been her father was Robert, the younger brother of Bill. Robert was gentle and courteous and the man Agnes's mother would love to the end of her days. They were betrothed in Edinburgh, but in the 1880s times were hard in Scotland; Robert and his brother set sail for Canada, where farmland was free and the future full of possibilities. As soon as he'd found work, Robert sent money for Jean to follow. I never thought to ask why the brothers ended up in a coal town on Vancouver Island instead of a farm on the prairies, that detail was so overshadowed by what happened when Jean disembarked from the sailing ship. Instead of her betrothed, there stood Bill, hat in hand, informing her solemnly that Robert was dead. An accident in the coal mines. She wasn't to worry about her future though. Bill would marry her.

There was no one for Jean to go home to in Scotland, and no one in the world she could ever love as she had loved her Robert. Alone and penniless, Jean accepted the older brother's proposal of marriage and bore the man seven children, yet never, for all that, did she accept him into her heart. Bill Baxter spent his days toiling in the dark underground and his dark nights above ground drinking in the public houses; the revulsion Jean felt for her husband couldn't help but infect her children. Listening to Agnes speak so glowingly of Robert as her true father, I too found myself easily thinking of Bill Baxter as the intruding imposter.

'Sometimes we grow up with the wrong father,' Agnes said. 'That happened to me and it happened to you. Neither of your fathers was the right man for you.'

I had in fact heard the drunken coal miner story and the heartbreaking tale of the lost true love, but before the day we sipped brandy together Agnes had never linked her story to mine. While we had both found our actual fathers wanting and yearned for someone finer, that was also, as far as I could see, where the parallel stopped. The man who raised Agnes—the man who also happened to be her biological father—was remembered as a drunken ne'er-do-well, while the father she yearned for—Robert Alexander Baxter, the one whose soul she was convinced informed her own spirit—was perfect. No one would ever have described Buddy McHenry—the man who raised me from the age of four—as anything so terrible as a drunken ne'er-do-well. Nobody ever said anything much at all about Buddy, unless it was that he seemed too much under the sway of his mother. Nevertheless it seemed somehow generally understood that he just wasn't quite up to the mark, and when, a year before my conversation with Agnes, Buddy had taken his own life, in a strange way he didn't really seem significantly more absent than he'd always seemed, even when he was right there. As for the father who was definitely physically absent from my life—

Earl Ryan, my biological father—he, by all accounts, had nothing in common with the saintly Robert Alexander Baxter.

I used to ask about Earl; I'd asked my mother, my aunt, my grandmother, even my uncle—the only people I knew who'd known him, but none of them ever had much to say. My mother waved me away. 'There's nothing to tell.' At most she made mention of his drinking and gambling, claiming that if we'd stayed with him we'd have been stuck in eternal squalor. My uncle said 'he was a jerk,' and my grandmother dismissed him as a 'dirty little sneak.' Even on the day Agnes wanted me to know about mistakes of birth she still had little to say about the man. She lifted her wasted hand with its bulging veins, and with tears in her eyes reached over to grasp my hand. 'It's like I told you,' she said. 'it's a mistake that man was ever your father; he wasn't worthy. You were such a well-mannered little thing and no one to really appreciate it. Now Magnus, *he* was a father.'

I've thought back on that conversation often. Why that day had it seemed so important to my grandmother to talk to me about fathers? And why as mistakes of birth? Did she worry that maybe I had been more upset by Buddy's death than I appeared to be?

Did it have something to do with my upcoming wedding? Or was it simply a moment for bonding, a recognition that both of us had yearned for and felt we deserved, a finer father? Obvious questions, but questions that only came to me later, after it was too late. That day the mention of Magnus sent my grandmother off on another tangent; she was anxious to join her husband in heaven. It had been too long. Had I been to his gravesite lately? Were they keeping it up? I did know, didn't I, that she would be buried next to him?

In fact I had been to the cemetery not that long before. On a spontaneously weird impulse I'd taken Ian—the man I was soon to marry—to the graves of my grandfather Magnus, my uncle Bob, and my stepfather Buddy. They were all buried in Ocean View Cemetery. I'd never known Magnus, he'd died three years before I was born; I was always uneasy around my uncle; and I'd honestly never felt very close to Buddy, and yet it had suddenly seemed important to introduce these relations to Ian, no matter I could only introduce him to their graves. And now it seemed serendipitous that I was able to tell Agnes that the gravesite she would be sharing with her husband was not only well-maintained, but was one of the prettiest spots there, shaded as it was by a lovely big tree.

'Big? It was supposed to stay little!' My grandmother's voice was so weak and anxious I could almost feel it scraping the bones of her throat. 'What if the roots have gone all the way down and wrapped themselves around Magnus's coffin? What if there's not enough room for mine beside him?'

I had not the slightest idea what kind of tree I'd seen, but since my sole intention had been to make my grandmother feel good about the gravesite, I assured her without hesitation that it was the sort of tree that had strong shallow roots.

She closed her eyes. 'Thank Heaven.'

It surprised me how easily she'd accepted my story. Had I really sounded so convincing? Or, more likely, was it just that Agnes needed to hear what she needed to hear? She let her head fall against the pillow and nodded off to sleep. Within a week she was in hospital, two days after that she'd passed away.

In between the day Agnes and I talked, and the day of her death, Ian and I got married; scarcely a month after Agnes died, my own mother fell down the front stairs of her home and suffered a severe brain injury. In the aftermath of my mother's fall, my aunt and I spent a great deal of time together in the hospital at my mother's side as we waited first to see if she would ever come home, and later, what condition she'd be in if she did come home. In the long hours of sitting I recalled my grandmother's "mistakes of birth" and asked Aunt Heather what she thought Agnes might have been getting at. 'Well,' said my aunt, 'she just never could understand Claire's choice in men. And your father, I mean Earl, well he really wasn't a very nice person.'

I told Aunt Heather that it felt bad that no one, not even she, could find a single good thing to say about my father. I had no personal memory of the man, but I felt oddly defensive. My aunt's brow came together in a deep furrow as she clearly searched for something nice to say. Finally she found it.

'He was good-looking,' she said. But then even my aunt was unable to leave it at that, adding, 'But he was kind of creepy too, he never looked you in the eye. And that place he took you to live was no place for a baby. To wash the dishes you had to go down the hallway to a shared bathroom. You never knew when someone would all of a sudden be standing there waiting to come in.'

I was in my mid-thirties before I even saw a picture of Earl. I was living in Atlanta and my mother, who by then had more-or-less adapted to being legally blind, had flown down for a visit. We were sitting at a table looking at photographs of my brother's wedding, an event pulled together in haste after his girlfriend announced that she was pregnant. No one had thought to invite me.

'You wouldn't have had the money to fly home to Vancouver,' said my mother. That was true, but still.

The wedding had taken place in her backyard; she wanted me to see the pictures.

'I thought you might want this too,' she said, casually sliding one last photo across the table.

I looked up, confused. It was a photograph of a bride and groom, but not my brother and his new wife. I knew the young woman was my mother, but the man wasn't Buddy—

'It's Earl,' she said. 'I didn't realize I still had it.'

I'm sure that was true; if my mother had come across a picture of Earl when Buddy was still alive she wouldn't have tried to hide it, she'd have tossed it out. But Buddy was dead now, and it occurred to her I might want a photograph of my father.

My mental picture of my mother's life with Earl was of dingy rented rooms, tattered clothing and tears, yet here she was in the most stunning white satin wedding gown, a long Chantilly lace veil and a smile that said, *I'm the luckiest girl in the world.* Everything about her, hopeful and innocent. Earl is older than Claire. He's trim, a look of stability in his dark suit, topcoat folded over one arm, my mother's arm looped through the other. If I saw that photo in a book somewhere and I didn't know who it was, I'd think how lucky those two were to have lived in an easier time, when love was safe. You look at them and imagine their storybook future. The children they'll have, the love they'll share. You see them old together, telling stories to their grandchildren. Nothing in the photo says shotgun wedding.

It was a peculiar feeling, seeing my father for the first time, or at least the first time that I had any sense of. I thought that my mother showing me the picture meant she was ready to talk.

'I look like him,' I ventured.

'You have the same high cheekbones,' she said. She was looking at the picture, not at me. 'And his dark brown eyes.'

There was something about Earl that seemed a bit exotic to me, or was that just my fantasy too? I'm darker skinned than anyone else in my family. I'd been told that I had Irish blood from my father's side but that didn't seem to explain my colouring. Once, in a text for a history class, I'd read something about survivors from the wreck of the Spanish Armada intermarrying with the Irish; looking at the photo of my father I could picture him as a Spaniard. I asked my mother if it would be okay if I tried to find Earl, now that Buddy was dead.

'Well I don't know why in hell you'd want to do that,' she said. 'Earl never wanted you. Buddy's the one who loved you.'

She reminded me that the first time Buddy asked me my name I'd answered *Nora Felicity Daughter Three Years Old,* just like that, all in one breath, and he'd laughed and asked Claire to marry him. 'He wasn't joking,' my mother said. 'He was utterly smitten, but you never appreciated Buddy, did you?'

She downed the last of her drink and asked if I wanted mine topped up; I'd had only a sip so she got up and poured herself another gin and tonic, leaving me holding the picture.

'You want to know something about Earl? I'll tell you something. You were almost a year old before he showed up on

Mom's doorstep spouting a bunch of baloney about how he was ready to be a father. Oh he was full of pride and praise that day. Weren't you just the most beautiful baby on the face of God's earth! Well, let me tell you, it didn't take a week before he discovered that babies aren't all cuddles and coos. You were in your crib screaming bloody hell because I'd put you down to sleep. When we lived at Mom's and I was working nights, Heather was the one who put you to bed, and even though I'd told her again and again that she needed to leave you to cry, she never would. She always walked you until you fell asleep in her arms. Now that we were living with your father, I had to train you from scratch.'

She sat down again, knocking against the corner of the table that was hidden in the blackness where once had been her peripheral vision. Her drink splashed, catching the edge of one of my brother's wedding photos, but luckily that too occurred in the black space that surrounded her and I was able to wipe it dry with my sleeve without her noticing. Like everyone who knew my mother after her accident I so easily forgot how little she could see until something happened that reminded me she had to move her head about to scan a scene that anyone else would take in at a glance. If she was sitting across from you and looking into your eyes she could not see your hands, though they were on the table in front of you.

'Earl yelled at me to make you stop screaming,' she said, unaware that her drink had even spilled. 'That's the one way Earl and Heather were alike. Neither of them could bear to hear you cry. I told him we had to leave you to cry, so you would learn not to fuss. And you know what he did? This man you're so eager to call your father? He yanked you out of that crib and he threw you across the room. You wanted a father-daughter memory? Well there's one for you. I caught you. I never caught a ball in my life, but I caught you. I swore if he *ever* tried something like that again, he wouldn't see us for dust.'

Not a tender father-daughter memory, obviously. Even so, I can't really say why I never tried to find him, given I was haunted by his absence. I knew Earl would never turn out to be the romanticized notion of the perfect father I yearned for, and yet he was part of me. When I was applying for a divorce from my first husband I'd told my mother that I intended to change my surname from his and to start using my birth name: Ryan.

My mother said, 'You sure as hell won't.' How could I even *think* of such a thing? What a slap in the face to Buddy, the man who had been there to raise me. If I was going to change my name back to anything it had better be to McHenry.

I'd gone all through school as Nora McHenry, but Buddy had never filed for legal adoption, claiming it would be a waste of money, that I'd just get married and change my name regardless, so technically, I wouldn't have been changing it *back*. Still, I hadn't meant it as a slap in the face; I'd just never truly felt like a McHenry. On the other hand, neither did I want to hurt Buddy, so that time I compromised and kept my ex-husband's name after all, but when I was getting my second divorce Buddy was already dead, I was living outside of the country and I was trying to find a name that was me. My birth certificate said *Nora Felicity Ryan;* I took back that name, but I didn't go looking for my father. From time to time I'd tell myself that one day I'd track Earl down and that I'd better do it before it was too late. After all, he'd be old now; whatever he'd done in the past I could surely find it in my heart to forgive.

When I returned to the hospital this afternoon Aunt Heather was perched on the edge of a chair next to Claire's bed. *Perched* is how my aunt positions herself on a chair these days, her body so light, her balance so tentative. She's six years younger than her sister, but so fragile and battered by Parkinson's, a person could be forgiven for thinking it was the other way around. 'A little white-haired sparrow of a woman,' someone said the other day, speaking of Aunt Heather.

I stood for a moment partially hidden from view by a curtain dividing my mother's bed from the next bed, now vacant. It chilled me, seeing that vacated bed. The day before it had been occupied by a man writhing and groaning and pleading for God to just take him; a heavily bejewelled woman had clung to his hand, insisting he had to hold on, had to wait for their son. Now the bed was empty, the fresh sheets and the thin blue blanket tucked tightly at the corners. Flowers and cards and bottles had been disposed of, all signs of the man eliminated, the bed ready for the next battle.

Aunt Heather sensed my presence, looked up, smiled tremulously. 'The only thing she's asked for is perfume,' she whispered. 'And I can't bring it to her.'

My aunt's eyes filled with tears; my mother had been mumbling on and off all afternoon, but the only words my aunt had been able to make out were *Heather* and *perfume*.

'I tried to tell her perfume's not allowed,' she said, 'but she kept repeating *perfume* and drifting off.'

My mother was snoring lightly, lips slightly parted. People often describe my mother as a big woman—big in body, big in life, too. When Aunt Heather is introduced as Claire's sister you can sense their unasked questions. Stepsisters? Adoption? Heather, petite in stature, demure in manner. Claire, larger than life. But lying there this afternoon, without her teeth, without her persona, my mother seemed almost tiny.

Aunt Heather got up and moved to the foot of the bed, wordlessly offering me the chair. I stroked my mother's hand, her eyes opened and she smiled. She squeezed my hand and garbled words tumbled out of her mouth. I smiled. I didn't ask her to repeat what she'd said because I didn't want to be always telling her I couldn't understand. She mumbled again. I squeezed her hand, squeezing back my tears.

'Chantilly,' she said.

This time the word had been crystal clear; both my aunt and I heard it.

'You see,' said Aunt Heather. 'Chantilly. Oh Claire, you know I'd bring you perfume if only they'd allow it.'

I said when I heard Chantilly I didn't think of perfume, I thought of the song. *Chantilly Lace.*

'The Big Bopper,' said Aunt Heather.

I didn't understand.

'That's who sang *Chantilly Lace*. He died in a plane crash with Buddy Holly and Ritchie Valens. It was so sad.'

The Big Bopper was what Buddy called Uncle Bob; I'd always thought The Big Bopper was a name that Buddy made up, not a real person who'd died alongside someone else named Buddy.

Except for on the radio, I can't remember anyone but Mom and me singing *Chantilly Lace*. When I was little she always sang while we did the dishes; she'd wash and I'd dry and when she sang *Chantilly Lace* she'd wiggle her behind and I'd shake my ponytail.

I looked at my sleeping mother and was struck by her beauty. Her face was yellow from the cancer and without teeth her cheeks were sunken, but what I saw was the beauty of her being. Earlier in the day I'd been remembering my grandmother talking about mistakes of birth and both of us having the wrong fathers; I'd thought the memory had resurfaced because Agnes had been so close to dying and now it was my mother's turn. Looking down on my mother's face, that seemed too simple. Perhaps the visitations of memories, like dreams, hint at things you know but dare not say aloud.

Agnes had been concerned, when she wanted to talk about mistakes of birth, with fathers, but at the time her choice of wording had reminded me of how she'd once tried to deny that Claire was her baby. What's more, I always knew that my grandmother never did quite approve of my mother. But then, for years, neither had I. Long before my mother's accident, when I'd wanted her to tell me about the past or to talk about the future, she'd wave me away, saying *now* was all that mattered, and I'd silently fume that she had tunnel vision. If something wasn't right in front of her, it was as if it never existed.

But looking at my mother in the hospital today and being so struck by her beauty I realized I had been suffering from a peripheral vision problem of my own. I'd spent years trying to imagine my absent father, but somewhere along the way I seemed to have become incapable of seeing my mother. Or at least it seems that *all* I'd been able to see for far too long were the peripherals: the drinking, the layers of makeup, the weight that accumulated year by year, the sharp bite of sarcasm when she was annoyed or frustrated. Her refusal to talk about things I needed to talk about. Her refusal, I now see, to be anyone other than who she really was. Unlike Earl, my mother was always there in person, but I'd stopped seeing *her*.

'I love you,' I whispered.

My mother's eyes were closed. I didn't know if she could hear. That's been part of the problem for a very long time, her never seeming to hear what I try to tell her.

Today she surprised me. Her eyes opened and with the trace of a smile she said, 'Yes, you do.'

At first I thought she might be mumbling to someone in another dimension, but she was looking right at me. She said, 'Now why was it so hard for you to say that before?'

When I was seven we washed the dishes together and my mother made it fun for both of us. Our difficulties came later.

Even at the age of seven I was impressed by how my mother could remember all the words to every song. She remembers them now, though most of her other words have fled. She closes her eyes and sings *Chantilly Lace,* and I remember how it used to be so easy for me to tell her, 'I love you.'

– 4 –
Heather

Sixty years after our father's death and I still get anxious on New Year's Eve. Magnus didn't die that night, he wasn't even sick, but I can't separate what did happen from his death two weeks later.

Until midnight it had been one of the most perfect nights of my life; I was eleven and I had Dad all to myself. Mom always worked the evening shift; usually that meant she was off at eleven o'clock, but people who couldn't be together in person at the turn of the year wanted at least to talk, so telephone operators worked overtime on the holidays and Mom wouldn't be home until after one in the morning. Bobby was twenty and Claire seventeen, so of course they were out partying with their friends.

Dad and I were sitting on the top steps of the stairs leading down to the basement. It was the first time he had ever invited me to join him in polishing the family shoes and I knew it was an honour. For my father polishing our shoes was a kind of prayer, a task he undertook every Saturday night, sitting alone on the stairs, getting the shoes ready for Sunday church and for the week to follow. He said it was his time to give humble thanks for the gift of his family.

New Year's Eve that year was a Wednesday, so the shoes didn't really need polishing yet, but Dad said he couldn't start the New Year without tending to his family's footwear. He'd polished Mom's Oxfords before she left for work, and Claire and Bobby's dress shoes before they went out for the evening.

My father was so handsome, sitting there in his white shirt with the sleeves rolled up. Honestly, I can't remember my father ever *not* in a white shirt. He lifted one of my own shoes in his hand. 'Before you start,' he said, 'there are two things you must know about polishing shoes.'

'First you clean off the dirt and then you pick the right colour of polish!' I blurted out; I was so eager to prove I was ready to help.

My father smiled softly. That's how his smile made me feel, soft and warm.

'Those things are important, Lassie,' he said. 'Very important, but there are two things that come even before cleaning off the dirt and choosing your polish.'

He gazed down at the shoe in his hand. 'The two most important things to remember in polishing shoes,' he said, 'are tenderness and patience. In that order.'

I looked at how he was holding my shoe. I thought how he was the only person in our household who could hold out his open palm and one of the canaries he raised would flit down to land there. The rest of us tried, but the birds trusted only my father.

'Remember,' he said, 'everywhere you go, you rely on your shoes to get you there. We must take precious care of anything that looks after us so well.'

Shoes were lined up on the stairs below us. I saw myself stepping into my school shoes, walking out the door; I wouldn't feel a sharp pebble or the cold sidewalk because my shoes protected me. I pictured my father, a salesman for Guernsey Dairies, six days a week walking the streets of Vancouver, over uneven sidewalks, gravel pathways, sometimes through mud, knocking on door after door, walking all over the city in his shoes.

Tenderness and patience. Remove the shoelaces so that you can get at the tongue. Next, the part I'd known: gently remove any dirt with the off brush, then choose your polish. One week use wax for weatherproofing; the next week cream, to keep the leather supple. Wrap the corner of your polishing cloth around the first and second fingers of your hand. Apply a tiny amount of polish, then rub it into the leather, in slow small circles.

Once my father touched cloth to shoe, we both fell silent. I just knew it was the right thing to do. I watched the tiny methodical movements of his hands and mine, and glowed with pride at how much *my* hands were like his. Claire used to say it wasn't fair; *she* was the one who played the piano, *she's* the one who should have had Dad's long slender fingers. All the things that happened to Claire in her life, and that's the only time I can remember her saying something wasn't fair, the only time I remember her complaining about an injustice. I wonder now why it was that Dad and I never played the piano. Mom and Claire both did, both of them with their short stubby fingers. People talk like that, don't they? Say that someone with long fingers should be a musician. A piano player, maybe, or a guitar player. I see long fingers and I think of polishing shoes.

Later, after Dad had let me polish a pair of his shoes and thanked me for polishing them with such tenderness and patience, we set up *Crosby Derby,* our newest board game. We each had to choose a horse and I picked Whirlaway because I liked the sound of the name; Dad picked Seabiscuit because he said the little horse never should have won so many races, but he did because he never gave up. On the phonograph we kept replaying our new Bing Crosby *Merry Christmas* album until just a little before midnight when we switched to the radio to hear Guy Lombardo's band and the countdown to *Auld Lang Syne.* At the stroke of midnight we ran out onto the porch to bang our pots and pans and let the world know we were alive and ready for another year. Taffy, our little cocker spaniel who'd been sleeping most of the night, ran out onto the sidewalk, skidding and barking and announcing that she was alive too. On every porch of the neighbourhood people made their clattering noises and yelled out 'Happy New Year.' I remember feeling that after this New Year's Eve I'd never be a little kid again. We went back inside and everything was perfect. My father took my hands in his and we danced around the living room and sang *Auld Lang Syne* one more time. He swooped me up in his arms, twirling me about like I'd seen him do with my mother. 'Never forget,' he said, twirling me one last time, 'there's nothing more important than your loved ones.'

Am I fooling myself now when I say that's when I felt the first chill? A premonition?

The door flew open and Claire rushed in. 'Happy New Year, Dad. Happy New Year, Heather.' Her friend Patsy was with her. And a boy with blond hair.

'Daddy!' I panicked. I could scarcely breathe. 'They're girls, Daddy. Patsy and Claire are girls and the boy doesn't have dark hair.'

There was a knock at the door and Claire ran to open it. Our next-door neighbour handed her a chunk of coal and a coin for good luck. He wished us all a Happy New Year.

Too late. I knew it was too late. How could my father, of all people, not have noticed too? According to Scottish tradition, our tradition, the first person to cross the threshold of a house after midnight on New Year's Eve determines that household's luck for the coming year. A tall dark man brings good luck; a woman, or a man with fair hair, brings bad luck. Once the first person has crossed the threshold, the year is set in motion. Any visitors coming after that are welcomed in willy-nilly, gender and hair colour no longer matter, only the gifts do. Coal for warmth, bread for food, coins for prosperity, whisky for good cheer.

Claire understood my panic and tried to convince me we'd be okay. Dad and I had gone out onto the porch to ring in the New Year, hadn't we? Then we were fine; our father would have been the first person to cross our threshold after midnight and he was tall and dark.

Claire was wrong. I love my sister, but I don't think she's ever really understood tradition. For Claire New Year's Eve has always been a time to party; for a true Scotsman it is a crossroads—what you do at the turn of the year connects you to the past and sets your course for the future. The ritual is complicated. Regardless of whether I'd gone back in the house ahead of our father, we'd still have been in trouble: to be a "first foot" you have to be outside of the house *before* midnight; you can't go outside your own house after midnight like we'd done and then come back inside. That would be cheating. You could still visit a neighbour after midnight and bring *them* good luck, but you couldn't bring good luck to your own house.

Dad said I mustn't worry. We would put on our coats and shoes and go visit as many neighbours as we could right away and we'd make sure that Dad was the first to cross those thresholds. Each of us would carry some coal and bread and before you could say *Hogmanay* three times we'd have spread so much good luck we'd be guaranteed to have our best year ever. The surest way to have good things happen, he said, was to make good things happen for others.

I could never bring myself to say that my father was wrong; it would seem disloyal. And anyway, it was already a few minutes after midnight. Though we hurried to get into our coats and shoes, by the time we knocked at their doors, most of our neighbours had already welcomed their first foots. We were too late to accumulate the amount of good luck we were going to need.

Two weeks later my father woke up with indigestion. It was three o'clock in the morning. He told Mom he was going to warm a little milk and then he'd be back to bed. She was waiting for him when she heard a crash from the kitchen.

Mom screamed for Claire. I came running too. Where was Bobby? I can't remember. Maybe he wasn't home. Maybe he just didn't know what to do. Dad lay crumpled against the stove, his eyes wide open. I didn't know that people could die like that, with their eyes open. I'd never seen a dead person, but I knew my father was dead.

Claire was the only one who knew First Aid and she was on her knees, in her nightgown, rolling Dad face down, folding his arms, placing his hands under his forehead, the way she'd been taught in class. Mom was screaming for Claire to save him, but just like on New Year's Eve, I knew it was too late. Too late as Claire rocked slowly forward, her arms straight, pressing down on his back. Too late as she rocked back, sliding her hands to Dad's arms, tilting herself backwards until she raised his chest from the floor. Over and over while my mother wailed and I knew Claire couldn't save him.

Now I do remember; Bobby *was* there, yelling into the phone for an ambulance. Taffy was barking. I was crouched by the sink hugging Taffy and telling her it would be all right. There was so much noise. The only ones not making a sound were my father and Claire.

There was banging at the front door and I ran to open it. Why didn't Bobby go? Maybe he was comforting Mom. I can still see two huge policemen standing on our doorstep asking if something was wrong. Or maybe they weren't policemen, maybe they were firemen. All I know for sure is that there was no ambulance outside.

'My Daddy.' I was crying and couldn't say more but they didn't need me to explain. Mom was wailing for them to hurry and save her husband. They pushed past me to the kitchen and the biggest one knelt beside Dad and rolled him over.

'I'm sorry,' he said. 'It's too late. He's gone.'

Mom wouldn't believe him. She wailed for an ambulance, wailed at the policemen, wailed at Claire, wailed at Dad not to die. Later the doctor would say my father was dead before he hit the floor, but I don't think Mom ever believed that. I think she always believed it was Claire's fault, that Claire should have been able to save him.

And now it's sixty years later, the 8th of January, and I can't help feeling I'm partly to blame for Claire being here in the hospital. I should have been with her in her home on New Year's Eve. I know I couldn't have saved her; we all know she's dying, but it shouldn't have to be like this. She deserved more time at home.

Telford says I'm being ridiculous, that I couldn't have been two places at once and I've *always* been in my own home on New Year's Eve. Even when we were teenagers and dating I wouldn't go out on the last day of the year. After Dad's death I always stayed home to ensure that the first person to cross the threshold of my house in the New Year was a tall dark-haired man. Telford is tall and dark. At ten minutes before midnight on New Year's Eve I send Telford outside so that he can be our first footer. I send him out with coal, bread and coins. A hat and scarf, too, to keep him warm, but that's just for him, not for Scottish good luck. People in the family tease me, insisting that not even in Scotland would they be so obsessive; even so, my family has always honoured my need.

Lately I've worried that Telford is no longer the right man. I don't mean as my husband, of course; I've been blessed there, I've always known that Telford was the man for me, even on days when he's grumpy and doesn't seem to remember I'm the woman for him. I still see the tall dark-haired man he used to be, although the wispy bit of hair remaining on Telford's head is white now, and I worry that the gods of fortune may look upon him with different eyes. But Telford has never suggested changing our tradition and I could never be the one to remind him that he's not the man he once was. Sometimes I even wonder if we haven't created our own charm, if our house isn't blessed each year simply because it's Telford crossing the threshold. Maybe his hair colour never even mattered.

But I should have been there for Claire. We could have locked our door and gone to my sister's and been there at midnight. We could have guarded her door and then come home and Telford would still have been the first to cross our threshold.

'Claire wouldn't have wanted you there,' Telford said. 'She needed to be with her son.'

Claire *was* with Jimmy on New Years Eve. Claire lives in her basement now; Jimmy and Tina live upstairs. Claire even sent Nora home before dinner. 'Jimmy needs some time alone with me,' she told her daughter. 'There have been so many people. You go home to Fred.'

Nora called me the next day. Beside herself.

'They just left her there,' she said. 'They left Mom alone on the front porch. Just left her outside in the cold and the dark and all alone.'

- 5 -
NORA

I was three and we were living in a rented room in Sophie's house. The room had a hotplate for cooking but when my mother was working, or had other commitments, I ate with the other children: four of Sophie's own and a varying number of foster children. Sophie's husband, Carl, mostly stayed upstairs. 'Dying,' said my mother. From time to time he'd appear in the kitchen doorway, never joining us, just standing there, tall and skinny. A hush would descend, but the minute he left, chaos returned, with children screeching and squealing and food flying and Sophie threatening everyone to smarten up or else.

I was squeezed in at the table between Sophie's slobbering

twins. 'They're disgusting,' I said, feeling so much more grown up than all the others. 'They need to be taught proper manners.' I'd heard my mother use those exact words in describing the chaos of these mealtimes to Aunt Heather. Now I added words of my own: 'Like Mom taught me.'

My manners included not just *please* and *thank you*, but table manners too; almost as soon as I'd learned to feed myself I'd taken to daintily wiping my lips with a serviette after each mouthful of food. Looking back I suppose I'd taken it to excess, but my mother's friends, charmed, encouraged my fastidiousness.

Sophie spun around from the sink. 'Manners!'

She started waving her dishcloth in the air like a winged weapon, lurching toward the table. The woman was as stout as her husband was frail, and though she jabbed pins in her hair every morning to keep it from her face, it was of no use; she was forever brushing strands of hair from her eyes, in the process streaking her forehead and cheeks with flour or even dirt from the garden.

Now she stretched out her beefy arm and yanked me from my chair, dragging me across the room, spluttering that *she* would teach *me* manners, snatching a bar of soap from above the sink.

I couldn't understand what was happening. Did she think *I'd* made the mess? Was she going to make *me* clean things up? I opened my mouth to ask what was wrong and Sophie plunged the bar of soap between my teeth.

'Listen to me, Miss High and Mighty.'

I was gagging but couldn't pull away. My ears rang with the injustice, while the twins, in the background, cheered on their mother.

'Just because your mother wears fancy high-heels and lipstick, don't think she can fool me. I know a floozy when I see one. It's no wonder you have no father.'

Sophie sent me to my room to "remember my place." I had hours to think about it, the taste of soap bitter in my mouth, waiting alone in my room until my mother got home late that night, but I just couldn't understand what I'd done that was wrong.

'What did you say?' my mother asked gently.

I repeated everything I'd said, word for word. In those days I never doubted that my mother had faith in me; once she learned what Sophie had done with the soap she'd march right up to her and demand an explanation. Other children had their mouths washed out with soap when they said bad words or when they lied. I'd only told the truth and tried to help.

My mother smiled gently and said I shouldn't have told Sophie her children were disgusting.

But that's what she'd said to Aunt Heather.

Mom hugged me to her breast. 'Sweetie, I'm so sorry, I shouldn't have said that. It's true, they are disgusting, but it's not the sort of thing you can say to a mother about her children.' She tilted my face so that we were looking into one another's eyes. 'Listen, Sophie had no right to wash your mouth out with soap. I'll tell her if she ever does that again, we're moving.'

It felt so good to be held by my mom; even years later, when we had our problems, no one hugged better than she did. I didn't want to hurt her, but I had to tell her everything; if I didn't, wouldn't it be like keeping a secret between me and Sophie?

'Mom, Sophie said something else.'

'Oh sweetheart.' My mother stroked my hair. 'What else did she say to you?'

Until then I'd been too indignant to cry, but when I told her exactly what Sophie had said and I saw my mother's face, I knew it was as bad as I'd imagined. 'What does it mean, *floozy*?' I sobbed.

'It means we've been living here too long.'

The day we moved I was sitting in the rumble seat of Mr. Henderson's car with boxes packed around me; my mother said she'd be just a second, she had to run upstairs to say good-bye to Carl. Sophie was standing in the front doorway, arms extended, hands gripping either side of the frame, blocking all passage. 'Over my dead body.'

I cried out for my mother to come back. She turned. 'Nora, it's okay.' She returned halfway back down the sidewalk, not retreating, seeking a better angle to call up to the second floor window. 'Carl, I'm leaving now. I wanted to thank you, but your wife won't let me come up.'

A face appeared at the window. 'Wait.'

My mother waited on the sidewalk; we all waited for Carl to make his way down the stairs. He was so frail and skinny it seemed like a wind might blow him over, but when he appeared at the door his wife silently lowered her arms and made room for him to pass.

Carl met my mother in the middle of the sidewalk and hugged

her. Then he came over to where I was tucked into the rumble seat.

'You take good care of your mother.' His lips touched my forehead and I felt a shiver of fear. I thought he was warning me that Sophie would be coming for Claire.

The next house we lived in was quiet; Seth and Hanna had no children. Every morning Seth and my mother left for work. I think Seth was a mechanic; he dropped my mother at the bus stop so she could go to an office. That left Hanna and me waiting at home. During the day Hanna cleaned the house or wrote a letter and once a day we'd walk down the big hill to the post office. Sometimes Hanna would ask me if there was anything I wanted to do. I wished I could think of something to cheer her up; she always seemed so sad, but the one time I suggested we play dolls she hadn't known how to talk to them. She stood them up and looked at them as if they weren't real. I felt sorry for my dolls and I felt sorry for Hanna. So mostly I'd say she didn't have to play with me; I was okay by myself. If we'd already been to the post office Hanna made dinner and set the table. She took a long time setting the table.

Most evenings it was just Hanna, Seth and me for dinner; on evenings when my mother got home in time for supper we all ate together and Mom would talk about her day. When she didn't come home in time I'd go out to the street curb and sit there waiting for her. Sometimes she got home before my bedtime; I could see her as soon as she turned the corner and started up the hill. She'd open her arms wide and I'd run down to meet her.

The nights my mother got home after bedtime were a problem; Carl had warned me to take care of her; it was bad enough that I had to let her out of my sight during the day, but when night fell I panicked. I couldn't tell my mother how I worried; worrying annoyed her. She'd scolded Aunt Heather more than once. 'It's a waste of time,' she'd say. 'People who worry never have any fun. And if they had their way, they wouldn't let the rest of us have any fun either.'

You can shame a worrier into keeping their worry to themselves, but that won't ease their panic. Carl had said Claire needed taking care of; he was a dying man, he must know what he was talking about. Maybe Sophie was the reason he was dying. What's more, it was my fault that Sophie was so mad at my mother. If I hadn't told Sophie that her children were disgusting we wouldn't have had to move, Mom wouldn't have needed to say good-bye to Carl, Sophie wouldn't have threatened her, and I wouldn't have to worry that my mother would never make it home again.

So I'd lay awake. Waiting. Some nights she didn't make it home. The next morning she'd explain that it had gotten too late. 'But I knew you were here safe and sound with Seth and Hanna,' she'd say. How could I tell her *I* wasn't the problem?

I think we lived with Seth and Hanna for about a year, though I remember little more than a quiet house, walks to the post office and the panic of waiting for my mother to come home. Mom met Buddy while we were still living there and sometimes we all went to Stanley Park. And then one day, the September after I turned four, we moved into the house where Buddy lived with his parents.

Now we lived with them too and I was supposed to call Buddy *Dad* and his parents *Gram* and *Grandad*. It was easy enough to say *Grandad*, the man was so gentle and with his bald head and semi-circle of grey hair below the hat line, with his smell of tobacco, he was the perfect storybook grandfather. I never once heard Grandad speak harshly of anyone. Gram could have stepped out of the pages of a storybook too, but with her mean yellow eyes and angry voice the story would have been a fairy tale, and she the evil witch.

For the first time in my life I slept in my own bedroom; my mother slept in another room with Buddy. That was hard. Even though Mom hadn't come home every night, the nights she did come home—most nights—were the best times of the day. We'd climb into bed and she'd snuggle me against her body. 'Like Kanga and Baby Roo,' she'd say and I'd say 'Yes,' though most of the time we were Christopher Robin and Winnie-The-Pooh.

Mom would open the book and turn to the picture at the front where Christopher Robin is coming down the stairs, holding onto the railing with one hand, clasping Pooh's paw in the other. 'Here we are,' she'd say. 'Are we ready?'

'Ready.'

Christopher is a boy's name, but the illustration is of a young child with long bangs and the kind of shoes and socks I associated with girls, so I always felt like it was me. Pooh sang songs and got stuck in rabbit holes and needed Christopher Robin to watch out for him; my mom sang songs and wore big dangly earrings and had no idea that I had to watch out for her.

Every child knows the rhyme about sticks and stones and how they can hurt you when names can't, but every child also knows that the rhyme isn't true. Words can hurt. Like Sophie, Gram had it in for Claire, and like Sophie she didn't hesitate to tell me exactly what she thought of my mother. 'She doesn't fool me,' she said. 'The only reason that woman dug her claws into my boy is so as she wouldn't have to keep paying people to look after you.' There was more: how Claire wasn't near the doting mother that she wanted Buddy to think; how she thought she was "somebody" the way she dressed; how she'd be the ruin of poor Buddy. 'Such an innocent boy.'

But I was older now than when we'd lived with Sophie, old enough to recognize there'd be repercussions for both my mom and me if I told her everything bad that I heard. We'd moved when she heard that Sophie called her a floozy; I didn't want to leave Grandad's house, and I was pretty sure Mom didn't want to leave Buddy, and I didn't think Gram would let go of Buddy. I learned to keep quiet.

I've never understood why Gram let us live in her house, or

why she had me call her Gram; in her mind Buddy and Claire were never married. Thinking about the wedding photo of my mother and Earl the other day it occurred to me I couldn't remember what she'd worn when she married Buddy. I couldn't remember *anything* about their wedding, so I hunted up a photo album that Aunt Heather, the custodian of family records, had put together for me. There are pictures of my mother as a little girl, of me as a little girl; there's that wedding photo of Claire and Earl, and lots of pictures of Claire and Buddy, but nothing that looks like a wedding photo of Claire and Buddy. I phoned Aunt Heather to ask if she had one in her album. She didn't. Nor, she was surprised to discover, did she have any memory of the wedding. Neither of us doubted that Claire and Buddy were legally married, but it gave us pause to wonder. Was the lack of evidence somehow Gram's doing? Had Gram destroyed everything? Or had Buddy and my mother been forced to marry quietly before a Justice of the Peace?

Gram always said she wouldn't be happy until Claire and Buddy were divorced, something that trapped her in an odd bit of logic because Gram didn't believe in divorce in the first place. She might not go to church, but she was Catholic; in the eyes of the

Church, and therefore in the eyes of Gram McHenry, Claire would remain the wife of Earl Ryan at least until death did them part and on that basis Gram had forbidden her son to marry Claire.

Yet they must have married and even though Gram never gave it her blessing, she must have acknowledged the fact at some level; otherwise, how did we end up living in her house? Everything about that arrangement seems so strange, yet there we were, all living in the same house, my room at one end of the hallway, Gram and Grandad's at the other, and Buddy and Claire stuck between. The end rooms were proper bedrooms with heavy wooden doors, but the room where Buddy and my mother slept had been the dining room, and the door was a simple wooden frame surrounding a see-through glass oval that was covered, but not obscured, by a shimmer of white lace.

The summer before I started grade two Mom, Buddy and I moved into a new house built on a piece of land subdivided from Gram and Grandad's property. Mom still lives there, in the basement, now that Jimmy and his girlfriend have taken over the main floor. Gram and Grandad, both long dead, had moved out of the neighbourhood a few years before Buddy killed himself. From time to time I've suggested to Mom that she might be happier in an apartment, where there'd be better light and air. She's always replied they'd have to take her out of her own house feet first.

We'd barely moved into the new house before other people started to arrive: Uncle Bob moved in, then one of his friends; when that friend moved out, another moved in. When I was ten, my brother was born, and since there were only two upstairs bedrooms and one of them was needed for the new baby, Buddy built me a bedroom in the basement. He'd already built one room down there for Uncle Bob and whichever of Bob's friends was living with him at the time.

I was afraid in the basement. Between my room and Uncle Bob's it was unfinished—a ceiling of exposed floor joists and a bare cement floor. My room was at the farthest corner from the stairs and when I had to go upstairs at night to use the only bathroom I was terrified that some kind of evil was lurking outside my door. I never told anyone how terrified I was. After all, there was nowhere else in the house to put me. What else could they have done? Besides, my mother never had any patience for 'silly' fears.

When Jimmy was a year old Mom went back to work. It was hard for her; she loved her job and she loved her baby. A neighbour looked after Jimmy while I was at school, then I'd pick him up on my way home. 'Thank heavens,' said my mother, 'I've got you to take care of your little brother.'

Christopher Robin didn't just watch out for Pooh, he looked after Piglet and Eeyore and all the others too. I tried to watch out for my mother, to look after my brother; I was the babysitter for all the kids in the neighbourhood, but really I was nothing like Christopher Robin: he was fearless, I was always afraid. Christopher Robin lived in a forest surrounded by animals that turned to him for wisdom and protection; I lived in a house surrounded by adults who believed they were protecting me, adults who scared me sometimes without meaning to, and of course my mother, who would, no doubt, have been shocked to discover I felt the need to protect her.

Take care of your little brother.

A year after our marriage, Dave (my first husband) and I moved to Australia. We wanted to take ten-year-old Jimmy with us; we didn't think it was right to leave him in the house. My mother was drinking by then and Buddy had his own problems, but we couldn't find the courage to raise the issue so we left my little brother behind. Certainly Claire never would have let him go anyway; she was his mother and she loved him fiercely. Still I've always felt guilty for leaving without him.

As for Claire's drinking, that was a problem no one talked about.

Now my little brother is almost fifty and my mother still can't let go. 'Go home,' she told me on New Year's Eve. 'I need some time alone with Jimmy.'

It broke my heart to leave her; she'd been diagnosed with pancreatic cancer four days before Christmas and suddenly, after years of denial and deliberate forgetting, I realized how much I loved my mother, how desperately I needed her company. Every moment she had left on this earth I wanted to be there, like Christopher Robin, looking after her.

But that night I wasn't the person my mother needed.

'Come back tomorrow,' she said. 'We'll have a nice family dinner with you and Fred, and Jimmy and Tina.'

Of course, Jimmy never made it downstairs for the alone time his mother needed. Sometime around ten or eleven he did invite her to join him upstairs where he and his friends were well into party mode. Jimmy's friends have always accepted Claire as a part of the group; she could always be counted on to join in for a drink, and no one objected when she paid. This New Year's Eve she wasn't drinking; I wonder if anyone noticed, I wonder if they even knew that she was dying.

Later the party moved to the schoolyard at the end of the street where they planned to set off fireworks at midnight. Mom was feeling weak and Jimmy said she should stay behind and watch from the front porch.

Jimmy and his friends had been drinking all night; Mom had to wait a very long time for the fireworks to begin.

'It was cold,' she told me the next day. 'And I couldn't really see anything.'

- 6 -
CLAIRE

'You'll never drive again.'

That's what they said. After my aneurysm everyone was ready to write me off.

Only Jimmy believed in me. 'Get back out there in the convertible,' he said. 'Show them who you are.'

I'd have gone, too, if his licence hadn't been suspended. What if I'd run into trouble? Jimmy would have taken over and he had problems enough; he didn't need to risk getting caught without a licence again. Oh, he'd have done it; he loves me that much. And who knows, if I'd gotten right back behind the wheel, maybe I'd still be driving.

Okay, I'll admit now that they *were* right about the driving. But Dr. Chubb said I couldn't cross a street on my own either. Like I was suddenly a two-year-old? Jolly good thing you don't need a licence to walk or they'd have plunked me in a wheelchair with a bib around my neck and left me to die. They didn't know Claire McHenry. Twice a week for twenty-five years I walked two miles each way to volunteer at the Margaret Fulton Centre. That's got to be some kind of a record. And not hit by a car once. Okay, it's true I had a couple of falls on the sidewalk and once I walked into a ditch, but that never slowed me down before now.

Well, I suppose this time they're probably right. Only place I'm walking now is up Jacob's ladder to the pearly gates. Of course Jimmy doesn't believe that either, but he is going to have to get used to it. I must remember to tell him when he comes this afternoon—

No, that's not right. He was already here this morning. Or was it yesterday? It's so hard to keep track of time when time doesn't mean anything. Look at the nurses rushing about with their watches, charting their observations to the minute.

Hello! We're dying here. Time doesn't matter anymore.

Nobody listens. Just this morning I had to tell the nurse that the man in the next bed didn't want to be interrupted. Couldn't she tell he was deep in conversation?

'There's no one else there,' she said. 'He's only talking to himself.'

I tried to explain to her that just because *we* couldn't see his visitor, it didn't mean he didn't have one. 'If you'd just be quiet a minute and listen,' I told her, 'you'd realize that he is most certainly not alone.'

'There, there,' the nurse said, patting my hand.

Idiot.

Well, no doubt I used to be as silly as everyone else, talking about things as if they had their moment and then were gone. Now I lie here and wait for my family to come. Sometimes Magnus appears, and sometimes Jimmy. Sometimes they're all here together: Nora and Heather and Buddy. Earl too, the other day.

Oh, I don't know. Maybe I am talking nonsense. The doctor says I get confused and I suppose I do get confused from time to time. Ashes to ashes, time to time, rum ti tum. That's good. *Trailing clouds of glory do we come ...*

I bet Nora forgets that I used to quote poetry. Not often, but always by heart. *Trailing clouds of glory do we come, from God, who is our home, rum ti tum, rum ti tum.*

I'm going home now. Well, well, well. Is that why I lie here in bed, talking away, even when no one is listening? Time to put my life in order. There I'll be, Claire Jean McHenry, knocking at the pearly gates, trailing my story. Rum ti tum. Or maybe in the big register I'll still be Claire Jean Sinclair. The name my father gave me.

It snowed yesterday, I'll tell them. When Nora came inside her hands were cold as a snowman's, and when she bent to kiss me a snowflake fell from her hair.

Oh, I was upset when the doctor told me two or three months.

'That's not enough,' I said. He just nodded his head.

By the time I sat down with Nora I'd gotten hold of myself. It will be good to see everyone again, I told her. And I meant it, but that didn't stop her from crying.

Magnus, how I've missed you. What will you think of your head-strong daughter now? And who will you see? A blind old woman? Mostly blind, anyway. I don't even have my teeth in.

Is that any way to greet a father? Or will I still be seventeen in your eyes? Forever how I was the night you left us? Mom crying and crying for you not to die. I did everything I'd learned in First Aid to make you come back. Do you remember? They've changed the rules since then; nowadays you're supposed to lay a person face-up. The doctor said it was too late, anyway. You were already gone.

Bobby was here this morning. He didn't say anything, just stood there at the foot of the bed looking at me. I wonder if he was sent to make sure I'm coming ... Gosh, what if he was talking to me and I couldn't hear him? I had a really great conversation with Heather the other day; then later I heard her tell Nora that all I'd done was mumble. It seems my sister can only understand me when I sing. How odd. Something must be happening to her hearing. Maybe it's related to her Parkinson's.

Heather isn't the only one though; people drift in and out and most of them can't seem to hear properly. How peculiar that they think I can't hear them. I suppose I should be used to it; ever since my aneurysm people raise their voices at me as though I'd lost my hearing as well as my sight. I hear better now than I ever did.

Maybe I should stop talking, it tires me out. There is so much still to say. I need to tell Magnus who I was. And I have to make Heather and Nora understand about Jimmy. I wish it were easier for them to hear me.

Listen to me! Who ever said life was easy?

Everyone wants to dwell on the past. Especially Nora. 'Tell me about Earl. Tell me about the little girl you put up for adoption.' Good God! 'Tell me why you're in a bad mood.' If I was in a bad mood sometimes, it was *my* mood and nobody's business. Everyone always wants to know *why, why why*. Heather and Nora: 'Tell us about the day you fell down the front stairs.' Dr. Bartman: 'Tell me how you feel about Buddy leaving you that way.'

None of that matters. Twenty-five years ago I had an aneurysm, I fell down the stairs, my life changed. End of story. Life with Buddy was a long time ago. Earl was Chantilly Lace. No, that's not right. Chantilly perfume. Balderdash, what does it matter? The baby girl I put up for adoption? I was pregnant and alone. I had Nora to look after. Abortion wasn't an option.

We don't always have choices, just the choice to get on with it. Listen world: I don't remember what happened the day I fell down the stairs. I don't remember and it doesn't matter. It's over. What matters is Jimmy. How can I get them to hear? How many times do I have to tell them: I fell down those stairs, I lost my job and my vision and half my brain and none of it matters. I just need someone to watch out for Jimmy.

It was one thing for Buddy to kill himself, but to do it while I was away was so unfair. I told Jimmy to keep an eye on his father. How could I have been so stupid? If Buddy was going to kill himself, he was going to kill himself. It wouldn't have made a damn bit of difference if Jimmy had been sleeping in the house. But Jimmy still blames himself because he wasn't there.

'Mom, you asked me to come home and I failed you.'

I'll think he's finally accepted it wasn't his fault, then we'll be having a late night drink and he's back to the same old story: 'Mom, I let you down.'

I'm not one to lay blame, but if anyone let anyone down it was Buddy. That damn suicide note with all its talk about the *wonderful years we spent together* and how he didn't see a future because he didn't know how to adapt like I could. Well, that was true enough, if only he'd left it at that, but then he had to add: *I hope our son becomes versatile like you.*

Versatile? What the hell did that mean?

And that's not the word that bothered Jimmy.

'He called me *our son,*' Jimmy howled. 'Like he didn't even remember my name.'

Nora said, 'He called me *our daughter.*'

I know she was trying to be helpful. Buddy had written that *our daughter* was clever, but it wasn't the compliment that set Jimmy off; Nora wasn't Buddy's flesh and blood. Jimmy was.

I can't recall Nora's reply. Did she say that Buddy was the only father she'd ever known? Or did she concede that it *was* different? After all, when Nora divorced she wanted to take Earl's name, not Buddy's.

I suppose that's how life goes, Buddy always wanting Nora to pay him more attention and Jimmy wanting more attention from Buddy. The truth is, Buddy was always a little jealous of Jimmy. It didn't help that by the time Jimmy was a teenager he was a good four inches taller than his father. Not that I cared a whit about Buddy being shorter than me. Hell, when we met what I noticed was how the man could dance, took me to the Commodore Ballroom and swept me right off my feet. As far as I was concerned I'd never met such a gentleman, all flowers and holding doors. And never the slightest pressure to get me into his bed.

Well, well, how was I to know *that* wasn't going to change after we got married? For three years I believed him when he said he just couldn't do "it" with his mother sleeping in the next room. The bed was squeaky, I felt self-conscious too, and I wouldn't have put it past old Ma McHenry to come banging on the door, but even after we moved to the new house Buddy said it still felt wrong, he respected me too much! *Playboys* all over the house and he respected me too much? Good God, I swear the only night we made love was the night I conceived Jimmy.

Well, I don't suppose it boosted Buddy's ego any when Jimmy started referring to his father as *Twinkle Toes*. I don't know if Jimmy even meant anything particular by it. 'Quiet,' Jimmy would say. 'Twinkle Toes is sleeping.' Did I laugh the first time he said it? Not knowing why?

It was the shift work, poor Buddy always trying to get some sleep. Me in the middle, pacing back and forth with the baby in my arms, trying to keep him from crying, and later, when Jimmy was a little boy needing to play, always having to shush him because his father was sleeping. We all got so used to creeping around our own house it didn't even seem strange, but that doesn't mean we liked it. *Your father's on graveyard, don't make any noise. Your father's on dayshift and he's cranky. Your father needs quiet. Go outside.* The only shift any of us liked was the four to midnight. Even Buddy liked it best. It never mattered that I didn't get to bed before two in the morning; I never needed much sleep. I used to think sleep was for when you were dead.

Well, I guess I'll find out if that's true soon enough. Everyone knows I'm dying but none of us knows what it means. Maybe I've got time all wrong. I was thinking that when I reached eternity time would run together, that everything would happen at the same time, the way they say white includes all of the colours even though it doesn't look like any colour at all. But what if I'm wrong? What if there's only the past? When Bob dropped in to visit he looked like he did when he was alive, he and Magnus the same age because they were both fifty-three when they died. Except when Magnus is here he seems older. I see him at my bedside and he's still my father and I'm still seventeen. But who does he see, I wonder? Can

I really be nearly eighty years old?

At times everything's so clear: I'm going home. And then a moment later I'm not so sure. I'm lying here worrying about Jimmy and all I know is that soon I'll be the one who's gone. When Buddy died it seemed so simple. His days were numbered, I said. And I meant it.

Dr. Bartman told me I was angry; that was two years after Buddy died. Dr. Bartman was talking nonsense; I was never angry with Buddy for killing himself. When your time's up, your time's up. If it hadn't been for the aneurysm and the fall and losing half my brain, I'd never have gone to a psychiatrist in the first place. I certainly didn't run off looking for help just because Buddy killed himself; that was about Buddy's problems not mine.

I do wonder now though if it was a mistake, leaving Jimmy to see that other psychiatrist on his own. But what was I going to say? Jimmy was twenty-one and he'd announced that now Buddy was gone, he'd be taking care of me. As if I ever needed taking care of. But Jimmy wanted to take care of me. How would it have seemed if I'd said: You're the man of the house now but I'm coming to hold your hand when you go to see the psychiatrist?

I'd already set up that appointment for Buddy and then when he'd killed himself before meeting even once with the psychiatrist everyone seemed to think that Jimmy should take the appointment. They were all so sure Jimmy needed help. So Jimmy went. When he came home he said that the man told him he was handling his father's death just fine, no need to go back. And yes I believed him; *I* was fine and Jimmy is my son. Why wouldn't I believe him?

According to Nora no psychiatrist would say Jimmy was okay after just one visit. 'Jimmy *has* to feel guilty,' she said.

God, that made me mad. Nora wasn't the only one insisting that Jimmy *had* to feel guilty. Yes, Jimmy helped Buddy fill out the application for that ridiculous rifle, but there was no reason for him to think Buddy was going to kill himself. The man was depressed. Lots of people get depressed, but they don't buy a rifle and shoot themselves. They smarten up and get on with it.

The trouble is Buddy didn't know what to do with himself; it was such a shock when Kraft Foods shut down the plant. Twenty-five years of Buddy grumbling about shift work and then one day his job gone. Just like that. He was convinced he was all washed up—'Who'll ever hire me after I've been stuck in the same boiler room for twenty-five years?'

And then lickety-split the union sent him straight off to a job at the university. All dayshifts and a heck of a lot better pay than he ever got at Kraft. What a godsend, we all said.

A week later it was Buddy whining: 'I'm too old to learn.' Complaining he couldn't make head nor tails of the instruction manual. 'I'm not smart like you.' I told him a new job takes time, but in his second week he smashed up the car on the bridge coming home. 'I can't do this.' Good grief! I had my own job to manage; I didn't have time to babysit Buddy too. I told him, 'Take some time off, you've earned it. Collect unemployment insurance for a while, no need to leap into your next career without taking time to think about it.'

By *think about it* I didn't mean mope around the house talking to his dead mother. The man was driving me crazy. Then one day he opened my *Joy of Cooking* and announced that as long as he wasn't working he'd take over in the kitchen. Of course I'd managed to do all the cooking *while* I was working; all the same, it would be a step in the right direction for Buddy and it would be a nice change for me, coming home to dinner on the table.

Well, I hadn't bargained on all the damn phone calls. There I'd be, working to a deadline, hammering out the details of a contract and that silly woman, my secretary, would slip me a note saying I needed to phone my husband as soon as possible. At least she'd finally learned not to patch the calls through like she had just after he'd crashed the car. 'I thought it might be important,' she'd say. I put a stop to that with one of my looks.

Oh yes, "the look." I was famous for that. Nora hated the look. She was always pestering me, asking what was wrong. Nothing, I'd say. Then how come I looked so angry? Well, isn't it just a pity she didn't like the look of my face. Terrible old me, not checking in the mirror every five minutes to make sure I had a big grin plastered to my face so that everyone around me could feel all comfortable and cozy. I *did* have things to do. Buddy was just as bad, grumbling that the look made him feel two inches tall. I certainly wasn't trying to do that; Buddy was short enough already, but sometimes I couldn't help myself. To hear people talk, the look defined me. My boss called me into his office one day and told me I had to do something about it; the women in the office couldn't handle my 'glares of disgust.' I asked what on earth he was going on about; he said everyone in the office talked about "the look." What a hoot. I never set out to create my so-called look; I've never even seen it. At least the men didn't get all tied up in knots if I had work to do and couldn't be coddling them every second. Maybe they didn't like it, but they respected me for it. Well, that's behind me now. For all I care, they can write it on my tombstone: *The look upset them.*

Eventually my secretary learned not to put Buddy's calls straight through, but the little hand-written notes saying I must telephone my husband immediately just kept on coming. If it wasn't to ask what I wanted for dinner, it was when would I be home? I was a bond underwriter, not a janitor. I couldn't just stop in the middle of a multi-million-dollar contract so Buddy's mashed potatoes wouldn't get cold. Jesus-H-Christ! He'd learned how to follow a recipe. Great. That didn't mean I could just walk out on my job. Somebody had to earn a living. Believe me, I'd already had my fill of Buddy the homemaker when Sheila called to suggest a Girls Long Weekend. 'You need a break,' she said. And I did.

Jimmy always understood it wasn't his fault that Buddy used the rifle they bought to shoot himself. Why do people find that so hard to believe? Buddy had taken up cooking and now he was taking up hunting. He'd talked forever about how he'd like to do that. Buddy was always wishing to be something he wasn't. Wishing he was a cowboy. Dressing up like that in cowboy boots and a cowboy hat. Buddy wouldn't have known the front end of a cow from the back end if he was staring straight at it.

Buddy told Jimmy they'd go hunting together. He'd been depressed; he was coming out of it. He'd never been any good at filling in forms; it made perfect sense for him to ask Jimmy for help with the application. And then after Buddy's death, everyone insisting that Jimmy must have suspected what was up, that Jimmy had to feel guilty.

Well, Jimmy does feel guilty, but not about the rifle. He feels guilty for letting me down, and sometimes he doesn't know how to cope with that.

People think I don't notice when Jimmy is rude. They think because my brain isn't what it used to be that I don't have a brain at all. Well, I don't have quite the intelligence I once had, but I'm not stupid; I understand perfectly well when someone slips in a comment about a TV commercial on elder abuse. I took an IQ test two years after my aneurysm and my verbal score was already back up to 119; if I'd taken the test more recently I'm sure I'd have scored even higher. I won't claim I'd be in the gifted range like I was in grade twelve, but I'd still score a damn sight higher than average. And I'm certainly smart enough to ignore the snide remarks of people who don't have the courage to plainly say what they really mean.

Jimmy loves me. Some people are just too thick to see what's what. I'll be the first to admit that my visual score isn't what it used to be, even though Dr. Bartman said scoring 94 was pretty marvellous, considering I'd lost ninety per cent of my vision, but I can see that Jimmy loves me. And anyway, instead of people being so darn sure I don't see what's in front of me, they might consider that I can hear what they can't. Don't they know that when one sense is damaged, another compensates? They hear Jimmy swearing at me, but all they understand are the words. I hear what's behind the words. I hear Jimmy's love. I hear a son's love for his mother.

- 7 -
HEATHER

Oh Claire, what a start you gave me when I walked in this morning.

'The name my father gave me,' you sang out. Your eyes were wide open and your grin made me think of the Cheshire Cat in *Alice in Wonderland*. Maybe that's why I was reminded of how you'd challenge me with one of your riddles when I was a little girl. 'Claire,' I answered, happy to play along.

But you kept repeating it: 'The name my father gave me,' and I realized you didn't even know I'd come into the room. Who did you think you were talking to?

Claire, why must you always terrify me? Do you remember

the time when I was five and you walked into the kitchen covered in a white sheet? 'I'm a ghost and you have to give me your piggy bank,' you said, and I laughed because it was funny, but then you made spooky ghost noises and I wasn't sure it was you anymore. I ran into the bedroom and came back with my pink piggy. You told me to put it on the floor, go back to the bedroom and count all my fingers and toes three times; you said ghosts were fair and if I did as I was told I'd find half of the money still in my piggy bank when I came back. If I counted too fast and came out too soon you'd have to punish me, just like you'd have to punish me if I told anyone where the money had gone. You hadn't put any holes in the sheet, so I couldn't see your eyes, and you didn't even reach out your hands when I tried to give you the piggy bank. I was sure it had to be you, but what if it wasn't? I ran back into the bedroom and counted my fingers and toes three times as slowly as I could. And then I counted them all over again in case I had counted too fast. When I snuck back out the ghost was gone. I checked my money, and sure enough, half of it was there. It couldn't have been much, maybe twenty-five cents; I don't know now, but I do know I never told anyone.

Claire, you have to promise not to leave me. Even if it means you have to come back as a ghost and haunt me.

Lord have mercy, what am I saying? You'd do it, wouldn't you?

> *Ashes to ashes*
> *Dust to dust*
> *Don't kiss a boy*
> *Or your lips will rust.*

Do you remember when you taught me that one? You were putting on lipstick and I was scared because Dad would never have allowed it if he'd still been alive. You sat me down and swore me to secrecy. You said you had to wear lipstick because you'd kissed a boy and your lips were starting to rust. You didn't want Mom to know because it would break her heart. You hadn't meant to kiss the boy, but it had happened and now you needed to cover the evidence. You hugged me and said: 'Don't let it happen to you.'

My dear crazy sister, is that why your lipstick kept getting redder and redder?

Oh I do wish you'd wake up. You scared me this morning with your wide-eyed rambling, but now I wish you'd open your eyes again. I wish it could be one of those days when you open your eyes and say, 'It's so nice to see you.'

Do you even know who you are? Claire Jean Sinclair. The name our father gave you. Remember the last time you were in this hospital? Twenty-five years ago and it feels like yesterday. It wasn't long after your fall and you still couldn't remember anything or anyone. Well, except for Jimmy. Nora was always here, but you never seemed able to take that in. It was all: *Jimmy was here this morning. Is Jimmy coming? Is Jimmy okay?* Oh sweetheart, we know you'd never forget Jimmy.

But Nora. I still remember the first thing you said to her. You opened your eyes, looked right at her and smiled. 'You've finally come.'

I told you that Nora had been here in the hospital every day since the accident.

'Who's Nora?' you said.

'This is Nora,' I said. 'This is your daughter.'

You looked at me like I'd lost my mind. 'Daughter? I don't have a daughter.'

I felt so bad for Nora, but then you flashed one of your big smiles and said, 'That's not a daughter. That's Boki the Magician.'

Nora and I laughed. It was funny and we thought you were teasing us, but you weren't. Like the first day you recognized me: 'Oh Mom! How nice of you to come.' Did I really look that old? Dear me, it took weeks for you to get us all straightened out in your mind.

Ah Claire, you look so peaceful now. It's selfish of me to want you to wake up. I should know that if you wanted to be awake you'd be awake. I'll sit here quietly and let you be. If you want me to talk, just say Boo.

Well, I can laugh now, but at the time when Claire mistook me for Mom I didn't think it was the least bit funny. Mom in her grave not five weeks; Claire and I co-executors of her will because Bobby was gone too. It had been one thing after another: first Bobby dead in that hotel room in Seattle; six months later, Buddy dead by his own hand; the next year, Mom gone too, and the doctors saying that if Claire did live, there was no chance of her returning to anything like her old self. Claire's face was all black and blue, and for the longest time one eye was swollen shut and we'd been told we'd just have to be patient to see if she'd ever regain any of her vision or ever again be able to carry on a basic conversation. I felt like I was losing my own mind, but every morning I'd walk into the hospital determined to look and sound optimistic. Then I'd go home and even there I couldn't allow myself to fall apart: Telford had his hands full with the parish, both of our kids were still living at home. Annie was fine, working hard in her first year of college, but Colin was a worry. We all think of Claire's Jimmy as the troubled youth in the family, but the year before it was our Colin who passed out, drinking with his school friends. We almost lost Colin that night, would have for sure if his friends hadn't found the courage to call an ambulance, if the doctors hadn't gotten to him as quickly as they did. As far as we could tell, Colin seemed to have learned his lesson and had settled into his last year of high school. Still I worried.

Worry's a waste of time. That's what Claire always says, but we were the ones left to deal with Jimmy when she was in hospital and all we were hearing from her was *Jimmy this and Jimmy that.* The only one she ever talked about was Jimmy. *Is Jimmy here? Is Jimmy okay?*

Jimmy, bless his soul, hadn't been to the hospital in days. He claimed it was too hard to see his mother lying there helpless. I'm sure it was, but that didn't stop him remembering he needed her money. He was twenty-two and the only work he'd ever done was swamping on call for a furniture moving company. He still lived at home, so there were the household bills for starters, and he had 'other needs' too. His mom always paid his car insurance, he told us, and until we found a way to get him some money he was forced to drive without insurance; that would be a problem because he already had two outstanding fines for impaired driving and he was afraid they'd put him in jail if he was picked up again. It wasn't fair, he said, because the impaired driving tickets weren't his fault.

People who knew the family said it's time he grew up, leave him to deal with his own mess. Maybe jail would do him some good. But honestly, how could I have done that to Claire? She'd certainly have given Jimmy whatever he asked for, but she could hardly be expected to write him a cheque when she didn't even know who she was herself. Much later, when we all got bank cards and PIN numbers, Jimmy would just help himself to Claire's accounts, but at the time the only way to get money to him was through someone with Power of Attorney. Nora insisted that I be that someone; there was no way she was going to be in charge of shelling out money to her brother. Jimmy said since *he* was the one living in the house, *he* should have Power of Attorney. That didn't seem wise to anyone except Jimmy.

It felt unnatural that I'd ever dare take charge of Claire's money, but something had to be done. When it came time to visit the bank manager I told Nora she had to come with me; I couldn't handle it alone.

We were still waiting in the bank's reception area when Nora caught sight of our reflections in a mirror: we were both wearing black t-shirts and burgundy wrap-around skirts. 'We look like the Bobbsey Twins,' she said. And she started to giggle. How we'd managed not to notice until that moment is a mystery; it was July, we weren't wearing coats, and by the time we arrived at the bank we'd already been together for at least an hour. Well, that was back before my hair turned white, so the notion of Nora and I looking like twins didn't sound quite so silly as it would today. Nora was already in her thirties and I was still on the young side of middle age, the two of us sitting there in identical outfits looking closer in age than we ever would again.

I started to giggle too. Then there was no stopping us, not even after we'd been ushered into the bank manager's office where we were trying to impress upon him that I was more fit than Claire to be in charge of her finances. Every time Nora and I happened to glance at one another we'd start up again, and even though I explained that we were under a lot of stress but I certainly understood the serious nature of my responsibilities, I'll never know why that man didn't have us hauled off to the funny farm right then and there.

I suppose it's because we'd already seen a lawyer and everything was legal, but Lord help me, I was in way over my head. In addition to keeping Jimmy happy, now I was expected to handle Claire's debts too. How was I supposed to manage that? Claire and I didn't think anything alike; we never had. Claire so grand and expansive, me so cautious. There was a *Final Notice* for taxes to be paid on a piece of property in Texas that Claire and Buddy had purchased some ten years earlier. As far as I understood it, their "lot" still lay submerged in the Gulf of Mexico, the promise being that one day it would rise as a spit of land from which they could step directly into their boat and sail off across the ocean. They had "discovered" the property when a telemarketer offered them an all-expenses paid vacation to Corpus Christi: "No strings attached." Preparing to board the plane with Buddy, Claire cheerily assured Nora that although they had no intention of buying, they'd be fools to pass up a free vacation. Buddy and Claire never did own a boat and after purchasing their underwater get-away had only managed to get back to Texas to take a look one time. Now there was a *Final Notice* for American taxes. I had been given Power of Attorney, but what was I supposed to actually do?

My niece and I had the same old-fashioned approach to money: save up until you can afford to buy. Nora didn't even have a credit card; Telford and I had always paid the full balance on our card the moment it came due. I know Claire's not unique in how she handles her money, but at the time I could hardly have been more distressed by the bills arriving in the mail than if I'd discovered my sister was embezzling funds from her employer. What was I supposed to say to the American government? *How* did one even talk to the American government?

My instinct was to sell my sister's underwater paradise so

that we could get a handle on the rest of her life. I also knew that if Claire *did* recover, the last thing she'd thank me for would be meddling in her affairs. It felt like I was in a terrible position because she'd have been equally furious if I'd refused to take on Power of Attorney and left Jimmy without access to her money.

In fact, although she would never be the same again, Claire was gradually recovering from the accident. One morning the doctor informed us that in a day or two they'd be moving Claire to Rehab. Claire was not pleased.

'I want to go flowers,' she said.

'Flowers?'

'Home.' She glared at me with her famous look: how could I possibly be so stupid as to mishear *home* as *flowers*.

The hospital had issued a day pass for Claire a few days earlier so that Nora and I could take her home to see how she might manage in her own environment. Claire had lived in the same house for twenty-six years, but when we drove up she didn't know where she was. Inside was no more familiar. 'Everything is so dark.' It terrified me to see my big sister so lost. She tried to guess which door might lead to the bathroom, the kitchen, her bedroom.

Claire's vision had improved a little, but the doctors were warning us that that *little* was almost for sure all she'd ever get back. Still, we were in a kind of hopeful denial, as though if we didn't say the word *blind*, it wouldn't be true. Assuming my best wife-of-a-pastor's voice I told Claire that in Rehab they'd be able to teach her a few tricks to make life easier while her brain continued to heal. I wasn't about to suggest that rehabilitation was to help her adapt to being mostly blind.

'I'm inhelpative,' she said.

Claire had always insisted on the right word. 'Don't use *can* when you mean *may*; *irregardless* when you mean *regardless* ...'

Now she was inhelpative.

As she recovered Claire became a stickler on word usage again, in particular, while the rest of us referred to her accident, Claire always spoke of her aneurysm. Certainly when Nora and I talked to Claire's doctor he'd said nothing about an aneurysm and in fact I don't ever recall Claire actually attributing the diagnosis to a doctor. With the exception of Jimmy, everyone else was equally certain of a very different and very clear reason why Claire had tumbled down those stairs. However, that didn't make Claire any less certain of her own interpretation of events.

A neighbour, Joyce Duglan, had been first to telephone Nora with the news that Claire was in the hospital in critical condition. 'She fell down her front stairs,' said Joyce. 'There was a party at the house, but she wasn't drunk.'

Nora had never discussed Claire's drinking with Joyce or with any of the other neighbours; she had never discussed her mother's drinking with me. That didn't mean we were blind, it's just that we mostly tiptoed around the topic. There was that one time, shortly after Telford had been ordained into the ministry and assigned to his first parish, when he felt he should be more direct. We were living in Manitoba, and of course Claire was in Vancouver, so he wrote a letter telling her he was concerned she might have a problem.

In those days long distance phone calls were for emergencies only, so when Claire called and asked to speak to Telford, the letter never even occurred to me. For a long distance phone call I could only imagine the worst. 'It's Mother isn't it?'

Claire snapped that Mother was fine and would I please just do as she'd asked: 'Put Telford on the line.' It was clear even through the telephone wire that my sister was wearing one of her looks.

Claire gave Telford an earful. Who was *he* to be lecturing *her?* He was still a pastor, he hadn't been promoted to God. If *he* couldn't handle anything stronger than tea, that was *his* problem, not hers. He'd never have dared write her that letter had she been a man.

When Joyce Duglan phoned, Nora didn't prolong the conversation to explore the veiled allusion to her mother's drinking. Nora rushed to the hospital and learned the few details that were known: Claire had been at an office picnic at Ambleside Beach most of the day, sometime around dusk a few of the picnickers headed back to her house for a drink, some neighbours arrived as well. The party was on the back deck. Sometime around nine o'clock someone noticed they hadn't seen Claire for a while and went inside to look for her. Someone else remembered they'd last seen Claire when she was going out front to say good-bye to Gary and Linda. A third someone went out front to see if she was still saying good-bye. *That* someone—and all these "someones'"somehow managed to remain anonymous—discovered my sister lying in a pool of blood at the foot of her front porch stairs. By the time the ambulance arrived it was estimated she had been there between thirty and sixty minutes. There are nine cement stairs leading down from Claire's front porch; she had fallen from the top step and smashed her skull on the sidewalk when she landed.

Piecemeal information, but truth be told, I think we all felt we knew the most important detail: Claire's drinking had become a problem and even the neighbours had noticed. According to Nora, some of them had hinted that Claire's drinking might have been what put Buddy over the edge. Of course others blamed Ma McHenry; others still, a changing economy that saw Buddy turfed out of his job after twenty-five years of loyal service. When a suicide note doesn't offer an explanation, everyone offers a theory. When it came to Claire though, there wasn't much disagreement; even the hospital staff appeared unanimous in their certainty that my sister was in hospital because she was some kind of drunk. I remember running up to the front desk that first night, bawling my eyes out, frantic to get to my sister. The nurse looked at me, cold as ice. 'You know she'd been drinking?'

An old lady and a drunk, not worthy of their time, that's what they'd decided. Sure, they kept her in ICU for a week, but in all that time they didn't order so much as a CT scan. And then one morning Nora and I discovered that Claire had been moved out of ICU in the night because, they said, 'We've done all we can for her here.'

My sister was blind and had no idea who anyone was but because she could mumble the odd word they'd decided that was good. 'You'll need to start thinking about a long-term care facility,' they said. 'She'll never live on her own again.'

I can hardly bear to remember how eager they were to inform us that Claire would probably remain blind because the optic nerve had been irrevocably smashed and about how she'd need constant care. So eager they were to share all their dire warnings, but there was nothing to warn us that when we walked into the new ward we'd find Claire in a coma. In ICU she hadn't known *who* was at her bedside, but at least she'd known *someone* was. Now Nora and I tried to wake her, to elicit even a flicker of response, but there was nothing. I ran to the nurse's station and alerted them: 'You need to call a doctor immediately.'

One of the nurses slowly raised her eyes from her clipboard

and stared at me. 'Please calm down. Mrs. McHenry has been sedated,' she said. 'She's fine, she just needs a little rest.'

I was furious, I told them I could tell the difference between resting and a coma, I was not some hysterical woman and my sister was a precious human being. I told them if someone didn't check on her immediately I would have them charged with negligence. I don't know where on earth I got the nerve to threaten anyone like that, but I must have looked like I meant business because one of the other nurses agreed to take a look. Next thing we knew, a doctor had rushed in and Claire was scheduled for surgery at six o'clock that very night. A Sunday night. They told us to call any family members who might need to say good-bye.

I phoned Telford and told him to bring the kids. Nora phoned Jimmy. I can't remember if she phoned Ian. Nora and Ian had only been married for two or three months at the time and I really didn't have much sense of who he was. What I do remember is that the surgery was to cut away part of Claire's skull to release the swelling and pressure on her brain; I remember all of us huddling in a little room near the elevator. I have no sense of how many hours we were there. The doctor came by at some point and said the surgery had been successful but Claire would be in the recovery room for another couple of hours. We should go home and get some sleep. Telford said, 'I'll take the kids home.' He knew I wouldn't be leaving until I'd seen Claire for myself.

Nora stayed too. Just the two of us. Sometime in the night my niece dozed off and I thought about all the times I'd watched her sleeping in the first year of her life. That's when Claire stopped treating me like a little kid; many nights she and I would sit on our bed with baby Nora between us and we'd talk almost like we were friends instead of sisters. Now Nora was in her thirties and only a few days ago Claire was a vibrant fifty-three. It looked like Nora and I might be taking care of Claire forever.

All evening long, every time the elevator door opened I was ready for it to be Claire, even when I knew it couldn't possibly be her because she'd still be in surgery, but sometime in the early hours of the morning it really was my sister they were wheeling into the hallway.

'Nora,' I whispered.

She woke with a start and we hurried to Claire's side.

'Sweetie, we're here,' I said.

'Oh.' The faintest smile trembled on Claire's lips.

'It's me, Heather,' I said. 'And Nora. We're here.'

Claire uttered the quietest little, 'Hi there.'

Did she know who we were? At that moment it really didn't matter. She was alive, she'd heard someone talking, and she'd responded.

Why am I so obsessed with remembering *that* time? That was 1983, Claire survived, she recovered that crucial ten percent of her vision and she made a whole new life. But now she really is dying. Even my sister can't beat pancreatic cancer. So why can't I be here in the moment? Hold on to these last moments we have together?

Or is that it? I need to remember because I can't hold on. Dad, Mom, Bobby. All of them gone. And now Claire. Dust to dust. Everyone disintegrating into oblivion. When Claire is gone I'll be the last one on earth who knew Dad. How can people disappear before we've even begun to know who they are?

I was so angry in 1983 when people wrote Claire off as a drunk, but if I'm honest with myself, how much better do I know my own sister? When I was young she was my big sister. When

I had my own family she was my older sister who enjoyed life and maybe drank a bit too much. Then she was my sister who fell down the stairs and had a brain injury, my sister who got on with the business of life and scolded me for worrying. But now she's getting on with the business of dying and suddenly I realize I don't know who she is.

I can't put out of my mind something she said in 1983. It was a few days after the surgery. She still didn't have much of her sight back but sometimes she'd turn her head to face someone and her eyes would be blank but wide open and it was just the eeriest feeling. On this day I was the one in her line of vision, whatever that may have meant, and suddenly, out of the blue, she said, 'Now we can try to clear up this darker serial part.'

Well I giggled. I thought she was imitating Bobby. My brother always used to say, 'Don't be so serial' when he thought someone was being too serious. It's true, I was serious. My whole life Bobby and Claire were after me for being too serious.

But that day Claire didn't smile, and what she said next was completely out of character: 'Evil lurks in the heart of man.'

It was more than words, it was the way she said it. Even now my body shivers with the memory, the way it does in the presence of the uncanny, the disturbing. Nora was there too, and we both heard what Claire said. The words were out of character; they resonated in the moment and they still resonate today.

My entire life everyone has treated me like an innocent: *Heather, Claire's naïve little sister. Heather, the perfect little minister's wife.* Sometimes that bothers me, but I suppose it's not so far from the truth. And yet, there's something about being with Nora that brings out the devil in me. She says I bring out the same in her.

I'd seen so little of my niece when she was growing up, mostly at family dinners, major occasions at Mom's, or at Claire and Buddy's, but the chaos of my sister's life had thrown us together again, and now we were expected to fix things there was no way of fixing. One way we coped was by collapsing into fits of giggling as we had in the bank manager's office. Another was by fabricating wild and devious tales of intrigue.

'It seems very strange to me that Claire's friend Linda never visits her in the hospital,' I commented one day.

In the last three or four years it had seemed that whenever I phoned Claire, Linda would be with her. Linda, a divorcée, had at first been living in a basement suite next door to Claire and Claire had been helping her to get back on her feet. Claire was always helping someone that way, and as far as I could tell, that usually meant supplying free drinks and giving them money. When Linda remarried she and her new husband moved into a home only a couple of blocks away, but it seemed to me that Linda still spent a surprising amount of time at my sister's.

Nora had noticed Linda's absence too. 'In fact,' she said, 'I'm pretty sure the only time Linda did visit was the very first day after the accident.'

'Don't you find that ...' I didn't know what word to use. I don't think I'd worked out what I was thinking.

'Odd?' said Nora.

'Yes, odd. For years she's been at Claire's practically every other day and now all of a sudden she disappears.'

Linda and Gary were the people Claire had been saying goodbye to at the approximate time of her fall. They'd reported that Claire was still waving to them from the porch as they drove away. Odd then that a good friend like Linda had come by to check on

Claire's condition only the one time.

I don't remember which of us was first to blurt out that perhaps it was because Gary and Linda had pushed Claire down the stairs. Whoever it was, the minute the idea was put into words we rushed to assure one another that we knew we were being preposterous, knew we were just releasing pent-up anxiety by fabricating an outrageous murderous plot that we in no way mistook for reality. Where was the motive? People don't push their friends down the stairs for no reason.

'More likely it was the butler,' said Nora.

'The butler, on the porch.'

So later, when Claire came out with that line about evil lurking in the heart of man, even though we'd made a joke out of our suspicions, Claire's words sent a chill through my body. I took Claire's hand in mine: 'Is there something you're trying to tell us?'

Claire closed her eyes, and then she was asleep. And never again to my knowledge did she mention evil. Or reveal anything about the day she fell.

Claire didn't remember. She didn't want to remember. As time went by and her brain began to heal she was very clear that she wouldn't be trying to piece together the details. 'The past is the past. I had an aneurysm. It happened. There's nothing more to say.'

It had been out of character for Claire to speak of evil and, I suppose, easiest for me to believe it meant nothing. But sometimes I wonder: what does *out of character* even mean? People are so sure they know my character. Heather the innocent. But now my brain is scrambling to piece things together: both times Claire was on her porch, both times Jimmy was there too. Or at least close by. Jimmy was at the house party twenty-five years ago when Claire fell down the stairs. Jimmy left her standing on the porch this New Year's Eve. Four days later Claire was here in the hospital. The doctor says it's not the cancer, but a fever that made her so suddenly delirious. Did we miss the clue? Has it always been easier to believe in an aneurysm or an accident than a cry for help?

Now I'm the rambling, inhelpative one. Claire, I'm sorry. I didn't mean anything by it. I've always had this overactive imagination. Of course Jimmy was there. He still is. He's lived with you at that house all this time.

So it must have been the butler. Oh Claire, I wish you'd wake up and laugh at me. The butler on the porch. I just can't for the life of me solve what he used for a weapon.

- 8 -
NORA

Friday, December 14, 2007: the first day of my extended Christmas holiday, the day my mother and I went looking for an angel. The beginning of the end.

I'd gone to Mom's house straight from the language school. Many students complete their term in time to return home for Christmas; to accommodate the short-term drop in enrolment teachers are encouraged to take a little extra unpaid time off and I'd jumped at the chance. I'd been teaching for only a year and a half, had in fact started my new career the very month Fred moved into my apartment; since then I'd had chronic bronchitis and recurring bouts of laryngitis. It hadn't been an easy time.

Fred and I are both in our fifties, of course there's baggage. "His and Hers," but not exactly a matching set. Mine was bulging with unfulfilled dreams and the residue of multiple marriages; Fred's was overflowing with grief.

After four husbands and four divorces my life had finally begun to feel like my own; I'd been single for ten years and had discovered to my surprise that most of the time being single suited me better than being married. I had just completed my certification to teach English as a Second Language. I'd always planned on completing an advanced degree in Literature so that I could teach at a university but somehow temporary jobs and temporary marriages had become my full-time life so that I never did get that PhD, but from the moment I walked into my first class as a teacher of English to foreign students I knew I'd found the work I'd been longing for. It felt like I'd finally found my stride: rewarding work and no relationship drama. Until Fred came along I'd felt almost settled.

A too recent widower, Fred had been married only once and had three grown sons. Fred and Teresa had been making plans to celebrate their twenty-fifth wedding anniversary in France when

Teresa was diagnosed with pancreatic cancer. Barely five months later she was gone.

I'd met Fred, and through him, Teresa, some six or seven years earlier when I was working in one of those so-called temporary office jobs. Fred commuted to Vancouver from their home in Nanaimo on Vancouver Island. After I changed jobs I'd kept in casual contact with both of them, a few random phone calls or emails throughout the year. I suppose I knew Fred the best from our having worked together though in fact I felt a little more comfortable with Teresa, probably just because she was a woman. Even so, I was surprised when Fred telephoned one day to say that Teresa had asked if I would take the ferry to Nanaimo to spend the night with her in the Palliative Care ward at the hospital.

At the time I had no idea of just how many close friends Teresa had, and therefore no sense of the extraordinariness of her request. I'd thought maybe there was no one else she felt she could ask and I was honoured. Or maybe it had something to do with my own health; over the last couple of years I'd had a few bouts with strep throat and I thought perhaps she wanted to warn me to take care of my health. But after the hoards of visitors, both family and friends, finally left for the night, Teresa made it clear that only one topic of conversation would be taboo: that of health.

'I want to hear about other things,' she said. 'I want to feel *life*. Tell me about Mexico.'

And so I told her about my recent holiday, and from there we talked late into the night about our lives. Superficially they looked nothing alike: Teresa had been married to Fred for almost a quarter of a century and they had three sons who were the centre of her world; I'd been married and divorced four times and had no children. But Teresa and I weren't just having a casual visit; she was a woman facing death who wanted to talk about life. We discovered we had more in common than not. She too had a complicated relationship with her mother, and in her case, with not only one, but two brothers. I learned that she had been divorced, though only once, and that she also had just completed a degree that would have allowed her to start teaching in September. I told Teresa things I hardly ever admitted to people I knew much better: the exact number of my divorces, a romance that I'd mostly kept a secret, an abortion that I'd been pressured into. She'd also had an abortion, long before she met Fred. A dark time in both of our pasts. We talked long after lights out. We made a date to go bicycling in the springtime. Teresa said, 'I know the bicycling is make-believe. I know I won't be around that long.' She said she could almost accept her fate. She said, 'And I know Fred will be fine. He'll find someone.' It was her boys she worried about. 'I won't be here to see them marry,' she said. 'I'll never meet my grandchildren.' In the darkness of the Palliative Care ward that was the only time Teresa cried.

After Teresa's death Fred came to see me. He'd put on weight. He couldn't concentrate. Nothing made sense anymore. Fred said Teresa was who people turned to if they had a problem. Teresa was one of four siblings and the centre of her family. Fred had five sisters and a brother, all of them with children; they all knew that if they needed someone to talk to, Teresa was a discreet and reliable listener.

I was a good listener too, but sooner than felt comfortable, Fred wanted me to be something more.

I liked Fred, but as a friend. It felt wrong to think of anything more. And besides, I needed to focus on my new career. I wanted to send Fred away for a year while I learned how to do my job. I wanted him to go away and grieve and come back when I might be ready. When he was ready.

But there was the catch, Fred was grieving and he didn't want to do it alone. He was still crying over the loss of Teresa but he wanted us to start a life together in Vancouver *and* he wanted me to spend as many weekends as possible in Nanaimo to be with his youngest son who was still living in the family home while attending the local university. So much for feeling settled. On top of everything else it was embarrassing. Everyone except Fred knew it was too soon, and don't people always conclude it's the woman who's swooped down to snatch away the man who has become suddenly available?

'The men most eager to remarry after the death of a wife are the ones who've had good marriages,' Uncle Telford told me. From his years in the clergy he'd witnessed the beginnings and endings and in-betweens of thousands of relationships; he was even the officiating minister for my first two marriages, yet he never appears to have judged me or anyone else. He didn't pretend to know what I should do about Fred. 'Every life has its complications,' he said. It was up to me to figure things out.

Fred moved into my apartment. On weekends he lived in Nanaimo and as often as I could manage I joined him there. Very soon my tiny Vancouver apartment became too tiny; together Fred and I rented a larger one. Fred was still grieving, I was still trying to figure things out.

In the midst of all this uncertainty and emotional turmoil I was more than ready for the comforts of tradition when I went to my mother's on the 14th of December to help put up her Christmas tree. When Mom was a girl the tree didn't appear until Christmas morning, delivered by Santa Claus along with all the presents. That sounded magical and exciting to me when I was a little girl but I was always happy that our family tradition was to buy the tree together and that when we came home we each had a role in its decorating. Buddy secured the tree in its stand, I tested the strings of lights and replaced the burned out bulbs, then it was Buddy's turn again, draping the lights over the branches so that Mom could then rearrange them to make them look beautiful. Jimmy got to hang the first ornament, and then my mother and I hung the rest. Next came the tinsicles; at my friend's house they just stood back and threw handfuls onto the tree, but Mom and I hung each one strand by strand. The job took at least two nights of meticulous teamwork—the work of Christmas—and my mother and I were responsible for making it perfect. We always played our two Christmas albums: Bing Crosby's *Merry Christmas* and Harry Belafonte's *To Wish You a Merry Christmas*. Mom said Bing Crosby's was the first album her dad ever bought.

My mother's dad, *my* grandfather. I've always loved him, though he died before I was born. What's more, I can hardly disentangle the image of Magnus Sinclair that I hold in my mind from that of Bing Crosby, the pictures I've seen of both of them have so many striking similarities: the steeply receding hairline, the perky wing-like ears, the kindly smile, the twinkle in the eye. Bing Crosby famously wore hats and was known for his whistling; my mother says my grandfather never left the house without a hat and that you always knew when he was coming down the street because you'd hear him whistling a happy tune. And then too there's Christmas, the two of them so deeply embedded in the magic of Christmas.

When I moved from Atlanta back to Vancouver Jimmy said, 'Good, now you can help her decorate the damn tree.' That was a dozen years ago and the start of a new tradition. So on this first night of my Christmas holiday, while Fred was off to his home in Nanaimo, I'd headed to Mom's to help her put up the artificial tree purchased after her accident. We'd already hung the lights and were in the process of unpacking ornaments when Mom paused, the treetop angel in her hand.

'Poor old thing,' she said. 'She's looking rather shabby, isn't she?'

The angel never had been elegant or ethereal; she was more of a chunky little doll with sturdy blue silk wings, but she'd held the place of honour at the top of Mom's Christmas tree for something like thirty years. I couldn't remember when the angel hadn't had that smudge of charcoal on her face, or when her blue wings hadn't been slightly frayed and drooping.

'Not just shabby,' I said. 'She looks sad.' Inexplicably, I felt tears welling up in my eyes.

My mother plunked the angel down on the coffee table and lifted her glass of rye. 'Well, if she upsets you that much, I guess

I'd better get a new one.'

'I don't know why I'm feeling so emotional,' I said. 'I'm just tired. Of course the angel doesn't look sad. She's lovely.'

We had history, my mother and I: without meaning to I'd say something that made her feel bad; she'd come back with a thinly veiled sarcasm; I'd say she'd taken it the wrong way; she'd say she didn't know what I was talking about; and the two of us would retreat to restrained civility. Misunderstandings materialized out of nothing, anytime, anywhere. I was always on edge in her presence. Even at Christmas.

'No,' she said. 'I really would like a new angel.' I was caught off guard, she seemed sincere, the fleeting recrimination of her first remark already gone.

'Why don't we go look for an angel tonight?' she said cheerily. 'Finish up our drinks and go. And we could drive around and see all the lights while we're at it.'

Then I really was crying. I told her the real reason must be because I was happy; she made Christmas so magical. We finished our drinks and sat quietly listening to Harry Belafonte sing *I Heard the Bells on Christmas Day*. A perfect song, a song that admits to despair but ends with bells ringing out a message of hope. The record ended and off we went, in search of an angel.

When we told the clerk what we were looking for she informed us we'd left it far too late in the season: 'You should have been here before the end of October.'

'That's ridiculous,' my mother said, 'how can we be too late for Christmas when Christmas is still ten days away? We'll just have to find something ourselves.'

With Mom in the lead, we strode the ravaged aisles of picked-over wrapping paper, discounted cards, boxes of ornaments with an item or two that were broken or missing. And because I was with my mom, a woman who knew above all else how to make Christmas magic, we were *not* too late. It's true we didn't find an angel in that store, but we found something even better: shoved to the back of an empty bottom shelf was our old friend Winnie-the-Pooh with his pal Tigger. They were grinning, perched astride a red and green locomotive coupled to a railcar loaded with brightly wrapped boxes tied down with a string of miniature coloured lights. I pulled the engine forward and pressed a red button on the bottom of Pooh's foot. The lights flashed, Pooh and Tigger began bobbing back and forth, Pooh brandishing a copper bell in one hand. There was a little chuckle and then a long jolly chortling rendition of *We Wish You a Merry Christmas.*

'Oh,' said my mother. 'I have to buy it for you.'

The tune ended and I pressed Pooh's foot again. Right there in the store my mother and I sang along with Pooh and Tigger, wishing everyone a Merry Christmas. I was flooded with love. Love for Winnie-the-Pooh, for the Christmas season that made it all right to sing out loud in public, and most of all, for my mother.

It felt good to see her so happy. Over the last few months I'd been more than usually concerned, she'd seemed so easily upset. From my perspective there was plenty for her to be upset about; she lived in a madhouse. When Jimmy's current girlfriend Tina had moved in she'd come with more than the customary baggage: Reg—Tina's ex-husband's best friend—and his yappy little Shih Tzu had moved in too. And that was just the start of it. My mother said, 'I can't have any dogs in the house.' Tina said Reg's dog was tiny and would be no problem. My mother reminded Tina that she was mostly blind; she'd step on a Shih Tzu before she'd see it. Tina assured her that "Uncle Reg" kept the dog close to him at all times. Shoo-Shoo would never be allowed downstairs into Claire's suite. Of course once Reg was established in the house he fetched his other dog, the one Tina had neglected to mention. Bones was white and big, at least two feet tall, one of those dogs that are muscular and dangerous-looking. Reg swore Bones would never hurt a flea, but how could any sane person believe him? Emboldened by Uncle Reg, it wasn't long before Tina and Jimmy decided they needed a family too: Tina bought a pair of Pomeranians, Jimmy a Chihuahua.

After living like this for more than two years and repeatedly insisting that Reg and his dogs had to go, my mother enlisted Doreen, a long-time friend, to post an eviction notice on Reg's bedroom door. The notice was ignored. Jimmy said what could he do, Uncle Reg was like family to Tina. When Mom told me about it she said really, finally, what could *she* do: Jimmy loved Tina and my mother wasn't about to lose her son over his miserable little girlfriend. There seemed no possible end to the chaos, but things could, it turned out, get worse.

I received a phone call from Doreen in late November. Doreen was one of the very few people who maintained a friendship with my mother from before her accident. Doreen was worried about Claire's drinking getting out of control again. She said: 'I think you should talk to her doctor.'

Doreen's call had been precipitated by a chat with Tina that had been a follow-up to Doreen having dropped by for a visit with Claire the day before. Doreen had found her old friend on the point of tears, the pain was so bad. 'If it doesn't let up,' my mother said, 'please, God, just let me die.'

That wasn't Claire McHenry. My mother always claimed that doctors said she had the highest pain threshold of anyone they'd ever met. 'Dr. Nay said anyone else wouldn't be able to stand it,' she'd boast. She said this of her back when she'd fallen down her front porch stairs. She said it later of a broken collarbone, a broken toe, an arm burned on an oven element that she hadn't noticed was still on. My mother has lived on Tylenol 3 every day for years; when questioned why someone with such a high pain threshold would need so many drugs she'd snap that anyone else would have required morphine.

This time was different: Claire told Doreen that a few nights earlier she'd fallen into the door of her bedroom closet and the next morning every breath she took hurt so much she didn't think she could stand it. An x-ray hadn't shown any broken ribs and the doctor said that even if they'd missed a slight fracture there was really nothing to do but take pain killers and wait for the body to heal itself. As to *why* she'd fallen into the closet door, Claire wasn't concerned about that. Since her accident she often bumped into things. 'That's what happens when you lose ninety per cent of your vision.' It might have been another aneurysm, she said. A small one that caused her to black out for a minute.

Tina had a different explanation. She'd been at the window when Doreen drove up and she was on watch for when Doreen was leaving. She intercepted her at her car. 'Claire was drunk,' said Tina. 'She's been drinking way too much lately and that's why she crashed into her closet door.'

Tina knew this because she'd been downstairs having a 'couple of drinks' with Claire that night and she'd noticed how Claire was 'really putting it away.' Tina heard the crash moments after she'd gone back upstairs for the night. It hadn't surprised her. Tina herself had been through detox more than once; now, she told Doreen, she knew how to handle her alcohol, but clearly Claire did not. 'And Jimmy,' said Tina for good measure, 'he's an alcoholic too.'

Doreen wanted me to go to my mother's doctor and tell him why she'd fallen, something I wasn't about to do. If I was going to talk to anyone it had better be directly to my mother, and the occasion would have to present itself.

That wasn't likely to happen. Years ago, when she was visiting me in Atlanta, I'd suggested to Mom that her drinking might be impeding her recovery from the brain injury. The conversation hadn't gone well. When she returned to Vancouver she told Jimmy I'd accused her of being an alcoholic. Jimmy said no surprise, ever since I'd left Dave he hardly recognized me as his sister. He assured our mother *he'd* never abandon her like I'd done, moving to Atlanta, the way I did, a year after her aneurysm. And now, on top of everything else, I'd gone 'all self-righteous.' Together my mother and my brother bemoaned by hardened heart.

Still, that was almost twenty years ago and there did seem to be something upsetting my mother. I would watch for an opportunity to talk about what was going on. Why she was drinking more.

Whether she was drinking more. I'd told myself I'd have to be vigilant.

Which is why, perhaps, there in Canadian Traditions, when Winnie-the-Pooh and Tigger stopped singing and I leaned forward to hug my mother, I noticed, really noticed, the state of her coat. Under the bright fluorescent lights the coat, like the old angel back at the house, looked shabby and sad. When had my mother stopped wearing her majestic grey cape? It struck me that I hadn't seen it for some time. This grimy white ski jacket, torn at the pockets, was something she'd picked up in a second-hand store.

My mother's sense of style had been rooted in her work life. In offices of the 1950s and 1960s that had meant high-heels, girdles, clothing that defined a woman's figure, styles that pleased men and made women like Sophie and Gram suspicious. Through the 1970s until her fall in 1983 Claire had moved steadily upwards through the ranks of the insurance industry; it was a world where men made deals over drinks and the rare woman who made it into their ranks necessarily developed a style that showed she was almost equal yet definitely still a woman. Never small-boned, over the years my mother added on substantial weight, but always she'd carried herself with style. Even after her accident she walked tall and if she had to buy clothes that fit more loosely, they were the clothes of a woman with flare and confidence.

Tonight though she appeared smaller, diminished by that sad, sad jacket. Just like when I was a little girl, I wanted to wrap her in my arms and protect her. I felt awash with regret, for all the time I'd wasted, all those times I'd been so angry and allowed myself to forget how much I loved this woman. We hugged and as we pulled away, smiled, looking into one another's eyes.

That's something else that had and hadn't changed after her accident; my mother had lost most of her vision but when she smiled her eyes still lit up. She was smiling and I was looking into her eyes when I noticed that the whites of her eyes were now yellow. Under the bright fluorescent lights it now registered with me that her skin was jaundiced as well.

I'd been looking for an occasion to talk to my mother about her drinking. Here it was. Alcohol was destroying her liver, poison was seeping into her blood, turning her skin and eyes yellow. There was a Walk-In Medical Clinic across from the store; knowing that my mother has always listened to doctors I guided her to the waiting room.

Five years ago when a doctor told her she had to stop smoking, she did. Just like that. No wavering. She'd smoked since she was a teenager and was dismissive of anyone who suggested it might be bad for her health, yet when Dr. Nay said she had to quit, she did and never looked back. Unfortunately he never did suggest she give up drinking; on the contrary, he'd told her that a glass of wine in the evening could be healthy, and since my mother never saw herself as having much more than a glass, no problem.

In the week following her visit to the Walk-In Medical Clinic my mother had been through a flurry of tests; now it was the Friday before Christmas and she'd gone off to her own doctor to get the results. I'd offered to drive her but she scoffed at the idea; she'd seen the doctor once a month—on her own—ever since her accident. I'd never understood why she had to go so often but she looked forward to her appointments, and really it was none of my business. But this felt different; it felt like we might be able to get a handle on the drinking. It felt like a turning point. I didn't argue when my mother said she didn't want me coming with her to the doctor's, but there was nothing to stop me from being at the house to greet her when she came home. I was waiting there when the taxi pulled up; I opened the door for her to get out.

'Oh,' she said, startled to see me.

'How did it go?'

'I'll tell you when we get inside.'

We walked around to the basement door at the back of the house and went inside to the living room. My mother sat in her old recliner, erect, her gaze toward the Christmas tree. I knelt on the floor by her feet, searching her eyes for a sign, my hands resting on her arm. *The Little Drummer Boy* was coming over the airwaves. The basement is small but Mom's always kept three radios turned on at the same time, all tuned to the same station. The radios stay on whether she's home or not.

'I've always loved this carol,' she said.

We listened in silence. A carol about a little boy who believes his gift isn't good enough. And then finds out it's the most perfect gift in the world.

The song ended and another began.

My mother said, 'Next year you can have the angel.'

She meant the new angel, the one we'd finally found at the drugstore after our visit to the Walk-In Clinic. The angel looking down at us from the top of the Christmas tree.

'Next year I won't be here.' She inhaled deeply, then slowly let the air escape. 'I'll be dead in two months ... Maybe three, if I'm lucky.'

I heard a howl of anguish as though from a distant place. My mother sat straight and silent—eerily calm. That primal wail had to have come from me though I had no sense of my own body.

'I have cancer.' My mother still seemed so calm. She paused, waiting for the words to sink in. 'Pancreatic cancer.'

Teresa had died of pancreatic cancer. I grabbed my mother's hands. This couldn't be happening. The doctor was supposed to help my mother, not issue a death sentence!

Gently she extricated her hands from mine.

'It's okay.'

I was sobbing. She cupped my face in her palms; with her thumbs she gently swept the tears from my eyes.

'It's not okay.' I was choking, gulping for breath. 'I love you.'

'And I love you.' She looked down at me with that eerie

calmness, stroking my hair like I was five years old. My ears were ringing; it was hard to hear.

Still she held my face in her hands. 'I thought I would have more time,' she said. 'But I don't. Well, never mind. It will be good to see everyone. It will be good to see Mom and Dad.'

My hands had gravitated to hers; now she lowered both our hands, cradling mine in her lap.

'Sweetie,' she said. 'I need you to leave.'

That's what it sounded like, but she couldn't possibly have said that, could she?

'The doctor could be wrong.'

'No, I don't think so.' She moved her hands, laid them firmly on top of mine. 'Nora, I really do need you to leave. Jimmy is on his way home. He can't know that I told you first. He was so upset that you noticed the jaundice before he did. He said Nora always finds out everything before me. You have to promise me you won't let on you knew first.'

My mother was dying and I had to leave so Jimmy wouldn't be upset? Jealous because he wasn't the first to know? My mother had just told me she was dying and I was expected to rush to my car and drive away as fast as I could in case my brother saw me?

'I promise I'll phone you as soon as I've talked to Jimmy.'

How could she imagine I could leave her?

'You've got to hurry.' She looked anxious. Of course she was anxious. She'd just learned she was dying. But we both knew what was worrying her even more. She lifted my hands from her lap. She stood. She walked me to the door. She promised again that she would call me after she'd had time to talk with Jimmy. She reminded me I must never let on that I knew she was dying before he did.

The basement door opens onto the backyard patio. Bones, all muscle and menace, is between me and the gate. I'm terrified of dogs. 'Get out of my way!' I shout, but Bones doesn't move. 'GO!' I scream, releasing my pent-up rage, stamping my foot on the concrete with a force and a fury I don't recognize. The dog panics, turns, scrambles, falls as its nails slip on the sidewalk, escapes past me into the back corner of the yard.

I stumble to my car. I get in. I start the engine.

I picture my mother in her chair. Waiting for my brother. Alone.

How can I possibly drive away? My mother has just told me she has two months to live. I want to go back inside. I want to be with my mother.

But I do what I've been told. I pull away from the curb.

In my rear view mirror, no sign of my brother, just a giant inflatable snowman that grins and waves happily, lights swirling and flashing inside his jolly transparent tummy.

- 9 -
CLAIRE

It's cold out here. Where could he be?

Oh, look at the lights, so lovely, like stars all the way down the railing. But where are the cedar boughs? Buddy always wraps the railings with cedar boughs for Christmas.

How silly of me, of course, they've gone into the woods for branches. Buddy and Nora. I wish they did more things together. I wish … Good Lord, listen to me. Wish, wish, wish. *If wishes were horses. Fiddle-dee-dee. Fiddle-dee-dee.*

No, that can't be. Buddy's dead, Jimmy put up these lights … I don't know if I like how they flash on and off. They didn't use to blink. I liked them better when they just stayed put.

Like me. I have to stay put. Jimmy's gone to light the fireworks ... When did people start setting off fireworks at New Year's? All *we* needed was good old Robbie Burns. *Should auld acquaintance be forgot* ... Well, I'm an old acquaintance now. And soon I'll be forgot.

Good God, look at me. I'm crying. Well, next year I'll be gone. The lights will be here and I'll be gone ... My leg is throbbing. I should go inside ... I can't. I'll miss the fireworks. My last fireworks. Last everything.

For auld lang syne, my dear. For auld ... I don't think I can stand any longer—

Claire, get a hold of yourself. What's a little pain? You're here. If you go, you'll never see these lights again. And Jimmy will be upset if you miss the fireworks.

God how I've loved this street ... *For auld lang syne, my dear.*

Ah Magnus, I see you! Here I am, waving. Oh please hurry. You have to be first to cross our threshold. *Hogmanay.*

What do you mean I called you Magnus? Of course you're Jimmy. I think I would know my own son.

- 10 -
HEATHER

When Telford saw me enter the hospital cafeteria he jumped up to hold me in his arms.

'Gone?' He was so gentle. Almost like I remember my father. 'Oh my darling.'

I laid my head against his chest, sobbing. I wanted to tell him but I couldn't speak. I needed to feel his arms around me, needed the release that accompanies the tears.

'She won't be suffering now,' he said.

'No! Claire's fine!' Now I was crying and giggling all mixed up together. 'It's Nora. Nora's singing!'

Telford took out his hankie and wiped my face clear of tears.

'*Jingle Bells*?' He smiled, relieved. *Jingle Bells,* our family joke.

'*You Are My Sunshine.*' I started to sob again.

'Let me get you some tea.'

I nodded and watched Telford cross the room as the tears streamed down my face. I was crying for the tenderness of my husband of fifty years getting me tea without first needing an explanation, for the tenderness of my niece singing softly to my dying sister, for the tenderness Claire–and Nora too–had so often been denied. Claire abandoned by both her husbands. And Nora, who had abandoned each of hers. Who knows why Nora kept leaving? I felt sure she never took it lightly. To me she would always be the trusting little girl I had known so well in the years before Claire married Buddy. Always so hopeful, so eager to please.

I still can't help wondering how different all our lives would have been if Earl had just left us alone. After Nora was born we were all so happy; for her first Christmas Bobby brought home a beautiful tree, and Mom helped Claire and me decorate it. It was the first time since Dad's death that I'd seen Mom allow herself to be truly joyful at Christmas. The year before had been all about the scandal of Claire's pregnancy; a year later that very shame had transformed itself into the source of our family's joy. We had so much fun buying toys for Nora and then we all laughed when the present she liked most was an empty light bulb package.

And New Year's Eve! If only Dad could have witnessed Claire on New Year's Eve. In the morning Mom was washing up the dishes while the rest of us were still dawdling around the breakfast table, Bobby hunched over the sports section of the newspaper; Claire, with bare-footed little Nora on her lap, rhythmically counting her daughter's toes: 'One,' tap. 'Two,' tap. 'Three,' tap. 'Four' ... She wasn't playing *This Little Piggy*, she'd just softly tap each toe with her red fingernail. 'One,' tap. 'Two ...' Nora was perfectly quiet, mesmerized, as was I, by the rhythmic counting. Without looking up from her daughter's toes, Claire said, as if it were the most natural thing in the world: 'If you all line your shoes up on the basement stairs right after breakfast, I'll polish them before I go to work.'

It had never occurred to me to continue the tradition of polishing our shoes on New Year's Eve after our father died; nor, apparently, before that day had it occurred to anyone else in the family. But on that one New Year's Eve, with Nora on my lap, I sat on the stairs and watched my sister polish the family's shoes. How had she learned Dad's technique? I couldn't imagine her ever sitting quietly with our father; it seemed to me she'd always been out, or getting ready to go out, or coming home late after she'd already been out. The only thing I can distinctly remember Dad saying to Claire was: 'Young lady, I'm going to box your ears if I hear you've ...' Well, there was more than one reason Dad might have wanted to box Claire's ears. He never would have done that, boxed a girl's ears, but those words are what I remember. And yet it was Claire who polished our shoes that New Year's Eve. She wasn't silent like Dad—she hummed the whole time—but there was the same tenderness and devotion to her task.

And what did I say just the other day? That Claire never understood tradition? Sometimes I wonder if I have any idea of who Claire is.

The Valentine's Day that followed New Year's Eve was more in Claire's style. I'd come home from school to discover six red roses on our front doorstep, a florist's card attached with a ribbon. *To the two most beautiful women in Vancouver.*

I rushed inside calling for Claire. Mom would already have left for work but Claire had the night shift, an arrangement that allowed her to be with Nora during the day, and for Mom and me to be home with Nora at night. On this day, Valentine's Day, no one was home. Had Telford left the roses? I blushed to think of it. Two weeks earlier he'd told me he thought we should stop seeing each other. 'You're too young to know what you want from life.'

Telford was only two years older than me and I knew he was really saying that *he* was too young to be tied down. I'd cried the day he told me we had to break up but Claire assured me he'd be back. 'Telford and you are meant to be.' She said he was just being a guy; first he had to prove to the other guys that he was free to do what he wanted. I wasn't to worry, one day Telford and I would be an old married couple.

Even though my sister's marriage had been a disaster, for some reason I thought she knew what she was talking about when it came to Telford and me. Maybe I thought she could distinguish between a false love and true love because she'd experienced the first kind and she could see the difference when she looked at Telford and me. Or maybe I just wanted to believe.

To the two most beautiful women in Vancouver. That was something Telford would write. Somehow he must have known that Claire had faith in him and he'd wanted to include her in his gesture. It was a beautiful theory and when Claire arrived home with Nora—they'd been out 'window-gazing' so that on her first Valentine's Day Nora could see the florist shops and stores all done up with hearts and cupids—Claire agreed. Hadn't she always told me Telford would be back?

Telford arrived in person about an hour later. I opened the front door and there he was, offering me a box of chocolates. He said, 'I miss you.'

I invited him inside; I wouldn't have dared hug him on the porch, in plain view of everyone. 'The roses are beautiful,' I said. I could feel myself blushing as I pointed to them sitting in a vase on the piano. 'Are they from you?'

Telford's grin dissolved into a scowl. 'No.'

I felt my blush deepening as Claire walked into the room. 'Oh Telford,' she said. 'The roses are beautiful.'

Telford shoved his hands into his pockets. 'Heather already said that.'

Telford wasn't our secret admirer and I was frankly a little hurt at how quickly he got over the idea that the roses might have been meant mostly for me. 'I thought I had a rival,' he said, attempting a joke. 'It would have been weird though if some guy was wooing both of you at the same time. Must be Bob.'

Claire said Bobby would have included Mom in the note.

'What makes you think he didn't?' Safely confident now that I didn't have a new boyfriend, Telford was himself again and wanted to show he wasn't intimidated by my big sister. 'Maybe the roses are for your mom and Heather.'

It wasn't Bobby either; he made it clear that he had better ways to spend his money. And when Mom saw the roses she said that Claire had better watch her step or she'd find herself back out on the street so fast it would make her head spin.

That night before Claire left for work she told me she was beginning to suspect Telford all over again. 'I wish he hadn't been too embarrassed to admit it,' she said. 'Just look at the trouble he's caused.' She picked out a rose from the vase. 'It *was* romantic, though.' She smiled dreamily. 'I do miss romance.'

The next day when I got home from school Claire was smiling again. 'Look who's here!'

'Hello Heather.' Earl was slouched in Dad's old chair, as though he had some right to be there. 'I hear you liked the roses I sent my two girls. Next year I'll buy you some too.'

I wanted to snatch Nora from Claire's lap and run out of the room, but of course I couldn't do that. I wanted to say something clever to show Earl that I wasn't taken in by his smile, but the only response I could manage was a pitiful, 'Oh.'

Claire lifted my little niece down onto the floor. Facing Nora in Earl's direction, Claire held her by both hands, helping her to balance. In the last few days Nora had begun to walk. Hopeful, wobbly little steps.

'Hold out your hands and call your daughter,' Claire said to Earl. 'Go to Daddy, Nora.'

Daddy! Before that day Nora had never even seen the man.

Earl Ryan held out his hands. He smiled. He made his voice sound kind.

Nora looked up at Claire.

'It's okay, Sweetheart,' Claire said. 'Go to Daddy.'

My trusting little niece wiggled her chubby little behind and moved a foot forward. Claire let go of her hands. Nora managed two more steps before toppling to the ground. She was always trying to make her mother happy.

Claire moved out the next day, taking with her the bouquet of roses and Nora and all the joy from our house.

It wasn't until 1983, sometime in that first week after Claire's accident when she was still in the ICU, that I learned about my niece's fondness for *Jingle Bells*. Claire seemed to be coming, if ever so slightly, back into the world, though she was still completely blind and didn't understand who she was or who anyone else might be. That morning a family member of another patient had greeted us with the news that they'd heard Claire singing. That was lovely, the way we all kept an eye on each other's loved ones in ICU, reporting on anything one of us might have missed. As if we'd all become one extended family. A nurse said, 'Oh yes, that Claire is delightful. Our little canary. Especially in the night.'

Later, on the drive home, Nora and I talked about the blessing of song, how that capacity sometimes seemed to linger in people who had otherwise lost the use of language.

'Sadly, that won't be me,' said Nora, and she told me about her fear of singing, how in third grade when she joined the school choir—the school wasn't permitted to exclude anyone—she'd been told to mouth the words. 'I do love to sing,' she said, 'but only when I'm alone in the car. The trouble is, that's never allowed me enough time to learn anything by heart.'

The one exception was *Jingle Bells,* a song she would sing any place, any time of the year. I'd laughed because Annie, our own musically challenged daughter, has the same thin repertoire. And is equally inclined to share it on any occasion. When I told Telford about Nora and *Jingle Bells* he said he'd heard of blood relations sharing a talent for music, but a *Jingle Bells* gene was something else again.

Now Nora was singing a new song: *You Are My Sunshine.*

Telford and I had already driven in to see Claire once today. Twenty-five years ago I would drive to Nora's on my own and give her a ride to the hospital. Now, with my Parkinson's, I can't drive, so Telford does. It's hard on Telford—at his age he finds the highway stressful—but he's brought me here every day since Claire was admitted to hospital. When Mother was dying the only day I missed seeing her was the day she passed away. That's not going to happen with Claire.

We'd already returned from our daily visit and I should have been settling down in the living room with Telford for a quiet evening; instead, I was pacing back and forth in the kitchen. Claire has been singing up a storm ever since she was put in the hospital—*Chantilly Lace, You Belong to My Heart, Little Sir Echo* and snippets of other songs from our past—but this morning there was just one song: *Auld Lang Syne.* Over and over. And then she'd cry out for our father: 'Magnus, Magnus. I'm waiting for you.' She was shivering and no matter how many warmed flannel sheets I got from the nurse, I couldn't warm her.

The doctor assured me it will be better tomorrow. Tomorrow they will try and put in a stent to drain her liver. The doctor says that should make her more comfortable, stop the poison from going straight into her blood. He said I should go home, that I needed to look after myself too. But after dinner I felt my anxiety rising. Why was Claire calling for Dad? Was tonight the night? I needed to be at the hospital, yet surely it was too much to ask Telford to drive a hundred kilometres through bad weather for a second time in one day. It was raining and dark now too, and I know how hard Telford has to concentrate to see in those conditions.

I tried to calm myself. I called the hospital. They said there was no change in my sister's condition. I continued pacing back and forth in the kitchen, something I do these days without even noticing, but this time it wasn't just because of the Parkinson's. Telford was in the living room building a balsa model of Sam Whitby's house. That's Telford, bless his soul, he can sit in the same chair for hours, so focused on a project that I swear the house could burn down around him and he wouldn't notice. Yet tonight he suddenly appeared in the kitchen and asked, 'What's wrong?'

I started to cry.

Telford knew I'd already called the hospital, he knew there had been no additional bad news. He put his arms around me and said, 'I think we should go to see Claire.'

I told him that he was the most wonderful husband in the world and that it wasn't necessary to drive all the way back to North Vancouver tonight; it was enough that he had offered. I told him all that, but he got me my coat and opened the door of the car and drove me to the hospital to see Claire.

Having left Telford to wait in the cafeteria, I made my way down the hall alone. I was already at the entrance to Claire's room before I heard the singing. There are four beds in the room; Claire is in one of the two next to the window. I peeked past the curtain dividing the beds.

Nora was seated next to her mother's bed, her left hand clasping Claire's right; in Nora's other hand, the page of lyrics she was singing from. Nora didn't see me; tonight she was like Telford, completely focused in the present moment. It would have been wrong for me to enter that space.

When I finally managed to tell Telford what had happened, all my lovely husband said was, 'I'm glad we came.' No words about how the trip hadn't been necessary, about how we still had the long dark drive back home.

That's something Earl Ryan never would have understood. A good man, a man like Telford, doesn't need to sweet-talk a woman with roses.

- || -
NORA

'**G**ood God! Just have an affair. You don't get divorced over the seven-year itch.'

That was my mother's response when at the age of twenty-six I told her that my marriage with Dave was over. It's the most emphatic piece of advice she ever gave me, and the one I most thoroughly rejected. I divorced Dave, then Ian, then Dallas, then the one that was over so quickly that many acquaintances don't even know about it. Four marriages, four divorces. I never tried to prolong a marriage by having an affair.

Divorce had been my advice for my mother when I was only eight years old.

We were in the garden weeding. Buddy was inside watching television. My mother was annoyed at him for something and I seized upon the opportunity to protest against what I perceived to be the unjust distribution of labour in our household. Mom went to work and I went to school; on top of that we cooked dinners, washed dishes and clothes, cleaned the house all year round and in the summer had to weed the garden too. Buddy went to work. Period. Except in the summer when he cut the lawn and planted a vegetable garden. Planted, but never weeded. Everybody admired Buddy's garden. He got the glory, but day after day all summer long while Buddy watched TV we were in the garden doing the work.

I said, 'It's not fair.'

The last time I'd made a big deal about justice was when Sophie washed my mouth out with soap. That time Claire had packed our bags and we never saw Sophie again. This time I knew exactly where we should move to, an apartment in the West End of Vancouver, next door to Aunt Heather and Uncle Telford. We'd have a Murphy Bed, like they did, the kind that folded up into the wall in the daytime, and at night my mother and I would share the bed, just the two of us, like old times, only even better because Aunt Heather and Uncle Telford would be right next door.

'We need to get a divorce from Buddy,' I said.

My mother slammed her spade into the dirt. She grabbed me by both arms, shaking me violently. I was never ever to talk like that again! It's the only time I can remember my mother handling me that way.

I was as bewildered by my mother's fury as I'd been by Sophie's the day she dragged me from a chair to wash my mouth with soap. If ever my mother was upset with me, a look or the words *I'm disappointed in you* had always been more than enough punishment, but on the day I suggested she divorce Buddy she'd trembled with anger. Buddy was her husband. And my father!

'You don't leave people just because they annoy you.'

To my mother's mind, at twenty-six I still hadn't learned that lesson. I'd been grumbling about how it wasn't fair that Dave and I were both going to university and both working part-time, but I was the one doing all the housework and typing all his assignments as well as my own.

She'd stopped me short. 'You want a divorce because Dave doesn't do the dishes?'

I tried to explain it wasn't *just* about chores and fairness, the bigger problem was love. I reminded her that on the day of the wedding I'd told her I didn't want to go through with it; I'd realized I didn't feel what you were supposed to feel on your wedding day. She'd said I was feeling nervous, *exactly* what people feel on their wedding day. She gave me one of her tranquillizers; the guests were on their way and there'd be no more talk of backing out. I'd thrown the pill in the trash.

Seven years later my mother hadn't changed her mind. 'Sometimes an affair is the only way to save a marriage,' she said. 'Marriages seldom work out the way you imagine, but you don't walk away.'

Had I ever told Mom that the only reason Dave started dating me was because he was tired of taking the bus to see his previous girlfriend? Our house was only three blocks away from his, and besides, he felt more at home with us than he did in his own house where everyone except Dave was serious and quiet. Dave was the rowdy one who smoked and talked too loud and played goofy jokes;

at our house Dave was a hero, especially to Mom and Jimmy. My mother never took anyone seriously *unless* they enjoyed a drink and a cigarette. Jimmy, who was only five when Dave entered our lives, adored him. Dave always played roughhouse in a way that made Jimmy squeal and feel grown-up all at the same time. Two years older than me, Dave blended perfectly into our family, his role almost that of an older brother. But by the age of twenty-six I was no longer content with the kind of love you feel for an older brother. I was ready for passion.

My mother said, 'You want passion? Have an affair. The passion will fade soon enough and you'll still have a marriage. A marriage is about more than just you.'

I couldn't see the problem; we didn't have any children and Dave was okay with divorce.

'The problem,' said my mother, 'is you made a commitment. A lot of people came to your wedding and when you said *for better or for worse*, they took you at your word.'

I reminded her that she'd divorced Earl. I knew she didn't like me talking about him, but how could I not? She claimed a marriage was about more than just the two married people, so how come she'd divorced *my* father?

Not the sort of question to open up a gentle conversation. How dare I even think of comparing my petty grievances to what Earl had done?

Well what *had* he done? I was a baby when Earl left; I knew almost nothing about him because no one ever wanted to tell me anything. I knew a few things, but no coherent narrative. I did know there had been another baby after me. Dave and I had found that out a year into our marriage on the evening before we left for Australia with no plan to return; for some reason my mother and Buddy had decided we should know about my sister who had been given up for adoption. Buddy said, 'I just wish I'd met your mother before it was too late. Two little girls, that would have been perfect.'

Why tell me then? Did they think they'd never see me again?

I knew that Earl and my mother had been reunited on my first Valentine's Day. I didn't know that four months later when Claire told Earl she was pregnant he'd said he wasn't strong enough to raise two babies. He just didn't feel what he knew it would take. He was strong enough to insist on that.

Yes, she *had* divorced Earl, but only because there was no other way to feed the child she already had. Me, in case I hadn't noticed. If every last penny she earned wasn't to be lost to Earl's gambling or squandered on other women, she had to sever every connection with her husband. She'd been forced to make that sacrifice for me; it certainly wasn't a self-indulgent flight of fancy brought on by a bit of boredom.

'You tell me you need to feel passion,' she said. 'You think you don't feel what a wife needs to feel. Well, you came by that honestly.'

Is that what I inherited from my father? Brown eyes and an inability to feel what I needed to feel?

All those marriages and all those divorces. No affairs. No children. My divorces were bumpy, but never nasty, and now all my ex-husbands are as close to me as brothers. As close, that is, as I'd always thought a brother and sister should be. My relationship to Jimmy, my actual brother, is another story.

This morning I was in the hospital room when Jimmy walked in. Mom has been in hospital almost a week but it's the first time

Jimmy and I have been in her room together; generally he doesn't come by until late in the afternoon and since he never stays long I've always excused myself for the few minutes he's there. A chance for my mother and Jimmy to be alone.

'Hey Sis.'

I was focused on my mother, holding her hand. He'd startled me.

'You don't have to leave.' He wasn't looking at me; he was looking down at Mom. He said, 'Tina's waiting outside.' He was standing on the other side of the bed. 'I just wanted to see how Mom was doing.'

I told him she'd been sleeping since I arrived. He bent down and kissed her on the lips. That's always made me uncomfortable, but the fact is my mother likes to kiss people on the lips. I've always tried to avoid it, veering off at the last moment to receive my kiss on the cheek.

'Hey beautiful.' He spoke quietly. I'm not used to my brother speaking quietly.

'Yes,' said our mother. She opened her eyes. 'Time to go home.'

'Not today,' said my brother.

Her eyes fluttered closed.

Had she meant home to her house on Drayton Street? Or was she talking about her heavenly home? I wondered what Jimmy was thinking.

'How's Fred?'

I looked at my brother standing there on the other side of the bed. A good-looking man, though his face was puffy and haggard, his long greying hair in need of a wash. Normally Jimmy talks with an intimidating bravado that can make even a simple greeting sound like a threat, but this morning the mask, the person I'd taken to *be* my brother for so many years, was down. Jimmy was simply my brother, ten years my junior, grieving the last days of his mother's life.

On a normal day the language Jimmy used with her was crude and bullying; he'd squandered all her money, forced her to accept strangers and a pack of dogs into her home, leaving her cornered in the basement of her own house. But she was also the most important person in his life. I looked at my brother now and saw the nine-year-old I'd loved when I left home to get married at nineteen. My little brother, thirty-six years later, and he still hasn't left home. I wanted to tell him not to worry, that after Mom was gone I'd be there for him. But what would that mean? Right this moment he was my baby brother, but when we left the hospital room the mask would go back on, he'd be the bully again, the angry drunk, the victim. In what way would I be there?

'Good,' I said. 'Fred's good.'

Jimmy and I had been looking at one another; now we both looked down at our mother. She'd mumbled something, opened her eyes again. She turned her head to look at Jimmy, then at me.

'This is how it should be.' She spoke slowly, distinctly. 'My children.'

'Yes.'

Jimmy was holding Mom's other hand, each of us holding onto our mother.

'Gotta go luv.' Jimmy's voice sounded husky, shaky, like he might cry.

He pulled his hand away from Mom's. 'Tina's gonna be pissed,' he said, the mask in place again. 'She's driving around the block, there's no fucking place to park. And we gotta get Shi-Shu to the vet.'

He bent down to kiss his mother on the lips, then rose, turned and walked out the door.

Mom closed her eyes. I remained where I was, holding her hand.

Two nights ago I tried singing to my mother. She had been agitated, her breathing ragged and rattling, her legs restless; to soothe her I began softly singing a lullaby: *Lullaby and goodnight, with roses bedight.* But then, though I knew there were words missing, all I could remember was the refrain: *Lay you down now and rest/ May your slumber be blessed.* I tried to think of words to another song but the only other one that came to mind was *Jingle Bells,* which, in the moment, felt wrong. And so I whispered the three little lines of my one lullaby over and over until eventually my mother's breathing eased, the rattling grew softer and she drifted into what I hoped was a peaceful sleep.

At home much later that night I downloaded the lyrics to the lullaby and to one of my mother's favourite songs: *You Are My Sunshine.* I'd heard her sing the latter so many times and it had never failed to make me feel happy, but once I saw the words on the screen I had to face the sad truth that really I had *never* heard the song, only the chorus and the music. I'd heard the happy tune, but the song is a song of loss. I'd missed all the lines about awaking to find the loved one gone, about being left behind. I'd missed the part about shattered dreams.

I always thought I was the listener, the one who paid attention, that Mom was the one who didn't hear. By the time I'd reached my teens I'd given up trying to tell her what was really happening in my life because it seemed she was deaf to my concerns; if everything wasn't bright and cheerful she simply wouldn't hear about it. 'What's your problem? Get over it. Get on with it.' When she'd counselled affairs over divorce, I'd thought I heard her loud and clear. I rebelled. Now, after reading those heart-breaking lyrics, I find myself questioning my hearing.

A marriage is about more than just you.

This morning, looking at Jimmy on the other side of the hospital bed I'd seen the nine-year-old boy my brother had been when Dave and I got married. Jimmy was five when Dave came into his life, ten when we wrestled with the idea of taking him with us to Australia, sixteen when Dave and I divorced. Dave could have visited my brother any time, but he never did, and Jimmy blamed me for that. After I left Dave, my brother never trusted me again. When I moved to Atlanta with my second husband, Jimmy told Mom *he* would never abandon her the way I'd done.

Later, after Jimmy had married and become a father, *his* wife left him and their three children. The first time I met my nephew and two nieces they were living with Jimmy and his new girlfriend upstairs in the house I'd grown up in; Claire had been moved to the basement. I was only home for a two-week visit but in that time Social Services apprehended the children. I'm pretty sure my brother blamed me for that too.

Jimmy adored his four-year-old daughter Chelsea, hardly knew what to do with baby Willow, and threatened six-year-old Jake with adoption every time he didn't sit still. My cousin Annie and her husband had looked after Jimmy's children for a couple of weeks when Jimmy and his girlfriend went to the Calgary Stampede. Annie, an elementary school teacher as well as a foster parent, called me to say she was worried; when she'd made a move to brush Jake's hair the little fellow cringed. Eventually Jake admitted that his dad sometimes hit him. We all knew Jimmy's temper and I'd heard him threaten Jake with adoption. I phoned my husband in Atlanta hoping he would agree to adopt Jake, a conversation that we never successfully concluded.

Two days later the social worker took Jimmy's children into custody. The Ministry of Child Services was already familiar with them since Jake and Chelsea had been enrolled in temporary weekday foster care from the time Willow was born. I hadn't contacted Child Services and Annie swears she did not make the call either, but I admit that I *was* relieved to think that someone, somewhere, was looking out for Jake, though I'd have preferred that it hadn't happened while I was in the city. The timing was so unfortunate; how could Jimmy *not* have suspected me?

The more Jimmy felt betrayed, the greater the distance between my mother and me. In some ways that was a relief. I was trying to break free from my past and build a life on my own terms, knowing that my mother could never understand what I needed, what I was searching for. Still it hurt to be portrayed as the person who had let the family down. When Mom went back to work after Jimmy was born she'd told me to take care of my little brother. She wanted me to never ever stop.

A marriage is about more than just you.

But surely my marriage was also about more than providing a big brother for my little brother to play with. Jimmy was sixteen years old when Dave and I divorced; he wasn't a baby anymore. And I wasn't his mother. Dave and I had both needed to step back to move forward. In terms of one another, we'd divorced with grace and remained good friends. The night my mother told me she was dying, before shooing me out the door so that my brother could believe he was the first to be told, it was to Dave and his wife that I'd turned for comfort. Fred had already left for Nanaimo and I'd needed to be with someone who could understand. My relationship with Dave was a failure viewed only through the narrow lens of Jimmy's victimhood and my mother's rigid respect for the superficial formalities of a social contract. Dave and I had grown out of our marriage, but we'd made a good divorce; that was progress, even if Mom would have done things differently.

All of that is true, as true as the fact that my mother is dying, as true as the aching rush of protective love for both of them that swept over me in the hospital room when Jimmy bent down to kiss our mother on the lips and whispered to her.

'Hey beautiful.'

- 12 -
CLAIRE

Magnus, I don't know what to do. I'm ready to come home but Nora won't let me go. Nora! She was always so quick to find fault with me. Now she sits here hour after hour and holds my hand. Tells me over and over that she loves me. She couldn't always say those words.

She tells me I'm beautiful. God knows I've never been a beauty. Sure, I knew how to present myself in the best light, and I never went outside the house without putting my face on, but I always knew I was no beauty. Nora was beautiful, not me. Yet here she is holding my hand, telling me *I'm* beautiful and I can hear in her voice that she means it.

'I see your soul,' she says.

I want to tell her I see hers too. I want to tell her all the things she's been longing to hear. I try, but my mouth is so dry. The words reach my lips but I can't get them out, they quiver there on the edge, little puffs of air that no one understands. If someone manages to pick out a word or two they so quickly lose the thread. Then they act like I've gone somewhere. Where do they think I've gone? I'm right here, for heaven's sake.

Well, really, how could they understand when I don't understand what's happening myself? I see you there, Magnus, and it's perfectly clear to me that you've come to take me home. It's perfectly clear, but I don't know what it means. Magnus, I can *almost* remember. *Trailing clouds of glory* ... But what comes next?

I've forgotten my heavenly home. Is that what will happen when I leave this earth? Will I forget this home too? I don't want to forget.

Okay, some things I'm happy to forget. Why hold onto the pain? But Lord knows, I do not want to forget the good times. My 1967 Mercury convertible. I remember the day Buddy and I traded in the old station wagon and bought the convertible. I did love driving that car, my hair flying in the wind.

What am I saying? That's the movies! *My* hair never flew in the wind; I always wore a scarf. And all through the seventies we wore wigs. I wonder why we did that. They were less work than those beehives of the sixties, but God what a strange fashion.

And that time in Puerto Vallarta when I was swimming and that young man popped up out of the water right next to me with something hanging from the tips of his fingers. He held it out toward me. I thought it was a drowned squirrel and I screamed. Of course I did! People turned to look. The poor boy's face turned brilliant red: 'I think this belongs to you, Ma'am.'

Good Lord, it was my wig! I burst out laughing. He was just a nice young man trying to be helpful but I couldn't stop myself from laughing. I know it's the worst thing a woman can do to a man, but I wasn't laughing at him. He was too young to understand that sometimes we just have to laugh at ourselves. I wanted to thank him but he swam away so fast that he was gone before I got my breath back. Before I'd plopped the soggy mess on my head and stretched it back into place, acting like it had been there all along.

Well, well, and now I've had white hair for so long that's all anybody sees. White hair, white cane, white old lady. But Magnus, it doesn't matter, does it? There's no difference. It's all happening at once and I can choose to be six years old or forty. I almost believe that, but I don't believe it, too.

It reminds me of the night Nora and I were sitting in front of the fireplace talking about life. Such a long time ago. Was it before Buddy died? I can't remember. Nora and I were alone having a drink in front of the fire; I do remember that. It must have been after she'd divorced Dave; otherwise, if it was late at night he would have been with us. Certainly it wasn't when she was married to Dallas; we wouldn't have been sitting in front of my fireplace. Well, *when* doesn't matter, what matters is that Nora and I were close that night. My daughter thinks we never talked, but sometimes, late at night, when I could stop her from rushing off, we did talk. Not about things that couldn't be undone, but about life. I suppose I've remembered that night because since I've been in hospital Nora keeps telling me she can see my soul. Well that night I remember telling *her*: 'You're an old soul and I'm kind of a middle-aged soul, and Buddy and Jimmy, well they're just toddlers.'

We were so close that night, relaxed from the drink and warmed by the fire, and it felt right to acknowledge that Nora was so much older than me. But Magnus, is that true? And if it is, what does it mean? We're still given the roles of parent and child. Surely those are the roles we're expected to fill this time around. With Jimmy it's always been so easy. Yes he loses his temper, and he swears a little—well, far too much—but with Jimmy I know where I stand. And he knows who I am. He knows I'm his mother and I'll always be there for him. Not a bad thing for a mother. To know she's needed.

When Leanne left Jimmy and the kids, Jimmy came home. But Nora never would come to me, would she? She'd just go out and pick up another husband. After she divorced Dave she moved right on to ... Oh dear, who was the next one? The one who moved her down to Atlanta? And only a year after my aneurysm. *I have to go,* she said. *He's my husband.* As if that means anything to Nora. She'd divorced him within the year. And did she come home then? Not on your life, she just moved on to another man, going through husbands like a box of Kleenex.

I know she thinks she can't come to me for help. I suppose it started with that business about Richard, but how was I to know my eleven-year-old daughter was talking in riddles? *I'm tired. Richard stays in my room too long when he comes to say good-night.* Well I knew that Nora took her schoolwork seriously and I told Richard he needed to say a quick good-night and let Nora get her sleep.

I liked Richard. He was good to Nora and he was good to me. Of all of Bobby's friends who came to stay with him in the house, Richard was the only one who pitched in to help with chores. Why he even changed Jimmy's diapers! He seemed perfect. What was he? Twenty? Halfway in age between Nora and me, the younger brother I never had, the older brother Nora wished she had. Good God, in those days we didn't suspect every man of being a child molester.

I'd never dare say so to Nora, but sometimes I wonder if she didn't just get caught up in all that media hype about sexual abuse and what is it they call it? Repressed something or other. Memories, that's it. Repressed memories. More like repressed fantasies if you ask me. Why else would my daughter wait until her thirties to come out with it directly? It even occurred to me that she might have fabricated the whole thing just because she was angry that Richard had disappeared so completely from our lives. Well I missed Richard too, but people move on.

And even if it was true, even if Richard had been overly intimate in my daughter's room way back then, what did she expect me to do about it when we hadn't seen the man in twenty years? Was I supposed to track him down and have him sent to jail? Did she want me to beg her forgiveness for not having understood what she now said she had been trying to tell me? Why didn't she just speak plainly?

And why couldn't she just move on? I was gang-raped when I was seventeen. I told her that. Good Lord, I told her more than I'd told any other living being. Gang-raped. Not *possibly fondled* by someone who cared for me. I was raped and I did what you do when life happens. I moved on.

Oh dear, I never told you about those boys, did I, Magnus? What would you have done if you'd known? But if you really are here now, that means you must already know all my secrets. And if I'm only talking to a figment of my longing, well, no harm done.

Sometimes I'm so certain. Other times I think they're right, that all this is just the incoherent mumblings of a sick old lady.

No, of course you're here. How could I doubt it? You've always been with me. Do you remember years ago when Nora asked me who had been the most important person in my life?

'Magnus.' I didn't even have to stop to think.

Nora said, 'And Jimmy.' She was always testing my affection.

'Well of course Jimmy. Jimmy needs me.'

Nora could have said she needed me too, but she didn't. Why couldn't she say that? An old soul should have understood that it hurts a mother to feel she isn't needed.

Well, maybe a mother needs to tell her daughter she's important too. Now I can see how that was a bad business with her last husband. But at the time I was just so spitting mad. After eleven years my daughter finally comes back from Atlanta after divorcing husband number three and when I suggest that she move into the house with me and Jimmy she just says, 'No,' like that, without even bothering to give an excuse.

Doreen said, 'Well, how could she live in that house after what happened to her there?'

Doreen knew all about "the basement." That's how Nora had described it to Vicky, and Vicky passed the story on to her mother. Apparently Nora could scarcely stomach visiting me in the house because of "what had happened in the basement." Well, the way Doreen talked about it you'd think we'd just been the most horrible parents on the face of God's earth. Good Lord, it wasn't like that at all. Buddy worked damn hard to make that room perfect for his little princess. He painted the room all lavender and pink and put in bright white bookshelves and then Agnes bought Nora that little vanity with the ruffled pink skirt. Before Buddy died, never in my life had I had a room of my own, let alone anything as beautiful as Nora's, but she wasn't grateful, she just wanted to sleep upstairs.

Now I know it bothers Nora even to visit me because I'm living in that same basement, even though her room isn't even there anymore. After Buddy died I had the basement renovated into a suite and Nora's bedroom got changed into a bathroom. And it's a lovely bathroom too. You'd have to stretch your imagination pretty far to see what it is about my suite that Nora still can't stomach. But that's Nora, she dwells on things.

And then picks up another husband so she'll have an excuse

for not coming home. Why, the plane had barely touched down in Vancouver before Nora married Harold, husband number four, and then divorced him before the ink on the marriage certificate so much as had a chance to dry.

Oh that was a sorry business. Harold. I liked the man and I felt sorry for him, being treated like that, so of course I invited him to dinner. I asked Jimmy to come downstairs and join us. We told Harold he shouldn't take Nora dumping him personally; she was like that. We filled him in on my aneurysm and how she'd manipulated the doctor into saying that Jimmy needed to move out of the house. She told my doctor that Jimmy's drinking and short temper would be too much for me when I was recovering. Just because Nora has always needed everything to be so quiet she thinks everyone feels the same. Up and decides I'd be better off alone than having my son there to support me. Of course it would never have occurred to Nora that *she* might move in and lend a hand. I offered that. Said that even now we could find a way to make room. But oh no, Nora couldn't come home. She'd pick up another husband sooner than that. Not Jimmy; he loves our home. I told her that's why I'm leaving the house to Jimmy.

Well I can't remember what else we told Harold; it was a long time ago. I do remember the letter he sent me the next day. He'd been happy enough drinking my rye and eating the dinner I'd prepared and then he goes home and writes me that letter. What gall!

Your boast of refusing to give any comfort to Nora when Dallas left her, claiming she got back her own, says it all—you are hardhearted. You have made yourself forever incapable of knowing your daughter, which is sad; but your constant bad-mouthing of your own daughter to others is inexcusable. Shame on you!

Shame on *me*? Who was Harold Jacobs to be telling *me* how to treat my daughter? I was just being kind to the man after she dumped him and he has the audacity to tell me I should be ashamed? Why Nora's ex-husbands are so loyal to her is a mystery to me.

Later Nora asked if I'd received a letter from Harold.

'Why ever would Harold write to me?' I said, innocent as could be. I wasn't about to give her the satisfaction. And we left it there. I suppose Nora would say it's just one more thing I refused to talk about. Well, please tell me, what was there to say?

Oh Magnus, I hadn't intended to get so riled up. Here's Nora holding my hand and telling me she loves me, and next thing I know I'm all tangled up in the memory of Harold's awful letter. That's exactly why I don't believe in remembering the bad things. Just look where that leads.

- 13 -
HEATHER

'How ya doin'?'

I tripped, teetering toward the handrail, unbalanced by the hoarse abruptness of the voice, betrayed by my Parkinson's. Telford had gone to park the car and I was alone, walking toward the hospital entrance. I couldn't immediately see anyone else around.

'Kinda wobbly are you now?' A hand reached for my arm, clamped it firmly.

I sensed more than saw the man's long grey hair, his trampled features. He might be crazy, or on drugs, desperate. My heart thumped wildly. I had to will myself not to scream. Will myself to do what I always try to do when I fear a stranger. Remember my father's advice.

During the Depression men often knocked at our door after having spent the night in a trench on the edge of the park at the end of the street. There was long grass in the trench and Dad told me they slept there seeking warmth. I mustn't be afraid of those men, he said. The only difference between them and us was that for the moment they weren't as lucky as we were. No matter our father had to walk for hours and hours every day as a salesman and my mother had to work nights at the Telephone Company to make ends meet, in my father's eyes we were the lucky ones; nobody who came to our door in need was ever turned away hungry. One of the first verses I learned by heart was from the Book of Hebrews: *Be not forgetful to entertain strangers: for thereby some have entertained angels unawares.* I'd peek out from behind Mother or Dad's legs as they suggested a man might rake leaves or chop wood for the fire. Dad could have done those chores himself; it was a kindness to allow the men to give something in return for their supper. I wasn't afraid of them; I hung back because I was shy, believing any one of them might be an angel. Even the ones who might not be angels weren't frightening; I just thought it sad they didn't have a home. Today if a stranger were to knock at our door I would be afraid, even though I have Telford to protect me.

Where *was* Telford? What was keeping him? The stranger still had me by the arm. I forced myself to look him in the face.

'Where's Uncle Telford?' he asked.

Tonight I think of that encounter and I feel humbled. How would I ever recognize an angel at my door when I didn't know my own nephew? I could say it wasn't my fault; after all this time how could I have recognized him? The years have just slipped by; I never meant it to be so long.

No, that's not true. I meant it to be forever, after what he did to Colin.

The summer Colin lived with Jimmy and Leanne, Colin said his older cousin was a really nice guy. I keep forgetting that Jimmy ever lived anywhere except with Claire, but he did move out for a few years after her accident. Just long enough to have three babies. That's something I don't forget, though it breaks my heart to remember: Jimmy had three children and lost them all.

We aren't supposed to believe in curses, the sins of the fathers visited upon the children and all that, and I know Earl wasn't even Jimmy's father, but I can't help feeling that's where it all started: one child is abandoned and then another, down through the generations.

For the longest time Claire didn't let on that Earl was gone again. I think she expected him to come back, begging for one more chance, not that he'd have had to beg; I don't think Claire could ever have said no if Earl had just asked. I don't know that she ever got over him, no matter what she said. When they first met all she talked about was how handsome he was and how mature compared to the boys she'd gone out with before him. Well he *should* have been more mature; he was twelve years older than Claire, though that's not what he told her. Twenty-six, Earl said, which would have been true if time had stood still in the six years since he'd joined the army. Claire didn't find that out until they applied for a marriage licence.

'If I'd known the truth at the beginning I'd have realized he was a guy who was always going to squander his life away.' Claire said that later, though that doesn't explain away that she *did* know that before the marriage and she *did* know that when she took him back after they broke up the first time. Well, Earl did look young for his age; that's *something* good Nora gets from her father. He could have had his pick of any woman, Claire said, which clearly wasn't true, even if Claire needed to believe it at the time.

Well finally she had to accept that he really was gone. She kept her job at the Telephone Company as long as she possibly could, but she couldn't keep working once the baby started to show. Claire was running out of options and one night she told Mom she needed to move home again. Mom had already warned Claire there'd be no coming back after the last time, but I couldn't see how she could refuse; this wasn't just about Claire, there was Nora to think about and the baby arriving.

'Don't worry,' said Claire. 'I won't ever be going back to Earl. I'm getting a divorce.'

I've always believed *that* was Claire's big mistake; in our family no one got divorced, no one even talked about it. It simply wasn't done. When Claire tried to explain to Mother why she had no choice, that on top of everything else Earl was gambling away the last of Claire's wages, Mother cut her off.

'You made your bed, now you can lie in it.'

'I think you mean *may* lie in it?'

My sister never lacked nerve! Nor pride. 'We'll trouble you no more,' Claire said, pulling on her boots and buttoning her coat while I helped Nora into hers, zipping it against the late autumn chill, pulling the little hood up over her head to keep her ears warm and tying the strings in a bow under her chin. Mom watched the preparations for leaving, silent as a stone, until the door closed behind them; stood there silently until the sound of Claire's departing footsteps grew too faint to hear, then turned without a word and went into her bedroom, closing the door behind her.

The next day I went to Claire's apartment to give her the babysitting money I'd been saving; it wasn't a lot, but I'd bring more when I could. Claire asked if I'd still babysit for Nora sometimes, but she wouldn't take my money; she didn't need it. She said I'd never guess who was helping her, that I shouldn't guess anyway, because she'd promised not to tell anyone. I thought from the way she smiled that it meant she already had a new man in her life, but years later I got the feeling it had been Bobby. They'd never gotten along growing up, but after Claire and Buddy got their own house

Bobby moved in with them. I could have asked Claire after Bobby died but I didn't. I know my sister; if she says she's not going to talk about something she doesn't. Maybe it was Mom who gave Claire the money. Mom couldn't let Claire come home, because they both had too much pride, but Mom wouldn't have wanted Claire to go hungry either. I'll never know now, but I'd like to believe it was at least one of them—Bobby or Mom. Even if it's just my fantasy I'd like to think one them cared that much.

Sometimes I try to make up a nice fantasy for Claire's second baby, too. Imagine she was adopted by perfect parents who adored her and took her on glamorous holidays to Europe. In fact all I know is that the baby was a girl and she was adopted straight from the hospital. A good home, they said. What else would they say?

Still, though I'd never have dared say so to Claire, I couldn't help feeling it was wrong. You just don't give away a baby. Claire wouldn't talk about it. Not then, not later. *The past is the past. What's done is done.*

I'm sure we all thought history was repeating itself when Nora married Dave before she was even twenty. Well, weren't we wrong! Nora never did have children; it was Jimmy who made Claire a grandmother. 'I just hope they know I won't be babysitting,' Claire said when she found out that Leanne was expecting. 'I can't even see.'

Fair enough, I suppose, aside from the fact that Claire always got so angry if any of us implied she wasn't capable of doing the least thing after her accident. She was eager though to point out that it was Jimmy who finally provided her with grandchildren. 'Nora's too busy traipsing around the world, trying on different husbands for size.'

Then Leanne left Jimmy, before long Social Services stepped in, and the children dropped out of our lives.

It's so sad that Nora never had children. For years I believed it was because she didn't want any, but after she moved back home from Atlanta she told me that wasn't it at all. Her first two husbands had told her they weren't ready for a baby. They needed time. Well some women would have just gone ahead and gotten pregnant, but Nora wanted to be sure that the man who fathered her children was ready to be a father. If only she'd talked to me I'd have told her that most men have to learn to love their children. I learned a few things as a minister's wife, but lots of women could have told her that a baby teaches a man how to be a father. How could a baby do that before it was even born? Then again, maybe she was always thinking of Earl.

When Nora married Dallas, down in Atlanta, he already had a nine-year-old son from a prior marriage. Dallas's divorce was far behind him, he adored his son and from his first date with Nora he maintained that he wanted another child and he wanted to have it with her, but when they married and Nora got pregnant the very next month, apparently he panicked. His business wasn't making money; he couldn't afford health insurance; if something went wrong with the birth they wouldn't be able to afford care; his son was still adjusting to Nora. A baby so soon would be a disaster. Dallas convinced Nora to have an abortion, promising they'd have a baby the following year. Of course they didn't, nor the next year, nor the year after that. Eventually Nora moved back to Canada, divorced once again.

The day Nora confided in me she said, 'I've always supported a woman's freedom of choice, but I could never go on pro-abortion marches because I always knew that for me, it would be wrong.'

'You mean wrong to have an abortion,' I said. I wasn't sure I understood.

'Yes, for me, in my soul, it felt wrong.'

'Yet you had an abortion.'

The second the words were out of my mouth I regretted them; I could see the pain in my niece's eyes. How could I have blurted out something so insensitive? I said, 'If only I'd known at the time.'

Just what could I have done? Families fly apart and we hear ourselves say those words: *If only I'd known.* Claire's family had been disintegrating from the very start. First Earl. Then the second baby, lost to adoption so many years ago; Buddy, so critical of Earl for abandoning Claire and her babies, suddenly gone by his own hand, his family left to cope alone in the aftermath of his suicide. And on it went. Jimmy's wife gone to find herself, their three babies gone to foster homes, and in the end, adopted out of the family forever. Jimmy stumbling around in his own dark place, and all the havoc he caused from his pain.

And me, I'm not blameless either. I shouldn't have abandoned Claire for all those years. Wasted years, I know now, but at the time I couldn't see it. I just couldn't get past what her son had done to mine.

Colin was at work the day Telford answered a knock at the door to find Kyra, our daughter-in-law, standing on the porch with our two-month-old grandson. She was leaving Colin and she was leaving the baby too. She said, 'I know you and Heather will help Colin take care of the baby.'

That night Kyra phoned Colin to make sure he understood. She was with Jimmy and she wouldn't be coming back. Colin was shattered. 'I trusted him,' he sobbed. 'I trusted him.'

I'm ashamed to remember that because of what happened between our sons, I went ten years without seeing my sister. I simply stopped going to see her. Of course Claire could no longer drive so there was no danger of her appearing at our place. I never blamed Claire for what happened; I just said it would feel wrong to visit the house where Jimmy was also living after he'd done what he'd done.

'I don't know what you're talking about,' said Claire.

'Kyra.' It hurt just to say her name aloud.

'Kyra? Jimmy helped her move.' My sister was all righteous

ignorance. 'Well isn't that a most dastardly deed.'

The years slipped by. We spoke on the telephone from time to time. Neither of us ever talked about whether or not Kyra spent any time at Claire's; I couldn't have endured even those telephone calls if I'd thought the woman who had abandoned our sweet little grandson was sitting all comfy and cozy in my sister's living room. The first Christmas after it happened I told Claire I'd like to see her but I couldn't bring Colin's son to Jimmy's house. 'Oh for heaven's sake,' Claire said, but she didn't press the issue. As the years went by it was just easier to find ourselves too busy, and if Nora hadn't moved back to Vancouver, who knows when I'd have seen my sister again.

'It's so good to see you,' Claire said, arriving for that first visit with Nora. As though ten years hadn't slipped away between us.

We never again talked about what had happened between Jimmy and Colin, though I still couldn't bring myself to visit Claire at her home. Thank heavens Nora liked bringing her mother to our house. The first time I went back to Claire's was after she was diagnosed with cancer; it had been eighteen years since my last visit and Jimmy wasn't at home that day.

My nephew had become a stranger to me. Jimmy, my sister's son. He was no longer a little boy, no longer a swaggering youth drinking with his mother to wash away his father's suicide, no longer the young father who'd lost his children and led my son's wife astray. My nephew had become the stooped and prematurely old man who was now holding me and steadying me by the arm.

Be not forgetful to entertain strangers: for thereby some have entertained angels unawares.

'Oh, Jimmy,' I gasped in sudden recognition. 'How are you doing?'

Jimmy took a final drag on his cigarette and dropped it to the ground.

'My mom's dying.' He crushed the cigarette beneath his boot. 'How d'ya think I'm doing?'

- 14 -
NORA

Fred has been asleep since midnight and I know I should get to bed too, but I can't make myself move; if I'm not at the hospital this is the only place I want to be, staring out the apartment window. Even in the middle of the night, even now in the darkest month of the year, I won't have long to wait before a shape emerges from the dark, a figure hunched over against the cold, hurrying to the shelter of home. When one appears I'll follow the silent figure with my eyes until it glides out of range of my vision, dissolving again into the blackness. I don't need to know who these nameless people are; I don't even want to know them, I'm just grateful they're there. In the distance, across the bay, car lights flicker. More people. Each of us moving through our own dark night. Apart, yet somehow united.

I should sleep, but I can't. It's not just the anxiety of being away from my mother when we have so little time left that keeps me awake, tonight I'm also kind of excited. I want to be back at the hospital first thing in the morning. I'm taking my mom a surprise.

What can you bring a dying woman? She doesn't want food or flowers and she can't have perfume, but today it occurred to me that she'd be missing her music. At home she'd have all those radios on, all tuned to her favourite station, the one that plays the music of the 1940s and 50s. Doris Day, Dean Martin, the music of my mother's dancing days.

Tonight before I left the hospital I went to the nurse's station to ask for permission to bring in a radio. Mom is on the waiting list to be moved to Palliative Care, and as I told the nurse, there she'd be allowed to have a radio. Without glancing up from her paperwork, the nurse lifted her hand to interrupt me. 'Here too. You don't need permission for a radio.'

I'm going to take my Dean Martin and Louis Armstrong CDs as well because the radio has a CD player and even though Mom won't be able to manage them on her own, when I'm there I can play them for her. It's so hard to know if she can still hear what we're saying, or if what she hears makes any sense, but if there's any chance at all I want my mother to know that some of the things she loves are things that I love too. I wasn't eager to admit that for a very long time, not when it seemed so important to impress upon people how different I was from my mother.

'Claire the party-animal,' I'd say. 'Claire and her drinks.' 'Claire and her denial.'

I wanted everyone to know all the ways I wasn't my mother. I was resentful if they should so much as pay me the compliment of saying I had her smile.

What I wouldn't give to redo those years.

This afternoon a nurse paused at the bedside where I sat holding Mom's hand. 'You have your mother's hands,' she said. 'Even the same nail polish.'

Last week Mom and I had our nails done at a salon. When it began to look like she really wouldn't live beyond a few more months I'd resolved to pamper her as much as I possibly could; I'd informed the school where I teach that I was taking a leave of absence for as long as my mother needed me. For both of us the manicure was our first ever and it was supposed to be just the beginning; I hadn't imagined that within forty-eight hours my mother would be in a hospital bed, febrile and delirious, likely never coming home again.

The manicurist, like the nurse today, remarked on the likeness of our hands. We both have square fat hands, if someone had made such a comment a month ago, that's all I'd have heard. Tonight I look down at my hands and feel a sudden rush of gratitude, for as long as I live I'll look down at my hands and see my mother.

If only she could be here with me tonight, the two of us looking out this window, watching the figures below appear and disappear. She'd approve of those two passing by just now, laughing and talking too loud, oblivious to the cold, warmed, it's clear, by the after-glow from a late-closing bar. Together my mother and I could imagine stories for them. Maybe we'd remember our own ... No, that's wrong. If I could wave a magic wand I'd take my mother to her own home to celebrate Christmas over again, her favourite day of the year.

On Christmas Day Mom and I were in Nanaimo with Fred and

his boys; it had seemed like both the right and the wrong thing to do, which is to say it was complicated, like everything else seems to be these days. What a mess. By Christmas morning my mother was on the phone to Aunt Heather, sobbing, 'I want to go home.'

We never should have gone to Fred's. I told Mom that the day she got her diagnosis.

God, what a day that was. First she tells me she's dying and then she hustles me out the door so that Jimmy won't know that I knew first. How crazy was that? She'd promised to phone just as soon as she'd broken the news to Jimmy. An hour at most, she said. Then I could come back to the house and we'd work things out as a family.

I had no choice, she'd just told me she was dying; it was hardly the time to argue. I drove home in a daze, faster than should have been possible, afraid I might miss her call. There was no phone message when I arrived. Fred didn't even know what was going on; he'd already left for Nanaimo to get the house ready for Christmas.

All I could do was wait for my mother's call. Just like tonight I pulled my stool close to the window, but that day it was still light when I first sat down. And then it was dusk. And then dark. The Friday before Christmas, people passing by on the street below, hugging parcels to their chests, returning from buying presents or receiving them, returning from work or meeting with friends. In the cadence of their movement you could sense the anticipation of joy and surprise. I sat and watched and waited for my mother to telephone.

After three hours I couldn't wait any longer; if she was still with Jimmy she could talk in code. I didn't care, I needed to hear her voice.

The phone rang. And rang and rang. Mom doesn't have an answering machine. The ringing was making me crazy. I couldn't just drive over to her house; she'd told me to wait. I phoned Fred in Nanaimo. He wasn't at home. I phoned Dave.

In the thirty years since Dave and I divorced we've seldom lived close enough to just drop in on each other, but a few years ago Dave and his wife Alana bought a condo here in the West End. Before Fred came into my life I often phoned them when I was feeling a little down and they'd say to come over, Alana every bit as generous as Dave in her welcome. More family, or at least my romantic idea of family, than friends. Even now, especially when Fred is in Nanaimo, I'll sometimes call when I need a little cheering up; by the time I walk the four blocks to their home I often don't even need to talk about whatever it was that was bothering me. Just the fact of them being there when I call is enough.

There's a story I've told many times about Dave being there when I needed someone. For my sixteenth birthday he'd given me my own telephone; this was decades before cell phones and it wasn't even a private line, just an extension wired into my bedroom. On the night I'm remembering—well now it sounds ridiculous— I'd seen a long black insect crawl towards the head of my bed and disappear. I often found bugs or spiders in my bedroom; they came with having a room in the basement, and were just one more reason to be frightened at night. The only difference this time was that I had a telephone. I dialled Dave's number and of course his mother answered. 'Are you aware it's after midnight?' she said, but she got out of bed and took the phone to her son.

It was three blocks from Dave's house to mine. Fifteen minutes later he'd crawled under my bed and captured the intruder, a harmless centipede that he cupped in his palm and delivered outside. I used to say that's why I married Dave, my knight in shining armour. I turn it into a funny story, but it means much more than I let on. Forty years later it was Dave's wife, not his mother, who answered the phone.

'Come over,' she said.

I hesitated, what if Mom called while I was out? Maybe this time Dave and Alana could come to my place. But that never became our routine, initially I suppose because my old apartment was so much smaller than theirs, and the habit has endured.

I walked the four blocks to their apartment. Alana hugged me and handed me a glass of red wine. We found our seats. We talked about our mothers, Alana's gone when she was twelve, Dave's six years ago. When Dave's mother died he was totally distraught and that surprised me; they'd never been close. It was my mother he'd come to for validation.

'I didn't get it,' I said to Dave. 'I never understood what it meant to lose your mother. I'm sorry.'

Mostly we talked about Claire. The wine and the company settled me, but I didn't stay long. There was no voicemail when I got home. I dialled my mother's number and for the next hour redialled every few minutes. When finally she answered around nine o'clock that night she said, 'Oh, Nora! I'm sorry. I forgot to phone you. I was visiting Christine next door and I completely forgot.'

My mother said she'd felt better after talking to Jimmy; he'd reminded her that doctors kept forgetting who they were dealing with. He reminded her that when she'd awoken one day last spring to discover she was unable to control the left side of her face the doctors diagnosed Bell's Palsy. They said it might be a year before her face returned to normal. A month later she was fine.

'Jimmy's right,' she said. 'After my aneurysm they said I'd never be able to leave the house by myself again. Well, how many times did I fly down to Atlanta by myself to visit you? And what about that cruise I took by myself to Alaska? Jimmy's absolutely right, the doctors don't realize they're dealing with Claire McHenry. Maybe I do have cancer, but that's no reason to just lie down and die.'

Jimmy had left almost as soon as he'd gotten the news; he'd had somewhere to be and then the next-door neighbor had called to invite Mom over for a Christmas drink.

'All I had was a club soda,' said Mom.

I told her we didn't have to go to Nanaimo for Christmas; we could stay in town and have dinner with Jimmy and Tina.

'Nonsense,' said my mother.

If only I'd insisted, or at least insisted that we stay in Vancouver, but plans had been made back in early December after Tina insulted my mother. Whatever Tina had said, it was serious enough that Mom swore never to speak to 'that woman' again. Jimmy was caught in the middle; he told Mom she needed to consider the consequences: he'd come downstairs and visit her on Christmas morning, but unless she apologized to Tina, she would be on her own for dinner.

Apologize? For what? Tina was the one who needed to make an apology.

Tina wasn't apologizing.

And so the plan was laid for me to go to Nanaimo a couple of days early to help get Fred's house ready; Mom would come over on Christmas Eve. She couldn't come before that because she was having dinner with Doreen the night before.

But all that was before we knew Mom was dying. Given the tragic change in circumstances I said that of course we'd stay in town and have dinner with Jimmy and Tina. I didn't say, 'Because it'll be our last Christmas dinner ever,' but obviously that's what I meant.

Mom said, 'Nonsense, we're going to Nanaimo. Tina might be acting all nicey-nice, but she still owes me a mighty big apology. And anyway, what if Dr. Nay is right? How many more opportunities will I have to take a little trip?'

Her one concession was that instead of me going on ahead, we'd travel to Nanaimo together on Christmas Eve.

On Christmas Eve Jeffrey, one of Fred's long-time friends, showed up with a guitar, a good omen, I thought, as my mother and I exchanged a smile. When Agnes was still alive we'd always gone to her house for Christmas Eve and while Mom played the piano the rest of us joined in singing carols. But it turned out that *The Little Drummer Boy* and *Silent Night* were not what Fred and Jeffrey had in mind; their their idea of a jolly Christmas was banging out the tunes of the Rolling Stones and the Beatles and the Eagles.

My mother looked at me. 'Oh,' she said. 'It's not very Christmassy. And it's so loud.'

The next morning friends and family arrived for a brunch of crepes and champagne followed by a rowdy *Secret Santa* present exchange based on a complicated game of stealing each other's gifts. This too was a version of something we'd done for Christmases past, something Mom had always loved, but now she was flustered by the noise, by the high-decibel rapid-fire repartee that is part of any feast at Fred's. Even the presents, many of them gag gifts, seemed insensitive under the circumstances.

I sat beside my mother, holding her hand.

'If I could just use a phone somewhere,' she whispered, and I wanted to scream at everyone else to go away.

I couldn't of course; we were the guests. And this, I knew, was a family still struggling to go on: two Christmases ago had been Teresa's last. This was Teresa's house, Teresa's family. Teresa's presence was still so powerfully there, even in her absence. Fred had talked to his boys when we'd learned that my mother had pancreatic cancer, the same cancer that had so recently taken their mother. Would they prefer that Claire and Nora not come for Christmas? The boys said it wasn't a problem, but who really knew what they truly felt? Girls aren't the only ones who try to look after their parents.

There was a phone upstairs in Fred's office. The room was crammed with computers and computer parts, with Fred's papers, with Teresa's papers, with boxes of wrapping paper and ribbons and mounds of craft supplies that had accumulated over the last twenty-odd years. A futon lay on the floor, ever ready for overflow company. It felt like a storage room but at least it was away from the hubbub. Fred hauled an armchair up from the living room, wrapped a blanket around my mother and handed her the telephone before returning to his family.

I followed Fred downstairs, stopping part way to crouch in the stairwell, wanting to allow my mother some privacy while remaining close enough to hear in case she needed help. I was guarding the door at the foot of the stairs to ensure that others wouldn't blunder into our space. I wasn't there to eavesdrop, but of course I couldn't help hearing.

'Tina, Merry Christmas,' I heard her say. She didn't sound

sarcastic. 'I hope it's been everything you wanted.' She sounded friendly. She spoke to Jimmy next and I heard her tell him how it was all very nice in Nanaimo, but people should be at home at Christmas. She said she could hardly wait to see him the next day.

She hung up, then phoned Aunt Heather.

'Oh Heather.' My mother's voice shuddered and she couldn't go on. I heard her take a deep breath. I heard her say, 'I want to go home.' And then she was sobbing.

I couldn't hear my aunt, but I imagined she was crying too. Tears streamed down my own cheeks.

I wanted to go to my mother, but I didn't want her to know I'd been listening. And she'd needed to talk to Heather. I imagined my aunt telling my mother it was okay, to take her time, to catch her breath, there was no hurry to talk. I imagined my aunt telling her she loved her.

'Oh Heather,' my mother sobbed. 'I wet the bed.'

On Christmas Eve we'd given my mother the master bedroom; we were "the overflow," sleeping on the futon in Fred's study. Sometime in the night I'd woken with a start, not knowing what

I'd heard, but realizing I needed to check on my mother. I'd crept downstairs and peeked into the bedroom; she wasn't there. I went to the bathroom door and called softly to ask if she was okay.

She was not okay. I had to wake Fred, had to ask him for fresh sheets for the bed. While I changed the bedding, Fred and my mother sat in the kitchen; over a cup of tea Fred answered Mom's questions about what she might expect in her future based on what he'd learned from caring for Teresa. I was grateful that my mother had such respect for Fred. Of course Mom has always preferred men to women, but in this case Fred had the added authority of his experience at his wife's side while her body failed her in ways that my mother was now having to accept. My mother didn't cry, she asked questions. 'I see,' she said from time to time.

Recently I told a friend that Fred tends not to display much emotion, but he's someone you'd want around in an emergency. Simply, clinically, Fred talked about incontinence, about cognitive confusion, about ways to manage pain. There were bound to be differences between Teresa's experience and hers, but inevitably Claire's body would fail her. It was all part of life. The quilted mattress cover she'd soiled was waterproof, purchased for Teresa during her illness. Not worth giving it a second thought.

'I see,' my mother said again.

I want to stand up now from this stool and wave a magic wand, whisking my mother away to the safety of her own home to make everything right for her last Christmas.

Because everything hadn't been right. I'd crouched at the foot of the stairs on Christmas morning and listened to my mother sobbing, the broken words, the indignity.

'I wasn't even in my own bed.'

- 15 -
CLAIRE

I have a radio! Isn't that grand! I feel like me again. 'It's because they managed to bring down the fever.' That's what the nurse said. Well, I suppose that helped too, but I know darn well the radio helped even more. That radio was a wake-up call, I was ready to give up this world, but it's not my time. I know that now. I've still got things to do. I just needed my music to help me along.

Heather keeps reminding me that Nora brought the radio. 'Nora loves you so much.' My sister must have repeated that ten times today. Worried I hadn't noticed.

I know what she's getting at. After my aneurysm Heather was

always telling me how lucky I was to have Nora for a daughter. 'She was there with you every day in the hospital.' Heather must have said *that* a hundred times. Nora even stayed at the house with me after I went home, even though she'd only just remarried in the springtime. Well, maybe she did; I can't recall. What I do remember is Nora convincing the doctor I'd be better off without Jimmy in the house. Why is she always so hard on Jimmy?

Regardless, Nora's here now and Heather needn't worry that I haven't noticed. She looks so young, asleep on that chair. *Nora Felicity Daughter Three Years Old.* How Buddy loved to tell that story. And now Nora's older than Buddy ever was. I look at her and I still see my little girl though she's fifty-seven years old and there's some grey in that dark hair of hers. Not as much grey as Jimmy has, but then life has always been easier for Nora. No wonder people keep telling me she looks ten years younger than her brother and not the other way around. A fancy-free life, hopping from romance to romance.

Still, that's quite the thing, her bringing in Dean Martin and Louis Armstrong. You're right, Louis, it *is* a wonderful world.

And I do love my daughter. I know this has been hard on her.

I told her: 'Go home to Fred. Get some sleep.' I could see she wasn't going to leave until she thought I was settled down for the night, so I pretended to be asleep. My little girl was so tired, she dozed off herself and now I find myself watching her there, wondering who she is. If she really was so good to me when I had my aneurysm, why did she run off and leave me a year later?

But she cried when I told her I was going to die. I can't remember the last time I saw my daughter cry. Well, I suppose she gets that from me; I figured out a long time ago that crying doesn't get you anywhere.

Good Lord, I was what? Twenty-one? It had taken all my nerve to walk inside that grimy little office, but what choice did I have? Earl was never going to be the one to file for divorce. Why would he? So long as we were legally married he could chase women, gamble and empty my bank account any time he pleased. It was up to me to take care of things.

I started off by telling … What *was* that man's name? I see him clear as day. His hair plastered down with Brylcreem. Lizard eyes and hands like bear paws … Krept! That's it. Mr. Krept. I started off by telling Mr. Krept about how I'd already moved back home to Mom's before Nora was born, but then Earl bumped into Uncle Slim at the horse races and found out I was in hospital having his baby. Well it was bad enough him waltzing in at the last minute as if he still had the right, but what man would show up in the maternity ward with another woman and try to pass her off to the hospital staff as my mother! Did he think they were idiots? Agnes was already in the room with me and the nurse came in demanding to know what was going on. Well, Mom lit out of the room and caught Earl and his "mother-in-law" looking in at the babies, but they took off before she could give them a piece of her mind. Telling that lawyer the story I started to cry.

Hell's bells, I feel my face getting red all over again, after all this time. Mr. Krept raised one of those great big hands, palm faced toward me. 'Stop, Mrs. Ryan. You've been misinformed. I'm a divorce lawyer, not a nanny.'

I said I was sorry and he snapped right back at me that he was a busy man; he didn't have time for sorry. 'If you're here to blubber about life being unfair, there's the door. If you want to divorce your husband, let's get down to business.' He said I wouldn't have to pay him a penny; he'd collect his fees from my husband. I told him Earl didn't pay bills and he said, 'I offered you a deal. You stop crying, I'll take care of your husband.'

Oh, there's times I've wondered just what he meant by that. *Take care of your husband.* But the man kept his part of the bargain; I never had to pay a penny for the divorce. And I learned a lesson. I made it in a man's world when women weren't welcome and I sure as hell didn't do it by turning on the waterworks like some of the women would do.

Tears never get you anywhere worth going; Nora learned that part, but she never understood what fairness means for a woman in a man's world. Buddy should be doing his "fair" share of the housework. What did I care about that? *Equal pay for equal work?* That was a slogan people like Nora bandied about. They could talk all they wanted but equal doesn't necessarily mean fair. And even if it did there's no such thing as equal in this world, for men or women.

Nothing was ever equal for Jimmy. People warned me from the time he was born: *He's a boy. You can't expect him to be as well-behaved as Nora.* They still compared him though, didn't they? Still pointed out it was no surprise he never took to school. *Well, he's no Nora*, they said when he barely scraped through. When Jimmy was seventeen I bought him a van. Didn't I hear about that? 'You spoil that boy,' said Buddy. 'We never bought a car for Nora.'

Of course we didn't, when Nora was a teenager we didn't have the same kind of money. Circumstances change, but that didn't matter to Buddy. Besides, everything came easy for Nora; she never had to struggle like her brother. All the neighbours wanted her to babysit; and she was only in grade eleven when she started working weekends at SuperValu and earning union wages. Nora always had her own money; she never needed our help.

And then she just threw away all those advantages. Honours student of her high school graduating class and what did she do with that? Years going to university and where did it get her? Working clerical jobs she could have done with a grade ten education. My poor mother was heart-broken; she used to tell everyone that Nora was going to be a teacher. That had been Agnes's own dream before her father lost his job over the coal mining strike and the family had to move to Vancouver and Agnes had to drop out of school to help her mother run a boarding house.

Well that's how life unfolds, isn't it. In ways we can't control.

Honestly, the two of them, my mother and my daughter, both wasting their lives fretting about what *should* have been. All her life Agnes believed she *should* have had Robert for her father; she *should* have been allowed to finish school and become a teacher; and when that didn't happen, Nora *should* have taken up the dream. For both of them. Mom was so darn sure that if Robert had lived to marry her mother he'd have built an empire as big as Dunsmuir's. 'He'd never have stayed down in the mines,' she said. 'He'd have owned them.' Well, if he'd owned those mines it's damn sure her mother wouldn't have run a boarding house in Vancouver and Agnes would never have met Magnus. Now *that* is something worth being sorry about.

And Nora with all her *shoulds* about equality and justice and husbands, fretting about all the things that she couldn't make perfect, and then the things she *could* do something about she just throws away. Mom was right about Nora and teaching; from the time Nora learned to read all she wanted to do was play school. Not once did I have to tell her to do her homework; there was nothing she loved better. So tonight when she said right out of the blue that teaching English to foreign students is the only job she's ever loved, I couldn't help asking the obvious. Why did she wait so long? With all the opportunities she had, why wait until her fifties? Why hadn't she been a teacher all along?

She said, 'I was afraid.'

'For heaven's sake—' She'd never failed at anything.

She said, 'I was afraid I wouldn't be able to handle the kids who didn't fit in.'

I'd have thought she meant the wild ones, rebellious teenagers, maybe boys like Jimmy, but that wasn't it. She said it would have been the ones who were always standing by themselves that scared her, the ones never picked for the baseball team at recess; she'd have wanted to smother them with love, but she knew if she did they'd have even less chance of being accepted by the others.

Why does my daughter always have to make things so complicated? I wanted to tell her that she thinks too much, that the whole world isn't her responsibility, that we only do what we can. I wanted to say that sometimes bad things happen even when we try to do the right thing. That's just life. I wanted to say all that, but I didn't quite have the words arranged in my mind, the way they are now, and I was suddenly afraid I might say something to hurt her feelings.

'For heaven's sake,' I'd said a moment before, but for once Nora hadn't seemed to notice. I've always been quick to say what's on my mind, but tonight I stopped myself. I didn't know what else to say, so I closed my eyes and pretended I'd fallen asleep. In the hospital no one is offended if you nod off.

It occurred to me that maybe Nora was saying that *she* was the child left out. I know she was never good at sports, but did she have to be the best at everything she did? She was always the top student in her class and pretty as a button too. At fourteen she had a steady boyfriend, and a good one at that. Men always noticed her. I remember that time when she'd come up for a visit from Atlanta and we'd had such a lovely afternoon walking out at Jericho Beach and then we'd stopped for an ice cream somewhere on Fourth Avenue. The owner was older than me. Italian. When he brought our ice cream he said, 'Your daughter has very beautiful smile. Like movie star.' Nora was in her thirties then, and even though I should have known better, I couldn't help myself. 'Just like me,' I said. 'Yes, yes,' he said, looking at Nora.

I wonder if Nora remembers the Italian. I opened my eyes to

ask her but she wasn't in her chair anymore; she was at the foot of the bed adjusting the blankets around my feet.

'Was I sleeping?'

Nora smiled—she really does have a lovely smile—and she asked if there was anything she could bring me. 'Chocolate ice cream,' I blurted out, remembering the Italian. Nora hurried off to the cafeteria and when all they had was vanilla, ran all the way to the grocery store. I felt bad when she returned with the chocolate ice cream and I could only manage a spoonful; I guess it'll take a little time to get my appetite back. I should have expected that after New Year's Day.

That was a shock when I couldn't eat a thing on New Year's. The four of us sitting down to dinner: Jimmy and me, Nora and Fred. I'd been so looking forward to that meal. Jimmy cooked the turkey upstairs, Nora brought the pumpkin pie and mincemeat tarts and that left me with just the vegetables to prepare. A real family affair. Of course Tina was supposed to be there too, but wasn't it just like her to send Jimmy down at the last minute to say she wasn't up to joining us. Naturally I had the table set for five, but poor little Miss developed a headache just in time for supper.

Jimmy had to load up a plate of food and take it to her upstairs. You'd think *she* was the one who was dying.

Well, I shouldn't complain too much because it *was* nice not to have her at the table; we'd have had to hear her story all over, just like every other time she's graced us with her presence. *Oh poor little me, my mother was on drugs and we had to live in alleyways and get our meals out of garbage bins.* Then she'd have gone on again about how she was put into a bath of scalding water and her legs were scorched to a third-degree burn. Yes, it's tragic, but does she always have to yank up her skirt to show off those skinny little legs? One time I'd had enough and said I hadn't realized alleyways were so luxurious. They came furnished with bathtubs and hot-running water, did they? Jimmy was furious with me and the next time I saw Tina I had to say I was sorry if I hurt her feelings. I thought it was too bad the hot water left her with such thin skin she couldn't handle a little bit of a joke. But I stopped myself from saying that. I've learned to be careful with Jimmy's girlfriend. So when she didn't come down for dinner I was ticked off and grateful at the same time. I had my family: Nora and Jimmy. And Fred, but I like Fred.

Nora gave a little blessing and for a minute I thought everything was about as perfect as it could be. Then I took one bite of my dinner and I thought I'd be sick. I just couldn't make myself eat another forkful. I said I must have snacked too much while I was cooking, but the truth is, I hadn't eaten all day. It was hard to stay at the table with all that food piled up in front of me, but I wasn't about to walk away just because I'd suddenly realized that I actually was dying. That would be Tina's way, not mine.

And now I see that I *wasn't* dying, I was just sick.

'You've had a fever,' the doctor said this morning. 'Now that it's broken I expect you'll feel considerably better.'

Imagine, Claire McHenry ready to give up just because a bit of fever put her off her turkey dinner! Oh Magnus, what would you have said to that? Remember the summer before grade eight when you told me I couldn't join the ski team that winter if I didn't stop stuttering? I suppose I'd been stuttering since I learned to talk, but I wanted to be part of that ski team and I knew you were serious. So I stopped stuttering. If I want something, I just put my mind to it. This morning when I told the doctor I wanted to go home now he said let's see if we can get you eating a little before we think about that. Won't he be surprised when he sees me waving goodbye.

Well I don't want to wake Nora now, but I'm sure that by tomorrow I'll be ready for ice cream. I'll be ready to go home in a couple of days and that sounds pretty darn good to me. I wonder if the first snowdrops have popped up yet. And I've had so little time to enjoy my tree and sit before a winter fire ... It's time I took charge of my house again. I'll insist that Reg get rid of Bones. I want that dog gone before I get home. I'll tell Jimmy ... Good God, look at me, I'm almost giddy with excitement. I'm not done yet. No Peggy Lee, that's not all there is. Not for Claire McHenry.

Look at Nora sleeping there. When's the last time I saw my little girl asleep? Maybe she could come and stay with me for a few days when I get home. Didn't she sleep over a couple of days ago? When was that? I don't know how long I've been here. I could ask Nora, but I want my baby to sleep.

I am glad they put me in this bed next to the window. I think I see a star out there. I do miss my backyard at night. Going out to look up at the stars. That's what I loved best about skiing, that long trek down Grouse Mountain coming home in the dark. Nowadays people just jump from their cars into the gondola but back then skiing was only half the adventure. First it was getting up in the morning before it was even light so that we could catch the Number 17 streetcar to Victory Square; then we had to really hustle from there to catch the ferry across Burrard Inlet; then another bus to the top of Lonsdale; and after all that still a three-hour hike up the mountain. No chairlifts or rope tows in those days. You skied down and then you hiked back up for the next run.

Didn't I just love the sting of the cold on my face! The speed of the downhill, the dips and turns and almost feeling like an athlete, though Lord knows I was never a very good skier. But the part I truly adored was coming home in the dark, hiking down the dark mountain with our homemade lanterns held high. We'd have made our little lanterns at the start of the season, punching nail holes into the sides of jam tins. Empress Jam. Lord that was beautiful, the candlelight flickering through the sides of the tin, guiding us home. Poor little Heather, she'd be so worried about me. 'Are you sure there's enough wax left? What if the candle blows out and you can't find your way home?' I told her I'd carry breadcrumbs like Hansel and Gretel. 'But what if it snows while you're skiing and by the time you want to come home the breadcrumbs are all buried?'

I wonder why I never thought to make lanterns for my garden. Oh, it will be so good to be home. I'll teach Jimmy and Nora how to make lanterns out of jam tins.

Yes Mr. Armstrong, it is a wonderful world and I'm not done by a long shot. No siree, not by a long shot.

- 16 -
NORA

I was dreaming. A recurring dream I've had so many times I can't tell anymore if it was always a dream or if once it really did happen. I'm about four years old, my mother and I are in a warehouse, surrounded by long rows of green steamer trunks stacked one on top of another, several deep. Mom hoists me up, sets me down on one of the trunks. 'You stay right here. I'll be back as quick as I can.' She's happy. She says, 'These men will keep an eye on you.'

The men—there are eight or ten of them in sleeveless white undershirts—are sprawled about on packing crates and stepladders, smoking and laughing. I'm wearing my blue velvet party-dress with a white silk sash and my black patent shoes and I'm terrified. What if she never comes back? What if she comes back too late?

I follow her with my eyes as long as I can, my mother swirling away in her red skirt and scoop-necked blouse. At the end of the aisle she pirouettes, blows me a kiss and disappears. I have no choice but to stay where I am, perched on the trunk with the men in their undershirts laughing: 'You're such a pretty little thing!'

I don't feel pretty, I feel afraid. I stay on the trunk, stay in the dream, stay where I am until at long last my mother reappears, humming, swooping me up in her arms, flashing a grin of thanks at the men clustered around us.

But this time something is different, something subtle that takes a minute to register. This time my mother is not humming, she's singing.

'Mommy!' I reach out my arms for her to lift me down. 'Mommy!'

I wake up, disoriented and confused. I'm not in the dream anymore. It takes a moment to comprehend that I'm in the hospital room and my mother is singing to me, telling me to hold my head up high. How could she have seen into my dream?

Propped up by her pillows she is almost in a sitting position though her eyes are closed. Tears stream down her cheeks.

I tiptoe to the bed, not wanting to startle her but wanting her to know I am near. Faintly but clearly, verse by verse, my mother is singing for me *The Bluebird of Happiness.*

I stroke my fingers lightly over the back of her hand and she opens her eyes.

'Oh Nora! Magnus was here.'

My heart lurched in panic. I've heard so many stories of the dying seeing their departed loved ones when their own time is near, the spirits come from afar to lead them home. I'm not ready for that, especially after Mom seemed so much better today, after the fever had broken. She'd talked about going home to her house on Drayton Street. Fred has warned me of false reprieves, how the day before his wife died she'd suddenly become convinced her cancer was cured and had wanted to get up and work in the garden.

My mother slipped her hand from beneath mine, gave mine a

little squeeze. 'I'd been remembering candles and then Dad was here whistling *The Bluebird of Happiness.*'

She squeezed my hand again and sang a line from the song, a line about light creeping through.

'Sweetie, when I get home I'm going to teach you how to make tin-can lanterns. We'll punch nail holes in the sides. That's how the light gets through. That's why Magnus was here, to remind me to teach you about happiness.'

Now I was crying. Was it because my mother still had tears on her cheeks? Or was it because I so desperately wanted to believe in the light?

My mother lifted her hand to brush away my tears. 'Promise me,' she said, 'you'll look for the bluebird of happiness.'

'And I promise,' I said, making a joke, 'I'll always hang the toilet paper so it rolls down the front of the roll.'

She cocked her head, a little wrinkle forming on her brow. This was not the Claire of the swirling red skirt flashing a grin for the men. This was Claire without her bright red lipstick; her lips, without her teeth to give them shape, sagging inward, parched and shrunken.

'How else would you do it?' she asked, confused.

'You're right,' I said. 'How else would you?'

She couldn't remember what I can never forget, the night I hung the toilet paper in her bathroom upside down, the free end of the tissue against the wall, the way I preferred. I'd just assumed that's how she liked it too.

We'd had our nails done the day before and in the evening when I was leaving to go home Mom had said, 'Tomorrow I need a day to myself.'

She's always claimed we're alike that way, that we both need time to be alone. I could never see it. I saw my mother's partying, saw her drinking with Jimmy and his friends, saw her calling up neighbours on a whim to take them out to dinner, her constant need to be surrounded by people. She'd phone wanting me to come over; I'd say I couldn't, I was behind on an editing contract I'd accepted to supplement my income, I was scrambling to put together a lesson plan. My mother would point out that *she'd* always worked plenty of over-time but that hadn't stopped her from having a life too. I'd give in and agree to come by for a couple of hours, but even on the occasions when I allowed the visit to stretch into six or seven hours, it was never long enough for my mother. For years I struggled against her demands on my time, guilty if I resisted, resentful when I gave in. She seemed insatiable, all the while claiming she needed time alone. Now that she was dying and I was hungry to be with her, she needed space from me.

She said she'd call me the next day. Life had been intense for both of us since that night in Canadian Traditions; we'd have to learn to pace ourselves. My mother suggested that maybe I shouldn't come over for a couple of days. Maybe, as the doctor said, she had only two or three months left to live; or maybe Jimmy was right and she'd be around for a lot longer than that. Regardless, she had always been an independent woman and no matter that now all I wanted was to protect and pamper her, I needed to respect who she was.

So I said okay and I left. The next day I went for a long walk on the seawall and thought of all the places I wanted to take my mother when the weather warmed a little. Walks along Jericho Beach, fish and chips at Steveston Pier, the tulip festival in

Washington State. That would be more than two months away, but like Jimmy, I believed Claire McHenry would beat the odds. I didn't expect it to be years, but surely months. I went home and waited for her phone call.

By seven o'clock that night I could wait no longer.

'I can't find the potatoes,' she said, answering the phone.

Potatoes?

'I can't imagine what happened to them.'

The potatoes have always been kept in the cold room, a windowless concrete space under the front stairs built to store canned fruit and produce from the vegetable garden. Now that Mom lives in the basement she mostly uses the room to store her kitchen staples. Boxes of cereal, cans of tuna, rice. Potatoes.

I suggested Jimmy might have "borrowed" the potatoes. Jimmy has always, without feeling the need to ask, helped himself to whatever it pleases him to take from his mother's kitchen stores.

My mother said, 'Oh dear, I need to get dressed, it's already late.' She said she was still in her nightgown. That wasn't like her at all; others might lounge about the house in their pyjamas but my mother had always believed the minute you got up you got dressed. Today she hadn't, which worried me, and I couldn't really follow much of her conversation, which kept looping back to potatoes.

I couldn't tell her I was worried, she wouldn't have liked that. I said I missed her, I said I'd gotten used to seeing her every day. I was staring at the toy locomotive; Winnnie-the-Pooh and Tigger stared back at me with their big innocent smiles. I asked my mother if I could come over. I wouldn't stay long, I just really needed a hug.

'Oh, would you?' Her voice sounded weak, the voice of a frightened old woman. 'Maybe,' she said, 'you could help me find the potatoes.'

I packed a nightgown, hoping she'd let me stay. When I got to the house I knocked, then let myself in with the key she had given me just two days before. 'In case of emergency.'

I found my mother in her bed. I sat on the edge of the bed and told her how much I'd been missing her all day.

'Yes,' she said. 'I've missed you too.'

She closed her eyes and seemed to be sleeping; when she

opened her eyes a minute later she was surprised to see me. 'Nora!'

'I love you,' I said.

She smiled. 'I can't seem to find the potatoes.'

I told her I'd take a look and had just opened the cold room door when Jimmy appeared at the foot of the stairs.

'Hey Sis, how's she doing?'

'I'm worried.'

He said, 'I told her she needs to get up. That's not *my* mom, lying around in bed all day.' He called into her room: 'Hey lazybones, time to get up 'n at 'em.'

'Yes, dear.' I could hear the strain in the feebleness, the strain of trying to sound strong for her son. 'You're right. Up and at 'em.'

Jimmy raised his eyebrows, shrugged his shoulders. 'Just came down to pick somethin' up.'

The liquor cabinet is kitty-corner to the door of the cold room; as Jimmy reached for a bottle I asked if he knew anything about the potatoes.

'Shit,' he said. 'That woman can't remember a damn thing I tell her.'

He pushed past me and into our mother's room. I watched him

bend down to kiss her. 'Hey you lazy old bat, how many times I gotta tell you I'll get you potatoes tomorrow?'

He straightened up and headed for the stairway. 'Got company upstairs,' he said to me. 'I'll see you later.'

Mom was sleeping when I walked back into her room. I stood motionless, unsure if it would be better to perch quietly on the edge of the bed so that should she wake she'd know I was near, or should I silently back away? I was almost afraid to breathe, afraid I might wake her.

My bedroom had been in this basement in the days before it became Mom's living quarters. Now instead of a cement floor, bare light bulbs and exposed beams, there was carpeting, wallpaper and rooms crowded with furniture that had once filled the upstairs, but beneath the trappings of domestic comfort the basement ghosts were stirring.

Lots of children are afraid of basements, but I had been truly utterly terrified. At night I'd pull the blankets over my head, convinced a man lay in wait outside my door, a knife in his hand. I'd sense him entering the room. I'd try to lay bone still. *Please God, let him think I'm already dead.* I could feel the man standing at my bedside, knife poised, waiting for a telltale sign I was only pretending to be dead. If I dared breathe he would carve me into little pieces.

I've spent my life escaping from that basement, from the man with the knife who was only a figment of my imagination, and from the other man who was not a figment and didn't need a knife to leave his mark. I was in my thirties before I was finally able to talk about Richard, my Uncle Bob's friend, the man who came into my bedroom every night from the time I was eleven until he moved away when I was thirteen. It's only in the last few years that I've felt safe enough to admit to the recurring fears that have followed me, overwhelmed me even, for long periods of time. Those who now know about Richard often assume *that* also explains the fear, but it's not that simple. Whatever damage Richard may have caused, I was never afraid of him.

Richard was real and I came to think of him with the range of emotions a real person can evoke: anger and revulsion and confusion. And eventually, when I was very much older, compassion. He was the kindest man in a house that over the years sheltered many men—Buddy, Uncle Bob, friends of Uncle Bob,

Jimmy—yet he was also the one who taught me shame. I wanted him for a father; he wanted me for a lover. He believed he loved me; I believed he loved me, too, but in a way that made me want to die. Caught in the tangle of Richard's confused and dangerous affection I learned to perform a kind of balancing act with men. A flawed balancing act, I'm aware: four husbands and four divorces does seem to indicate something at least a little off kilter. Still, I always knew that Richard never wanted to harm me.

The dread that stalked me through my adult life did not flow from Richard's sexually misguided attentions; he was only a man, and in time I learned, as many women do, how to live with that kind of danger. Even after I'd married and moved away I was haunted not by Richard so much as by the imaginary faceless presence. If my husband (whichever husband) wasn't sleeping right next to me I relived the terror I'd felt in the basement. I never slept peacefully alone through the night until after I'd divorced for the last time and had moved to the 18th floor of an apartment building in Vancouver's West End.

My fantasy when I was a child living in my basement bedroom was that one day I'd live in a house like those in the storybooks where children climb the stairs at night to their beautiful safe bedrooms. Mother and Father follow to tuck them in and kiss them gently and wish them sweet dreams before returning down the stairs to the gracious living room, the crackling fire and a night of quiet reading. From time to time the murmur of gentle voices wafts up the stairwell, a reassurance of shelter and protection.

My apartment on the 18th floor, so high above the street, felt a bit like the house I'd dreamt of, and then when Fred and I rented a new apartment together on the fifth floor of another building I discovered the fifth floor was even better, high enough to feel safe, low enough to take comfort from the rustle of voices rising from the street below. A few months ago I realized that my feelings for the basement had finally shifted; I was able to visit my mother in her home without always feeling the old sense of dread. I'd thought the ghosts had finally departed.

But as I stood at the edge of my mother's bedroom I felt them again, the ghosts of all the people who had lived in that basement, the imaginary and the real. My heart ached for the child I had been, for that terrified little girl who was so eager to please, but also for the adults who, it now seemed to me, had just been stumbling through their own lives the best way they knew how. Sometimes showing affection in the wrong ways, unaware of the damage they caused. Sometimes so lost they didn't know how to show any affection at all. I'd wanted to feel safe, to feel sheltered and protected. But what about those people who were supposed to be the adults? What fears had haunted them?

My mother stirred. 'Jimmy?'

I touched her cheek. 'No, Mom, it's me.'

'Oh.'

Did she know who 'me' was? Should I tell her? Risk offending her?

She asked, 'Did you just get here?'

I said it hadn't been long. I told her the time and she said she wanted to get up to watch the news. In the living room I helped her into her recliner and tucked an afghan shawl around her shoulders. Mom had made shawls for most of her friends and for all of the women connected to the family, even Tina. This one was a pattern of green circles linking white and yellow daisies.

'I wandered lonely as a cloud,' I said softly, reminded by the yellow flowers of a poem my mother used to recite.

Without missing a beat she picked it up now. '*That floats on high o'er vales and hills, When all at once I saw a crowd, A host, of golden daffodils.*'

Mom had always been so good at remembering the lyrics to songs, but as far as I could recall she'd only ever recited from two poems, both by Wordsworth: this one about daffodils, and the other one where we come *trailing clouds of glory*. It scared me to think of that second poem, it was too close. I wanted to thank my mother for teaching me the daffodil poem but she shushed me sharply.

'The news.'

Any other time I'd have been offended, now I was almost pleased. A hint of the old Claire that quickly faded under the relentless pressure to engage with the worlds' problems. She said, 'They talk so fast. I can't understand what they're saying.'

I was having a hard time following the stories as well. Drug companies were more interested in profits than people. Was this suddenly news? My mother was dying. What did I care about elections or assassinations in distant countries? The newscast advances through "hard news" to "human interest": a dark spiral was observed descending from the clouds above Prince Edward Island; a couple had filmed it for more than half an hour. Neither Environment Canada nor the Transportation Safety Board was able to identify the phenomenon.

I wondered if the descending spiral had spoken to my mother as well, but she'd fallen asleep again, her jaw sagging open. All of my mother's teeth had been pulled when she was thirty; within a few weeks she'd adapted to the upper dentures but the lower ones never felt comfortable. This was around the time Jimmy was born; having neither the time nor the money to be running back and forth to the dentist, Mom had simply gotten used to having no bottom teeth. It had never stopped her from eating what she wanted, including steak. She was, after all, Claire McHenry.

We all simply got used to seeing her like that; it seemed so perfectly normal that I was surprised when she came back from her fiftieth high-school graduation reunion, imitating in a high squeaky voice the witless woman who'd said aloud: 'Oh, but you have no bottom teeth.'

'I should have told her, *Oh, but you have no brains*,' said my mother.

Instantly I'd bristled, hating that woman, but Mom said she didn't merit another thought, no one else had ever noticed her missing teeth; it was that woman's problem, not hers. Now my mother was asleep, her open mouth revealing her secret, and again I found myself hating that horrible woman who had been so rude to my mother.

My mother opened her eyes. 'Oh dear, I think I fell asleep.'

In hockey news the sportscaster was breathlessly recounting another shutout by the local hero.

'It's very loud, isn't it?' said Mom.

And in a moment: 'I think I might be ready for bed.'

Her new tentativeness unnerved me.

I settled her into bed and sat down in the living room to read. I couldn't concentrate. I turned off all the lights except for those on the Christmas tree. At the top of the tree was the new angel, the one we'd found the night this all started, the night my mother and I, and Winnie-The-Pooh and Tigger sang *We Wish You A Merry Christmas*. I recalled how my mother had shared her news when she returned from the doctor a week later: *Next year you can have the angel. Next year I won't be here.* Tomorrow it would be two weeks since she'd told me she had only two months to live.

I don't know how long I sat staring at the angel; at some point I heard Jimmy's friends exchanging boisterous good-nights and wondered if Jimmy would remember saying he'd come downstairs to visit.

He didn't come down. I didn't go up. Eventually I made my bed on the sofa, leaving the tree lights on. In each of her hands the angel held a miniature light-bulb candle. This angel with her gold gown and its trim of white fur, with her feather wings and the soft tilt of her head, had become such an intimate part of our journey, to extinguish her light would have seemed like an admission of defeat.

There's a little girl; I think she might be around five years old. She is surrounded by a flock of chickens but I can't tell if the expression on her face is one of awe or fear. I hesitate. If I run to rescue her will I be snatching her from a magical experience, or freeing her from terror? The anxiety I feel turns to dread. To do the wrong thing feels like a matter of life and death.

I wake up, look at my watch. It is 3:33 a.m. and I'm on the sofa in my mother's basement suite. The dread moves from the dream into my waking life. I rise to check on my mother.

There's a night-light in the bedroom; from the doorway I see her sitting on the edge of the mattress. I can't tell if she's returning to bed or just getting up.

'Mom…'

I go to her and sit carefully on the bed by her side.

'I have to get up,' she says. She doesn't move. 'Oh dear.'

'Do you need a hand?'

'Oh.' She looks at me, as if surprised I'm there. 'Oh,' she says again. 'I have to go to the bathroom.'

Again I offer to help.

It seems a long time before she answers. 'Yes, but I'm not ready.'

Another long pause before she sighs. 'Oh dear. I need a minute.'

I wait.

'I have to get up,' she says, not moving.

I put my hand under her elbow to lend support and she panics: 'No! I'm not ready.'

It takes us half an hour to move from the bed to the ensuite bathroom, to get her settled on the toilet.

'Don't leave,' she says.

'I'm here.'

I look away, preserving a tiny decorum.

'Oh,' she says. And then: 'What's wrong?'

I hear the rising confusion in her voice. I'm squatting on the floor next to her on the other side; I glance up, see her touch her hand to the paper to roll off the pieces she needs. The paper won't roll down. 'Oh,' she says again. And tries again.

I see the problem. Earlier that night I'd replaced the toilet paper, mounting it on the roller the way I always have, the way (I would have said) my mother taught me. I tell her now, 'You have to pull the paper from underneath.'

'But I always do it this way.' She tries again, but the paper won't roll down.

I apologize; I hadn't realized that I'd put the toilet paper on wrong.

She tries to unroll the paper towards her again; still she can't get the pieces to unroll. I explain again what I've done, how I've mounted the roll the other way around, but she can't follow my explanation. 'But I always do it this way,' she repeats. She tries. And tries again. Each time becoming more perplexed. Refusing my help. Redoubling her focus on this problem that is defeating her.

It takes most of an hour to finish in the bathroom, to get my mother back to bed.

In the morning I called the doctor to ask if I could bring my mother to see him. He listened as I recounted the events of the evening.

'Call the ambulance,' he said. 'I'll meet you in Emergency.'

- 17 -
HEATHER

I was at the entrance to her room this afternoon when I heard laughter. The procedure must have worked! Claire's dear friend Doreen was with her and Claire was back! Of course she's going home, she's Claire.

As I moved to join them the woman in the adjacent bed caught my attention, beckoning me closer with a crook in her finger. She'd arrived overnight and looked a hundred years old, a few little wisps of hair on her tiny head. When she spoke her voice was so weak I had to lean over very close to hear.

'A party,' she whispered. 'It's a party.'

A little laughter was hardly a raucous party, yet perhaps to someone that frail the laughter was a nerve-wracking jangle. Well, surely Claire deserved a little happiness. I'd felt myself bristle, but a pastor's wife learns to keep things inside. I said gently that the laughter wouldn't last long; the woman on the other side of the curtain was my sister; her visitor was her very best friend and it had been a very long time since anyone in this room had been moved by laughter.

'Oh no, you have it wrong.' The woman's face crinkled in a toothless smile. 'I love parties.' Her eyes squinched closed when she smiled, as if her wizened little face could manage only one feature at a time. Her eyes stayed closed as she struggled for a breath.

Now I felt bad, the little dear hadn't been complaining at all. She exhaled and opened her eyes. 'I used to have friends too,' she whispered. 'Lots of friends. We'd laugh and laugh...'

Now I wanted to cry. Who was this woman? Where were *her* loved ones? Why was she all alone? Would she like me to pull back the curtain and introduce her to my sister? Claire was having a good day. She wouldn't mind.

'Oh no, dear,' she said. 'I'm too tired to meet any more people.'

She stopped, closed her eyes, found another breath. 'Please thank them for their laughter. That's how I want to go, surrounded by the sound of laughter.'

Her eyes, briefly opened, were closed again. She seemed frail as a butterfly, as if she'd crumble at a touch.

'I'll tell them,' I said, lingering. My hands were trembling—the Parkinson's, everything that had been happening to my sister over the last few days, fear lest I injure this dear little soul, and yet how could I not at least stroke a finger against her hand, show her she still had a friend, no matter how fleetingly?

I held my breath, willing my hand to stop shaking. My finger against her skin was the lightest briefest touch, but it sent a shudder through my body. For a glancing flash I was looking at my own mother. Just as quickly, the unknown person returned to who she was, a little soul longing for laughter.

'My name is Heather,' I said.

'Evelyn,' she whispered.

She hadn't opened her eyes and I waited to see if she'd say anything more. She didn't and I didn't move; so long as I remained behind the curtain, concealed from view, Doreen and Claire might continue laughing. Like Evelyn I wanted to soak up the sound, to fill up the empty aching places with laughter.

Through the curtain I heard Doreen say, 'These days no one would dare.'

Then Claire's voice: 'They'd be horrified.' Followed by another round of merriment.

I had no idea what they were talking about, but I thought Claire's joyful laughter was just about the most beautiful sound I'd ever heard. For the last week she'd scarcely managed more than a mumble.

I heard her saying, 'Our daughters would have smuggled in water.'

That set the two of them off again, Claire giggling and Doreen in a full peal of laughter. I looked down at Evelyn. Did I detect the flicker of another smile? I couldn't tell, but I wanted to believe that if this dear wee lady really was going to die soon, the last sound she'd hear on this earth would be my sister's laughter.

I peeked around the corner of the curtain. Doreen had her back to me and Claire was focussed only on Doreen. Neither had sensed I was there.

Doreen said, 'Remember when you'd come over to my place when Buddy was working and Rod was out of town and we'd roll up the carpet and switch on the jukebox and dance all night.'

Claire started singing *Only You,* the old Platters tune, and Doreen raised her arms to embrace an imaginary dance partner, swaying as she moved her feet to the music. Now Doreen and Claire were singing together, filling their hearts, my heart, and by the look of the growing smile on her face, dear little Evelyn's heart, with love.

Twirling, Doreen spied me behind the curtain.

'Heather!' She swept me up in a hug. 'Isn't it wonderful! Our Claire is back!'

Doreen stepped back from the hug. I'd started to cry. 'Dance with me,' Doreen said, taking one of my hands and leading me into the room. '*Only you* …' she sang, stepping in, raising her hand high, twirling me around.

Well of course I was awkward—people with Parkinson's don't make the best dancers—still I would have kept dancing just to keep Claire singing, but Doreen didn't try to twirl me a second time; she led me to sit in a chair beside Claire's bed.

I took Claire's hand in mine; Doreen stood at my side, a hand on my shoulder. It felt good to be included.

'You know, Heather,' Doreen said, 'Claire is my very best friend.'

Every time we meet Doreen tells me that Claire is her very best friend and always will be. And then, as though I'd never heard the story before, she'll recall how her first husband left her with three children and no money and it was her neighbour, Claire, who came to her rescue. Claire had dropped by for a visit and Doreen started to cry because she didn't have any coffee to offer; she couldn't even afford to buy cereal for her children. My lovely generous sister opened her purse there and then, handed Doreen one hundred dollars and told her to go grocery shopping; she'd look after the children. One hundred dollars seems like an awful lot of money for anyone to have had in their purse in 1960, but that's always the way Doreen tells it. 'One hundred dollars.'

And then the story Doreen loves to tell even more, how if it weren't for Claire she'd never have ended up marrying Rod Macdonald, her great true love. She'd been on her own for a couple of years when Rod, a lawyer she'd worked for briefly, phoned to ask her out on a date. Doreen had three young children, the youngest a six-year-old boy in a cast from the waist down to correct a congenital defect. She'd never get a babysitter. Well, once again Claire happened to be in Doreen's kitchen at just the right moment. Claire overheard Doreen turning Rod down and called out plenty loud enough for Rod to hear: 'Of course she'll go out with you. I'll look after the kids.' That date led to a life Doreen had only imagined in her dreams; it seemed every time I talked to Claire, Doreen and Rod were off travelling in Hawaii or Russia or China or who knows where.

But even though Doreen went off to live the life of the rich and beautiful, she was the one friend who remained true after Claire's accident. They say brain injury patients suffer a double tragedy: first the physical catastrophe, and then they're deserted by their friends. Unless, that is, you're blessed with a friend like Doreen. Some fifty years after Claire and Doreen first met, I walk into the hospital and there they are, laughing together just like everything is normal.

Once Doreen had gotten through the retelling of why Claire would always be her very best friend, the two of them started in on how their forties were their very best years, how they'd go golfing and even though neither of them knew a birdie from an eagle from a bogey, they loved being out on those fairways or roughs or whatever it was, out in the glorious sunshine taking turns sipping from a single bottle of beer they'd tucked down the side of the golf bag. Doreen said they'd laugh and laugh. She said that's what it was all about, two friends laughing in the sunshine. Claire started singing *We'll Sing in the Sunshine*, and of course Doreen joined in.

All I could think of was how the song ends and I started crying again. But Claire was looking at Doreen and Claire looked so happy—

And then Jimmy walked in.

That slouch, that long grey hair. Doreen has to be thirty years older than him but I do believe a person could mistake Jimmy for Doreen's senior, instead of the other way around. Even nearing eighty Doreen is still petite, blonde and beautiful and so chock full of life. The contrast to my slouched nephew was startling, more so than it would have been if I hadn't already been feeling so guilty.

I've been wanting to phone Jimmy ever since that day I saw him outside the hospital, the day I didn't know who he was until

I finally came to my senses and recognized my own nephew. *My mom's dying. How d'ya think I'm doing?* I haven't been able to get that answer out of my head.

I wanted to telephone, but every time I think of telephoning I don't know what I'd say. It's not even about Colin anymore. That was such a long time ago now, and the irony is that if Kyra hadn't run off, leaving Colin to bring up Cai on his own, we'd never have bought this house so that we could ensure a safe place for our dear little grandson. What ever did we do to deserve the gift of Cai? His little feet padding down the stairs in the morning—'Nana, read me a story'—snuggling in between Telford and me. All the little drawings on the refrigerator, the bouquets of dandelions, his first day of school, the day he played the lion in the school play. 'Grrrrh.' Never was there a more heart-breakingly adorable lion in this world. *And the lion will lay down with the lamb.* Oh Cai, my sweet little lamb. And Telford and I there every step of the way. All the hours Telford and Cai spent building models of 1950s Chevrolets. The way Cai walked me through his high school holding me by the arm and introducing me to all his friends and teachers. The other teenagers made their parents drop them off a block away, but Cai was never embarrassed to be seen with his Nana. Who knows what really happened between Jimmy and Kyra? Whatever it was, it certainly didn't last. Lord knows I never would have wished for Kyra to run off, but I can't pretend that Cai hasn't been the great blessing of our lives.

Jimmy's life so different. First losing his father and then his wife and his children and now his mother is dying and I still don't know what to say. If I could, I'd offer him hope and peace, that's what I want to do, but I don't know how. How do you give hope and peace to someone like Jimmy?

'Auntie Doe. Auntie H. How's it going?'

I should be used to people tossing out that sort of greeting that leaves no space for a reply. Thankfully Jimmy wasn't expecting an answer; he was already talking to Claire, asking if the doctor had signed her discharge papers: 'We gotta get you home so we can get you some decent food.'

It was the first time I'd seen Jimmy in the room and I knew how important it would be to Claire so I excused myself. I'd just pop down to the cafeteria to check on Telford; I'd be back in half an hour. Doreen said she'd walk down with me. I don't think

Claire even noticed us leave.

In the cafeteria Doreen wanted to talk about funeral arrangements. She's Claire's executor, but Claire has never specified if she wants to be cremated or buried. Did we know?

I didn't, maybe Nora did. It made me uncomfortable, talking about Claire's funeral. I know we'll have to face it some day, and probably sooner than later, but now with Claire improving it seems like the wrong time.

Doreen said the only wrong time is when it's too late, and Telford agreed, so I promised that tonight I'd ask Nora. In the meantime shouldn't we be dealing with more immediate problems?

Doreen had already been thinking about how Claire could manage if she really did go home in the next couple of days. Claire would need a panic button, which in turn would require a medical alert lock box so that emergency personnel could enter Claire's suite if she was unable to get to the door. Doreen said, 'I've already called Pest Control to get rid of the mice.'

'Mice?'

According to Doreen, Claire has been living with a rodent problem for ages. Hadn't I ever noticed droppings on the carpet?

Before last week I hadn't been to Claire's house in years, and even if I had, it was inconceivable to me that Claire would live in a house with mice. Her home on Drayton Street was where the family had gathered for all the important celebrations: Christmas, Easter, Thanksgiving, birthdays, and plenty of plain Sunday dinners, too. No, not plain. That's the wrong word for Claire. Nothing my sister ever does is plain. No matter the occasion, everything — the house, the table settings, the food—was always as elegant as something you'd see in a magazine. How anyone could handle a high-powered job in the insurance world, raise two children, lead a hectic social life—and the drinking that went with it—and still keep her house absolutely spotless and elegant would have been a mystery to me if that "anyone" hadn't been my sister.

I'd started crying again. Some days it seems that's all I do. *Cry baby, cry baby.* That's what Claire would say when I was little and she wouldn't let me tag along with her and her friend Patsy. Well, why would an eleven-year-old want a five-year-old tagging along? Six years is such a big difference when you're young. But I wanted to be with Claire. I remember one time when I was crying and demanding to know why I couldn't come too, Claire answered:

'Because we're going to the Houses of Parliament and you're too little.' I believed her. I didn't know what they did in Houses of Parliament, but it sounded important. Of course my sister would be going there.

I excused myself from the cafeteria: Telford could work on the details with Doreen, I needed to go back to Claire. I'd just peek inside the door; if Jimmy was still there I wouldn't go in, but I didn't expect to see him. Nora says he drops by almost every day, but usually not for more than a few minutes at a time.

Nora had arrived and was holding Claire's hand. There was no sign of Jimmy. Claire appeared to be sleeping. Nora looked up and smiled, motioned me over to the bed.

'Before she fell asleep,' Nora said, keeping her voice low, 'out of the blue Mom said, *white satin*. I asked her, what was white satin, and for a long time she didn't answer and I thought she'd drifted off again. But then she smiled and said, *I should give you my wedding dress*.'

Oh Lord, I was weeping again. Claire's wedding dress. What a day. I can't seem to stop crying. I was remembering the night my Cinderella walked all the way home through the snow in her white summer loafers, hugging all her belongings in two wet pillowcases. That night, come bedtime, Claire and I were back together in the room we had always shared. At some point in the evening she'd slipped into the bedroom to spread her wet things along the brass headboard and on the back of the single chair. She'd lined her toothbrush and hairbrush and lipstick out on the dresser. Now she put her finger to her lips: 'Shhh.' She patted the bed for me to sit down beside her; she lifted a bundle lying on the bedspread and placed it in her lap. The bundle had been carefully wrapped in butcher paper, the only possession Claire had protected before packing the pillowcases. Carefully she undid the string, and then slowly folded back the paper.

Her beautiful dress. She grinned at me, pinched some material near each shoulder seam and stood. The brown paper fell away and the dress unfurled to the floor. Still grinning, Claire swayed her hips, her left arm holding the fabric to her chest, the right arm pulling the fabric in close under her swollen belly.

'But what will you do with it now that you've left Earl?' I asked her.

Claire shrugged. 'It's beautiful,' she said.

For Claire, that was reason enough.

Is it possible Claire still has the dress? I always thought my sister threw things out; I'm supposed to be the one who's obsessive about holding onto treasures and trinkets. Claire has almost no storage space in her basement suite. If she does still have the wedding dress, where would it be? In that awful cold room? I know Claire's put old lamps and dishes back there, but I can't bear to think of her beautiful gown in there too. The silk yellowed, the dress in tatters, and little mice feet scurrying all over it. Oh Claire, you deserved so much more.

- 18 -
CLAIRE

Damn, it was good to see Doreen yesterday. 'I should bring my jukebox here,' she said. Wouldn't that be something, hauling a jukebox into a hospital! I wouldn't put it past her either; Doreen could get permission to bring in a circus troupe if that's what she wanted. Wouldn't Heather's new friend over there be surprised waking up to a jukebox blaring, and me and Doreen over here belting out *Pretty Woman* at the top of our voices.

Oh I do miss fun. Christmas wasn't right this year; I never should have gone away.

Never should have! Since when did Claire McHenry waste time moaning about what's already past? Haven't I always said:

Do things or don't do them, but don't waste time regretting.

Well, maybe when I get home I'll just have to do Christmas over again. I've hardly had time to enjoy my tree, no need to rush taking it down, Valentine's Day is still a long ways off ... Now there's an idea, I'll invite everyone for Christmas dinner on Valentine's Day. Turkey and chocolate hearts. Wouldn't that be terrific! Nora could help with the decorations. Maybe Jimmy too, now that the two of them seem to be getting on. Wouldn't *that* be something, Nora and Jimmy at the table cutting out paper hearts together!

Tina would want to be included. I'll just tell her no, this is for my children. But the dinner would be for everyone: Jimmy and Nora and Fred, and Heather and Telford and the kids ... Even Tina, I suppose ...

Maybe it should be a party instead of a dinner. Nora could invite Dave. Jimmy would like that, and Fred seems to like him too. And Doreen and Rod, that goes without saying ... No, not Rod. Of course Rod can't come, he's in the nursing home. The last person in the world I'd have imagined ending up in a place like that. I'd have expected it of Buddy, always fussing over every little cold or fever when there was nothing in the world wrong with him. But Rod was a real man, healthy and strong as an ox. Good Lord. And it's been seven years already. Doreen visiting him every day for all that time, and never complaining about it either.

That's because Doreen's like me, no use trying to make sense of the troubles life deals us. All the more reason to have a party for those who can still come. Wouldn't it be wonderful if Jimmy's children could be there too. I'd love to see Willow! ... Wait a minute, didn't they move to Mexico? I'm sure her new parents are missionaries in Mexico. Stan and Charm. Who would think Mexico needed missionaries? But that's what Nora told me, that they packed up Jake and Chelsea and Willow and the three babies they had after they'd already adopted Jimmy's children and off they went to save the Mexicans. Well, I suppose that's what they think their purpose on this earth is, to save everyone, but it sure would be nice to have my own grandchildren at my last party. I haven't seen them as much as I should have ...

There's that word again: *should*. Well, how *could* I see them? I couldn't drive and they lived so far away. Nora said why didn't Jimmy drive me—that was before they moved to Mexico—after all, it was an open adoption and Charm and Stan said Jimmy was welcome to visit his children any time he wanted. But it's so hard for Jimmy; he feels he let them down. Nora should understand that.

Well that's just one more reason for me to have this party, bring everyone back together; maybe that's something I can do for my son before I leave this earth. What a pity I can't invite Beverly, my own little lost baby. Of course that's probably not her name now; they probably changed it when they adopted her. *Smith* is what they told me the family's name was, but I always suspected that wasn't true, that it was a made-up name they used for the paperwork to keep a person from asking questions. It didn't stop me from scanning the papers for news of Beverly Smith; I couldn't help myself. I didn't regret my decision to give my baby up for adoption, life doesn't always give you choices, but I guess I wanted to know that she was okay. Once I saw a Beverly Smith listed as a contestant in a teen beauty contest in Burnaby; the age was right and for all I know, she really was living that close by. Buddy said we should try to track her down, but life was pretty darn busy back then with work and with trying to keep the peace between Buddy and Jimmy. And honestly, what right did I have? Hadn't I signed away my rights when I put my baby up for adoption? There was no such thing as open adoption when Beverly was born.

I don't suppose I ever did forgive Earl for forcing me to give up my baby. I forgave him for leaving me alone in the hotel the first night of our honeymoon while he went off gambling and didn't come back till the next morning. And I forgave him for not being there when Nora was born. Hell, I even forgave him for swaggering into the maternity ward with another woman on his arm. And when he came back, pleading for another chance, I didn't hesitate, not for even a second. Well more the fool me. I hadn't been able to teach him the meaning of love, but I thought maybe his daughter could. And I honestly believed he'd be happy when I told him I was pregnant again. Fat chance of that. The same man who'd sworn on Valentine's Day he wouldn't have his daughter growing up like him, without a father, well, when he heard he was going to have another child the man left so fast you could have played dice on his coattails.

And there was Buddy, the total opposite. I half believe Buddy really did marry me so that he could have Nora for his little girl, and he'd have been a father to Beverly too, if there'd been any way we could have gotten her back. Sometimes it just made me furious how Nora could never seem to find it in her heart to love Buddy. So he wasn't perfect. Who is? Poor Buddy, I lay it down to Ma McHenry. Buddy pretended to ignore her when she said that in God's eyes we'd never be married, but I know that it ate away at him. Why else was he so afraid to have sex with me? 'I respect you too much.' What kind of an answer was that? What kind of a man *thinks* that way?

Good Lord, why am I thinking about all this? That's over. That's all in the past. What's important is right now. I need to think about the party. If it's going to be in February maybe it should be a birthday party for Mom as well. It's been ages since I threw a party for Mom.

Oh, for heaven's sake. What's the matter with me? Agnes has been dead for years.

- 19 -
NORA

I couldn't say no to my mother, but what do I say to her grandchildren? *Dear Jake, Chelsea and Willow, you are invited to Christmas dinner on Valentine's Day at the home of your Grandma McHenry...*

Or is it *Nana* McHenry? Cai calls Aunt Heather *Nana,* like I used to call Agnes until I started to feel self-conscious in my teens. Everyone else had *Grandmas*. Even *Gram*, the name I used for Buddy's mother, seemed more grownup.

And then there's me, what do I call myself? Aunt Nora seems a bit presumptuous given I scarcely know my brother anymore, let alone his children. On the other hand, I never knew my Aunt Nora, but it's always felt special that I have her name.

Anyway, it has to be me not Jimmy who writes to his kids because we can only contact them by email and my brother doesn't know how to use a computer. First I'll have to remind them who I am, then explain why they're being invited to Christmas dinner on Valentine's Day. *Your grandma is very sick and wants to see you.*

But just yesterday Mom told me she's not going to die until at least the fall. She's "decided". She'll clean up the backyard, plant dahlias, have the neighbours and friends and family for summer barbecues, so I can't mention the real reason she asked me to contact her grandchildren; it would feel as though I were jinxing her odds of recovery. And if I write that it's unlikely she'll even be alive for Valentine's Day, if I say it, and she dies, maybe I'm partly the cause of it happening. For not keeping the faith or something. I tell myself I don't believe that, but I can't shake the uneasiness. Well it's my problem now, Mom asked me to contact them and I promised I would.

She was so animated: 'We've never had a Christmas with all of us together.' She meant her and me and Jimmy and Jimmy's children. She said Aunt Heather and Uncle Telford and Colin and

Cai and Annie and her husband and their children had to be there too. 'Just like old times.'

And then suddenly she looked sad. One moment so excited and full of hope, the next so quiet, like all the air had gone out of her. I could have asked what was wrong, but I was afraid of the answer. What if she believed she wasn't going to live to see her Christmas/Valentine party? Did she intend the email to be an advance announcement for her pending funeral? I know she'd like her grandchildren to be there, she's named them in her will.

Or were the thoughts of a funeral my thoughts? Maybe my mother was simply remembering those 'old times.'

'You will invite them?'

I promised and she closed her eyes.

I wonder if Mom remembers that in the old days her tree would have been down long before February 14th. When I still lived at home that was a ritual for New Year's Day—everything to do with Christmas packed away and the house scrubbed from top to bottom, fresh and clean to start the New Year. But with an artificial tree everything can be extended; for years now she's left it up until

Valentine's Day, and even then is reluctant to see it go.

Christmas at Valentine's. Why not? If we actually reach that day together maybe I'll have a chance to make up a tiny bit for how I messed up the real Christmas.

Mom didn't blame me for the fiasco at Fred's house; she didn't have to. I'm never going to forget sitting on those stairs Christmas morning, listening to her tell Jimmy that people should be home for Christmas. My mother wasn't at home; she was in a strange house, disoriented, ill and humiliated because she'd wet the bed. And we'd gone there because I'd wanted to take care of her, give her the best possible Christmas under the circumstances. Instead it feels like all I did was rob my mother of the last Christmas she'll ever see.

I think now of how I raged at Jimmy's carelessness when he left Mom alone on New Year's Eve. How could he have been so reckless with her safety, leaving her there all alone on the porch in the freezing cold while he went off to whoop it up with his friends? But what kind of care did I give? Our mother on the phone to Aunt Heather, crying that she wanted to go home. She didn't ask me directly; of course she didn't, she's Claire, she's tough, she'd already said we'd have dinner that night with Fred's family. We put on our happy faces and stayed so we wouldn't make a fuss or hurt Fred's feelings and we left for home, as planned, the next morning.

On the ferry back to Vancouver Mom needed to use a washroom; I offered to go with her in case she couldn't find her way back. 'I think I'm old enough to go to the bathroom by myself.' The look flashing across her face, the sarcasm. Echoes of the old Claire. I let her go without me. I had to. But I kept an eye on her from a discrete distance, watching her stress rising as she became disoriented and couldn't find her way in the crush of travellers. I edged closer, pretending not to notice her, allowing her to believe she'd found me on her own.

Maybe she knew what I'd done; she'd never say if she did, never acknowledge the humiliation of needing my help. Of course if it had been Jimmy who offered to take her to the washroom she'd have been flattered by his attention. As she would have been with any man. So I was already feeling frustrated and disappointed, aware that I had let her down, when we arrived at the ferry terminal to discover that Jimmy—Jimmy who could do no wrong—wasn't there to meet us as promised. He has a cell phone but he wasn't answering and so we stood in the cold waiting for a taxi for nearly an hour. Not the best possible Christmas. Not like old times.

The old times were before people started dying. Everyone at the table: Buddy, Agnes, Uncle Bob, Gram and Grandad McHenry, Aunt Heather, Uncle Telford, Annie, Colin, Jimmy. The great aunts too: Agnes's sisters Etta and Nell.

The extensions are fitted into the dining-room table; there's a centrepiece of evergreen boughs, holly and candles. Claire is seated at one end of the table, Buddy at the other. At each place setting a chubby marshmallow snowman peeks out from beneath a red foil hat, little coloured pins for eyes, between its mini-marshmallow arms, a name card. Everyone has a name, everyone has a place.

Dinner is a success, Claire's dinners always end in success. The lead-up can be tense, but when we sit down everything is elegant and perfect: the polished silver, the good china, the linen napkins, the mountains of turkey and vegetables steaming on plates hot from the oven. Everyone dressed in their finest. Claire the hostess, Claire on top of the world.

This memory, my memory, includes all the family I've ever known, but that's not true for everyone. At the table others remember their pasts, Christmas dinners with their loved ones, since departed. Reminiscences. Over dessert Agnes speaks of her mother, Jean, and Gram McHenry of Buddy's father, her first husband, but most of the talk seems to revolve around Magnus. Agnes says that on the first Christmas they were married Magnus gave her the necklace she still wears every year; she is wearing it now, a delicate gold filigree with pinpoints of pearl surrounding her birthstone, an amethyst so small I can't make it out across the table.

Aunt Heather says the best present she ever got from Magnus was the puppy he brought home for her eleventh birthday. He'd picked the puppy up after work and because it was late, and because it was pouring rain, he decided to take the streetcar, something he would not ordinarily do. The puppy, whether from excitement or fear or motion sickness, threw up all over itself and all over Magnus. Magnus got back off the streetcar and walked to Hardy's Drugstore where Mr. Hardy washed and dried the puppy and tied a big red bow around its neck.

Uncle Bob says people are supposed to be remembering Christmases, not birthdays.

Aunt Heather falls silent.

Why does my uncle always have to be so picky? What does it matter if the puppy came in October or December? By January Magnus was dead and one of Aunt Heather's last memories of her father is of him bringing home the puppy with the big red bow.

My mother says, 'The best Christmas present I ever got was my Shirley Temple doll.'

Attention turns away from Aunt Heather and I am relieved; let my aunt be, let her remember what she needs to remember.

I'm intrigued, too; my mother so seldom indulges in memories of the past. Any time I press her for any kind of details she says she can't remember and doesn't want to; now here she is describing how she'd seen the doll in a store window on her way home from school, how the doll's green eyes were wide open, how it felt as though the doll was looking right at her, willing Claire to take her home.

'I knew I had to have her,' my mother says. 'I ran home and told Mom and Dad that if they bought me the Shirley Temple doll

I'd never ask for anything else in my whole life. I can see her now.'

My mother is holding her crystal water glass, staring into it as if it were a portal into the past. She describes a doll with thick blond ringlets, a white dress with ruffles and a scarlet sash. She looks up at Agnes. 'You said it was the Depression. You said dolls like that were expensive and you reminded me I wasn't an only child.'

Such a memory. Stored in such precise detail. I wanted to remember a Christmas like the old times, a Christmas of magic and joy when I was little and Santa Claus was real, but in this memory I'm already a teenager, already aware that behind every moment of magic lurks the doom of inescapable loss. The memory floods over me as I sit here in my mother's hospital room, hearing but not hearing the muted rustling of activity in the hallway, while the only sounds that register are the long slow exhales and the sharper short inhales of my mother's breathing. I know the ending of the Shirley Temple doll story and I'm living it again, my heart beating fast.

I'm watching as my mother stares into that crystal water glass. I'd seen *Heidi* and *Captain January* on television when I was the same age as Shirley Temple was in those movies and I'd always thought she was the same age as me. She was *my* hero—a little girl who took care of vulnerable adults, a waif whose smile and optimism always made the ending turn out happy. Now my mother is saying she too had known and adored Shirley Temple when she was a girl. She tells us how on her way home from school she'd stopped by the store every single day to check on the doll, how two days before Christmas it was gone.

'The two most anxious days of my life,' she says, and I feel a sympathetic stab of panic as my mother describes how she couldn't sleep for those two nights, even though she'd already told us the doll was her best ever Christmas present.

She looks up with the most beautiful smile, says to my grandmother, 'I'll never know what you and Dad had to sacrifice to make that dream come true, but I want you to know that I will remember that doll to the end of my days.'

We all turn to my grandmother. She has always been hard on Claire. I've heard from Agnes herself how she told the nurses at the hospital that Claire couldn't be her baby. Never has my mother managed to gain her mother's approval, no matter how hard she tries to make things perfect. Now I'm hearing a story in which Agnes had sacrificed to make a dream come true for Claire. I feel a rush of love for both of them.

Agnes places her teacup carefully in its saucer.

'It's a fine memory,' she says. 'But Claire, the doll was never *yours*. You were too old for dolls. We bought the Shirley Temple doll for Heather.'

She smiles across the table at my aunt.

'Isn't that right Heather?'

Later that night, doing the last of the dishes alone together, I tried to talk to my mother about her feelings.

'Well, I guess I was plain wrong,' she said. She jammed a handful of cutlery into the dish rack. 'I guess my *mother* would know better than *I* who they bought the doll for.'

I said Agnes must be wrong. She was cold and mean. I couldn't believe she could be so heartless.

The look flashed across my mother's face. 'Oh, for crying out loud! Why do you have to make everything into a tragedy?'

- 20 -
HEATHER

If Nora remembers the evening so clearly, it must be true. Why then can't I remember? Nora says it's probably because the emotions that stayed with me from that Christmas dinner were about Bobby making fun of me and my puppy. Poor little Taffy, I don't even think of you that often. What I can recall of your life is hardly more than three scenes. The night Dad brought you home with your big red bow. The night Dad died and you barked and barked while I crouched by the sink hugging you and telling you it would be all right. Well I was wrong about that, wasn't I? Dad died.

And then there was the night Earl was at our house and you

were sniffing around under the kitchen table and Earl kicked you. Oh my poor Taffy, you yelped and skittered under the chesterfield and I told Earl he was the most evil and nastiest man in the world.

Well of course I didn't say it out loud; I was too afraid of Earl. But I *thought* it, that's for sure. Mom wasn't in the room at the time and Claire just glared at *me*, letting me know I'd better well keep quiet. When Claire and I were alone in our bedroom later that night she apologized for Earl's behaviour, blaming it on the war, saying he'd suffered traumas we could never understand. His nerves were shot. Well maybe, but it was no reason to kick an innocent little puppy.

I used to remember everything. Something my niece and I have in common. At least we used to. Claire doesn't remember—Claire doesn't *want* to remember—she always wants to move on and put the past behind her, but Nora and I dwell on things and that keeps them alive. If that's so, how is it I have no memory of Claire ever wanting my Shirley Temple doll? How is it I can't remember the Christmas dinner Nora described to me in such detail the other night? Agnes was so cavalier, Nora said. The way she dismissed Claire's story. I had to admit I simply couldn't remember, but Nora didn't blame me at all, bless her heart, even though it felt like I'd let her down.

Tonight I asked Telford to go into the garage and find me the box of dolls. I always meant to pass them on from Annie to her daughters, but after Cai's mother abandoned him there hardly seemed time to be proper grandparents to Annie's girls as well. I feel sad about that sometimes, but as for the dolls, the girls probably wouldn't have been interested in them anyway; they already have so many things of their own.

Poor Telford, I could understand him being grumpy when I said I needed that box tonight: driving back and forth every day to see Claire is hard on him, but he still went out to the garage and heaved those cardboard cartons around until we found the one we were looking for. And then he carried it into the kitchen and cut through the packing tape for me before he left me alone with my box of memories. Annie's dolls, and dolls that had been mine before they were hers. Annie's *Barbies,* her chubby-faced baby *Thumbelina* and freckled *Chatty Cathy.* My *Raggedy Ann* was missing most of her red yarn hair; there was a doll I had named Elizabeth after the Princess. I'd forgotten how much I loved the teen-aged Princess Elizabeth, and to think, now she's been Queen Elizabeth for half a century.

One by one I lifted the dolls from the box. All those lonely little faces. Their tiny hands. Every doll brought fresh tears to my eyes. I pulled the ring on *Chatty Cathy's* back and the recording inside her tummy said: 'I love you.' I pulled it again: 'Please take me with you.' I must have sobbed out loud because there was Telford back at my side, wiping my cheeks with a tissue. He said I should put the box away for another day, that I didn't need anything more to distress me.

But I couldn't stop. I lifted out a doll with long pigtails and I remembered when my little Annie had pigtails. Now she's a mother with two daughters of her own. How can that be when sometimes I feel like I'm still only a child myself?

The next doll had grubby blond curls and faded but still vaguely rosy cheeks; her white dress had turned almost yellow, her scarlet sash replaced by a blue ribbon. I lifted her closer to take a better look and her eyes snapped open. I let out a shriek and the doll slipped from my hands. Thank heaven Telford was still in the room, curious in spite of himself; he caught the doll as it fell.

I feel so silly when I jump like that, but I've always been nervous and the Parkinson's makes everything worse. Telford set the doll on the table, trying to prop her in a sitting position; when she kept toppling forwards he went into the living room, returning with our big thick dictionary for support to keep her upright.

The dolls eyes were clouded, not the bright green eyes Claire had described to Nora, more a sort of milky hazel. Goose bumps covered my arms. I wanted to lay the doll back down, make the eyes close, but I couldn't. I thought of Claire's eyes. Mother always said they were the wrong colour for our family. Mother was already gone before Claire lost most of her vision. What would Mother have made of that?

Telford stroked my arm. 'Now that we've found your doll,' he said gently, 'can we please go to bed?'

It's been another long day and he knows I want to be at the hospital early in the morning but I convinced him I needed to sit up just a while longer. He sighed, went off to bed and let me be. Sometimes I fret that he worries too much about me, but I wouldn't trade my husband for all the tea in China. Well that's a silly thing to say. What would I do with all the tea in China? But I couldn't live without my Telford.

I've been sitting here ever since he went to bed. Trying to remember. Maybe Mother was wrong; maybe the doll wasn't mine. At least not at first. I used to get so many of my sister's hand-me-downs. She'd grow out of things, or be too old for them, or just get tired of them, and once she was done with something she never thought about it again. I was the one always trying to save our past. But what if this time Claire was the one who remembered it right? What if this was the one present that ever really mattered to my sister?

Now that I look more closely I see that there are a lot of fine lines and cracks on the face and arms and legs. I wish I could talk to Nora. Should I take this poor old doll to Claire, just as she is, or is it too late?

For sure at two o'clock in the morning it's too late to phone my niece. She's probably awake, sitting on her stool by the window, but even so, Fred would be sleeping and I'd hate to wake him. The poor man has to work in the morning and I can't imagine what all this must be doing to him: first his late wife, and now Nora's mother, what are the odds of both of them dying of pancreatic cancer? If the phone woke him I know he'd tell me it wasn't a problem, the man is a saint. Even so, I don't want to take advantage; I already worry that Nora doesn't appreciate him as she should.

Oh mercy, something else to worry about. I love my niece, but she's so used to running away from men. What would it take this time for Nora to see that she's found a good man? *Before* she leaves him. She always talks about her exes so fondly, claiming it's her fault she couldn't make it work. As far as I can tell, they seem to care for her, too. So why does she always leave? What would it take for her to stop running?

Maybe if Fred did what Dad did on his wedding night? Dad got down on his knees and thanked God for 'the gift of Agnes.' Then he prayed for God's help, that he never cause her any sadness. Mother often told that story.

When I reminded Bobby about it once he said, 'Sure, but Dad made her sad anyway, didn't he? She cried for months after he died.' I said that was different, but Bobby just made fun of me for living in a fairy tale. Sometimes I wish I could wake Bobby from the dead and ask him if he still feels so superior. Sons aren't supposed to die before their mothers, but he did, didn't he?

Listen to me! Arguing with my brother who's been dead for thirty years while my sister is dying right now. Two days ago I almost believed that Claire was getting ready to go home; it seemed like she really was getting stronger, but today she had that horrible rattling at the back of her throat. I know it's almost time.

If only I could phone Nora. I imagine her awake like me, but sitting at her window, looking out. She's told me how she'll wake up in the night, go to her living room and tell herself she can't go back to bed until someone appears on the street below, and then she watches until they disappear again. She says she finds those passing figures on the street reassuring: 'A testament to the ordinariness of our impossible lives.'

Well, if it were possible I'd be there with her now. I loved the little apartment Telford and I had in the West End when we were first married. If we could afford to, that's where I'd still want to live. I told him that the other day; he said he wouldn't go back there if you paid him.

Maybe *that's* what Nora needs, for Fred to tell her he won't take her away from the one place she's felt at home. But there you are, Nora's told me that's the one thing Fred *can't* promise, not when he raised his family in Nanaimo, not when it was only two years before his wife died that they bought *their* dream home, imagining a future with that house full of grandchildren. *That house is where Fred wants to live with Nora.*

Why is life so complicated? Sometimes it seems no matter how hard you try to be a good person, things get messy. Maybe that's something my father knew from before he married my mother, maybe his getting down on his knees that night and praying wasn't just romantic. He couldn't have always been perfect. There is so much we don't know about him. What if there was something in his past that had already taught him how easily we hurt the ones we love? What was the real reason he left Scotland in 1913, never to return?

But that's not quite true, he did return once. I have the photo.

What a night for memories. I went into the living room and found the album with the picture taken of Dad during his one trip back to Scotland. A family photograph. On the back, in Mother's handwriting: *Martha and John Sinclair, and Granddaughter*

Mattie with their son Magnus when he visited during the First World War. Sandwick, Shetland, Scotland.

I've propped the picture up alongside the doll. What am I doing to myself? First the doll's eyes staring at me, now the eyes in this photo are staring at me too. And everyone's dead. I don't know when John Sinclair died, but his wife Martha died on Mother's Day, 1941. Do I remember that because it became part of family lore repeated yearly on Mother's Day, or because the symbolism affected me so deeply even though I was only five at the time?

We were already dressed for church when the telegram arrived. Dad didn't read it aloud.

Without a word he laid it on the table, removed the red carnation from the lapel of his suit, and left the room. By the time we slipped silently into the church pew my father had found a way to replace the red carnation with a white one. Red for the living, white for the dead. I've never felt comfortable with carnations since then, even the red ones, only too aware of how suddenly they can change to white.

In the photograph my father is wearing an army uniform. It's a studio photograph: posed, not a snapshot. The people in the photograph are looking straight at the camera, and now I've been staring at the picture so long and so hard, it feels like they're staring back at me. Who do *they* see? An old lady with sunken eyes. I'm even older now than Dad's mother. His father looks so small in his dark Sunday suit; I expect it fit him better when he was a younger man. He seems to be challenging me, staring me down, as if to say: *Just who do you think you are? You call yourself my granddaughter but you're older than my son, older than me, too. My granddaughter is here beside me, seated on my son's knee.*

That's something that's always struck me as a little odd. The granddaughter, a little girl in a white frock who looks to be about four years old, is sitting on my father's knee. I was never able to find out what had happened to her mother, but it seems it was something disreputable, one of those hushed stories you weren't supposed to ask about. But why is little Mattie sitting on my father's knee, a man she'd never seen before and will never see again? The expression on her face is one of curiosity: *Who is this man who is holding me?*

Or is that just me thinking of Cai, thinking how I'd never have been able to pass him off to a stranger. Of course Dad was no stranger to Martha. But to that little girl?

I can already hear Claire: *For heaven's sake, Heather, you're being silly again. If the little girl looks curious maybe it's because she's wondering who you are. You, an old lady outside the picture, gawking at her.*

The more I look at the picture it seems to me that Dad has the smallest hint of a smile, as if he's always known that one day I'd be examining this photograph, searching for clues. His gaze is serene: *Don't worry, little one. Yes, life is complicated, but there is a logic to the unfolding, even if we can't understand it.*

Don't worry. That's definitely what Claire would say.

I look at the woman again, my grandmother, and I see a worrier. Martha had reason to worry: *something* had happened to her daughter. And her eldest son, a fisherman, had already drowned; her youngest had lied about his age and run off to the war, dead two years before he was legally old enough to serve. When Martha received the news of her youngest son's death she wrote to Magnus, her only surviving son, begging that he promise never to enlist. Magnus was living in Canada, in Jean Baxter's boarding house; on the very day the letter arrived he fastened a black armband around the sleeve of his best shirt and then he walked downtown to the recruiting office to enlist.

I see now I was wrong at first about the expression on Martha's face; she's not a worrier, I'm the worrier, always afraid something bad will happen. Martha is a fatalist; she *knows* bad things happen, so many of her worst fears have already come to pass. Sitting for that photograph I think she knows she'll never see my father again.

Magnus will survive the war but he will never again return to Scotland and his family. He will go back to Vancouver to the boarding house. When Magnus first came to the boarding house Agnes was only eleven years old, and Magnus, at twenty-two, was twice her age, but four years after his return from the war she will be nineteen, old enough to marry. On their wedding night Magnus will get down on his knees and pray to God he will never be the cause of his wife's sadness.

I got so mad at Bobby for saying Dad made Mother sad by dying, but I know he's right. After they took Dad's body away she set up the ironing board in the room where he died. It was still dark. I remember it as being four o'clock in the morning, but that doesn't seem right. It must have taken more than an hour from the time Dad woke up with indigestion until the time Mother began ironing his shirts. Watching my mother ironing scared me even more than watching my father die. She wouldn't talk; she just ironed his shirts until all the shirts were ironed, and then she lay down on the chesterfield and cried for four days. Later that summer I heard her tell Mrs. Conroy, the one neighbour she was close to, that there'd be no more crying. Magnus had come to her in the night. That's enough, he'd said. Agnes must get on with her life.

So I know she was sad when he died, but what about before? The problem is I honestly can't remember my parents being together very often. In all my memories from the age of six until my father died when I was eleven, Dad worked days and Mother worked from four in the afternoon until eleven at night. Dad made our porridge in the morning; later Dad and I made the dinner together. Where was Claire? Surely Claire helped with dinner too. But I can't find Claire in these memories. Only Dad and me.

The only conversation I can accurately remember between my parents wasn't a conversation, it was an ultimatum: 'You'll have to choose: gas for your car or food for your children.' The next day

I went into the garage and discovered Dad's Model T hoisted up on big wooden blocks; he never drove a car again.

I do remember my parents dancing: the third Friday of every month, mother's night off, Mother, Dad and I would walk to the White Rose Ballroom on Broadway for the Orkney and Shetland Society Dance where there were always live bands and long slabs of white and chocolate cake. I loved watching my mother and father, dressed to the nines, dancing the foxtrot and the Scottish reels. All the adults smiling and talking; there was no place like it. When I knew it was almost time to go home I'd pretend to fall asleep so that Dad would lift me in his arms to carry me. I loved us all going home together in the dark, me in Dad's arms. He was the perfect father, and he must have been the perfect husband too.

I know Mother loved him till the day she died, so it feels a bit wicked of me to even have this thought, but I always wondered just a little what would have happened if Dad's younger brother hadn't died. When Dad first arrived in Canada he was carrying a picture of his family that he showed to eleven-year-old Agnes. Pointing to Robert, his youngest brother, he said, 'One day I'll bring him to Canada too.'

'And I'm going to marry him,' young Agnes confidently declared.

Probably that never would have happened, but Robert was only three years older than Agnes and I can see how Agnes and Magnus might both have believed it at the time. One of Mother's jobs was to make the beds in the boarding house, and she told me that when she made the bed in the room where Magnus slept she'd always stop to look at the picture of Robert. She said: 'He had beautiful blond curly hair, and the same name as the man my mother was meant to marry.'

Claire, you can't die. You're the only other one still living who knew our father. I always thought you didn't care about things, but I was wrong. You're the one who remembered this doll. So what if her face has cracks running through it? You'd still love her, wouldn't you? At this age, don't we all have lines and cracks? Do you really still have your wedding dress? So many questions I have for you: Shirley Temple, our father, all those Roberts—the one who should have been our grandfather, the one who might have been our father, and the one who was Bobby, our brother.

Of Shining Fame: we thought that was hilarious, didn't we, when we found out that's what *Robert* meant. In our family, all those idolized Roberts and not a single one of them famous or shining or even a father except in someone's dreams. Such a waste of dreams. Jimmy, bless his heart, for all his griefs and troubles, became a father. But what's that got to do with anything?

Claire, you must have made me think that. Why else would I think of Jimmy now?

It's this doll, isn't it? Her eyes are getting to me, stirring up all these memories …

- 21 -
CLAIRE

See ya soon baboon. That's what Bobby always said. *In a while crocodile. What a smile ...*

Oh dear, what comes next?

Me! But not yet, no siree Bob! It's too soon. There are things I have to do. Jimmy, you'll be okay. I'll watch over you.

Tina drives me crazy, but Jimmy loves her and it's his life. I have to tell Jimmy that's okay by me. Ma McHenry could never do that; she said she'd never rest till Buddy and I were divorced. Well, Ma, you've had Buddy to yourself in heaven all these years. I hope you're happy.

Ma McHenry. I bet that's what Tina calls me. That's rich. God how I hate it when she calls me *Mom*. Jimmy's friends always call me *Mom*, but it sounds different coming from Tina. Smug. Well little Miss Smarty Mouth, don't be so sure that Jimmy loves you more than me. You should have heard the way Buddy moaned and carried on when *his* mother died.

What am I saying? I don't want that for Jimmy. I want him to be happy. I need to tell him it's okay to be happy with Tina.

And Nora, I want her to be happy too. I need to tell her she has things to do; she's not to be thinking of dying. She sat by my bed last night and reminded me of what we said to one another last Mother's Day. She probably thought I couldn't hear her but she talks to me anyway. Actually they all do, and I'm grateful for that. Even when I can't follow what they're saying I like to hear them. A lot of times I drift off to sleep and it's a great comfort when I wake up to the sound of their voices keeping me company.

Last night I heard Nora as clear as can be; I couldn't manage to open my eyes and tell her, but I followed her every word. 'You can go now,' she whispered. I guess the sound of my breathing makes her think I'm in pain. I'd tell her, if I could, that it's not the pain that's making my breath so ragged. It's just that this old body of mine knows it's almost time. I said it when Buddy died and I say it for me: when your number's up, it's time to go.

Nora needs to know it's not her time. I'm afraid she doesn't understand that.

On Mother's Day Fred was at his house in Nanaimo with his youngest son ... Now what is that boy's name? Ken? Cam? Cameron? That's it: Cameron. Well Fred was spending time with Cameron, and Nora came over and picked me up so that we could have dinner together, just the two of us. We started off with such a lovely walk through the rhododendron garden in the park before we went back to her apartment and opened a bottle of wine while Nora baked a salmon. It felt good, sitting there watching my daughter in the kitchen. Since she left home Nora hasn't shown much interest in cooking, but when she was still a girl and I was working, she was such a help; I'd arrive home and the vegetables would be peeled and the table set. On Mother's Day I told Nora that I was remembering how she'd always been such a cheerful little helper and I thanked her for that. I'm so glad that I remembered to thank her.

What troubles me now is what happened after our beautiful

evening of feeling so close, when Nora was driving me home. Out of the blue she said: 'I feel happy. If I were to die now it would be okay.' In that moment it made perfect sense and I said I felt the same. We both agreed we'd been blessed with good lives. We weren't longing to die, but each of us wanted the other to know that when it happened we wouldn't feel short-changed. Last night Nora wanted to remind me of that. 'I know you're ready,' she said. And I am ready, but I need Nora to know it's not her time. Fred's a good man. She needs to stay here with Fred and share some of that love she's got bundled up inside.

Or maybe Fred is the one I need to talk to. Nora's not as tough as she looks, I'd tell him. All those years when I thought she didn't need me I guess I was wrong. That's what I want to say: Nora needs to feel loved. I forgot that. I thought she was so strong. Fred, I'd say, tell Nora you love her. *You're Nobody 'Til Somebody Loves You.* Dean Martin had it right.

Let's see, who's next?

Heather! I have to tell Heather that Magnus and Agnes are waiting for me. Waiting for her too, but it's not her time either. The other day I thought she could see Magnus standing by the bed; I thought that was why she didn't come right up and kiss me hello like she usually does. I saw her staring at us and I called to her to come quick while Magnus was still here but instead she ran back out into the hallway dragging along the lovely Dr. Sugar. My, my, Dr. Sugar! What a name! Surely it can't be his real name. Perhaps he was a Zucker before he became a Sugar. Certainly he is a sweet man and I must say he's been good to me while Dr. Nay is on vacation. And I can see that my young sister is quite taken with the good doctor. Nora is too, for that matter. I might not see an awful lot, but I see the sparkle that comes into their eyes the minute he walks into the room. God knows I don't begrudge them a moment's flicker of joy; they've both been so good, coming to see me every day. And what a hoot when Dr. Sugar walked into my room that first day wearing a plaid flannel shirt, and his long grey hair tied back in a ponytail. My little sister was priceless. Good Lord, she can't weigh more than ninety-eight pounds but she just puffed herself up like a mother bear and demanded to know who he was before she'd let him get anywhere near the bed.

'Dr. Sugar,' he said, holding out his hand. 'I'm the on-call doctor this weekend.'

He said it was good of Heather to protect me. He was dressed that way because the power had been out in his home. A snowstorm.

Don't I miss the weather! In a hospital there's no wind, no sting of snow to remind you you're alive. I miss my backyard, going outside before bed at night and the wind howling through the trees. And all those stars, I've always liked to imagine that each star is really the spirit of a loved one shining down on us, watching over us, ready to guide us home when it's time.

There you are, that's what I think of when I remember Dr. Sugar's snowstorm. Heather was still sceptical about him until Dr. Sugar noticed my dry lips. He was the first person to know what to do about it. He popped out of the room and returned with those nice little tooth sponges; after that he could do no wrong. Heaven knows it brightens my day when he walks in here, even though I'm not his patient since I've been assigned to Dr. What's-His-Name. As far as I can tell, Dr. Sugar is the only one of the doctors who recognizes that I'm a person.

I know I'm getting things a bit out of order, but after I'd tried to tell Heather to hurry and come see Magnus and she'd run to get Dr. Sugar, he came over to the bed and asked me how I was doing. Magnus was gone by then and I'm not sure if I managed to say anything intelligent at all, but whatever I did say was clearly enough to reassure Dr. Sugar. He told Heather to come sit by my side. 'Your sister worries about you,' he said to me. 'She loves you.'

That's the other thing I have to tell Heather: *I love you too.* Well of course she knows that, but it's important to say it out loud. We all need to hear it.

And there was somebody else. Who *was* it?

Somebody, somebody, somebody... Doreen! I have to tell Jimmy that I want Doreen to have my box of Cascade dishwasher detergent. I just bought it and I want Doreen to have it.

- 22 -
NORA

'Good-bye my darling sister.'

Aunt Heather bent down to kiss my mother on the forehead. Her body trembled as she straightened up, she didn't even try to wipe away her tears. I could feel her heart breaking.

Half an hour earlier I'd gone down to the cafeteria with Uncle Telford to allow my aunt time alone with her sister, but now it had started to snow and Uncle Telford had sent me back upstairs to tell Aunt Heather they needed to leave. I felt the frailty of my aunt as I wrapped my arms around her, hugging her good-bye.

'I know,' I said.

There was no need to say more. I knew we were thinking the

same thing: today is the 13th of January, Magnus died on the 14th of January, at approximately 3:30 in the morning.

Uncle Telford appeared at our side; I suppose I'd been gone longer than I thought and he was getting concerned about the snow and the long drive ahead of them.

'Will you be okay?' he asked me.

I nodded, I would be fine. He put a sheltering arm around my aunt and walked her to the elevator. I worried about them having to drive in the snow but at the same time I was grateful that the snowstorm would allow me to be alone with my mother. Neighbours and friends had been dropping by all day, sensing the end so near, wanting to say their good-byes, but it was nearly dark now and the snow would keep others away.

In the morning I'd told Fred that I would be spending the night in the hospital. 'Would you like me to be there too?' he asked, and when I said no, he understood. He didn't try to talk me out of staying the night, didn't say that people don't usually die at an appointed time in commemoration of their deceased loved ones. He said, 'Call if you need me.'

I knew I could not possibly save my mother, any more than

she could have saved her father the night he died, but I wanted to be with her. As soon as Aunt Heather was gone I settled into the chair by my mother's bedside. She hadn't uttered a word all day; I doubted she knew I was there. At times she'd seemed in pain, her legs twitching and her brow wrinkled; the nurse had come by and increased the dose of morphine. Now there was only the sound of her breathing, long slow exhales that stretched out so long it seemed that each must have been the last, yet always followed by a surprising sharp gulp of air. Something between a gasp and a snore.

'We need a little Dean Martin,' I said. I couldn't know if it would make any difference to my mother, but I needed to hear that familiar warm voice.

You're Nobody 'Til Somebody Loves You: I hadn't recalled that being the first song on the CD; hearing it now I remembered my mother's words of the night before. She'd talked quite a lot last night, but mostly I couldn't make much sense of what she was saying. Her eyes would be wide open, looking straight ahead at the foot of the bed, no matter where I might be standing or sitting. She didn't seem upset, just focused. Every now and then I'd been able to make out a word: *cascade ... sugar ... wind.* For the most part there was no continuity, no context, nothing I could grab onto. When a phrase popped out intact it was all the more unsettling for being coherent amongst the gibberish: *See you soon baboon, in a while crocodile.* Hearing those words my head had jerked involuntarily towards the foot of the bed, as if I really did expect to see the ghost of my Uncle Bob saying good-bye, always the baboon and the crocodile followed by your mandatory reply: *See you later alligator.*

But it was the other phrase my mother had repeated at least half a dozen times last night that had me listening for even the slightest catch in her breathing that might provide a clue: *Somebody loves you.*

'Loves who?' I'd said. 'Loves me, do you mean? ... I love you too. I love you Mom.'

I hadn't associated the words then with Dean Martin, but now I watched, hoping, yearning, for some little sign.

Her breathing continued as before, those long slow exhales, the short laboured intakes between.

And then I knew something *had* changed: my mother and I

were together and Dean Martin was singing. When death is at the door, does it matter who loves you, as long as there is someone? I closed my eyes and let the crooning warmth of that voice drift over me. *Volare* ... *In the Chapel in the Moonlight* ... *Memories Are Made of This.*

Memories.

I wish I'd thought to tell my mother about the lesson I designed for my students using that Dean Martin song. A lesson on the imperative. The teacher's manual instructs us to have students write recipes; examples are provided: a recipe for salsa, another for an ice-cream sundae. Practical exercises to be sure, but my students are mostly young men and women in their late teens or early twenties; romance, not cooking, is uppermost in their minds. I have my students listen a couple of times to Dean Martin's *Memories.* They get it: it's a recipe! First they identify the ingredients: a kiss, bliss, grief, joy... The verbs are there too: stir, fold, serve. Now they're ready to write their own recipes. I suggest possible topics: *How to Introduce Yourself to Someone You're Attracted to in a Coffee Shop; Recipe For a Perfect Date; How to Break Up With Someone While Trying Not to Hurt Their*

Feelings. The assignment is to prepare written instructions but two young Venezuelan boys took it to a whole other level, singing and strutting their instructions for *How to Pick Up a Girl at Starbuck's* with all the flair and swagger of the original Rat Pack.

Mom would have loved watching that performance, or me sharing the story of it with her, but before she was diagnosed with cancer it never would have occurred to me to talk to my mother about my lesson plans. Now we were together and listening to Dean Martin, and though I feared it was only magical thinking on my part, I wanted to believe that somehow she knew what I wanted her to know. If she could sometimes see visitors that were invisible to me, I could at least hope that she could see into my heart as well.

The music played on. *Smile, Smile, Smile. The Door is Still Open To My Heart* ... Every song speaking aloud the words my mother and I had so often found difficult to believe in, to share. I let the hope, and the hopelessness, flow over me. My eyes filled with tears of gratitude that I'd had the gift of these last few days to realize just how deeply I loved this woman. They were tears of grief, too, for how long I had been blind to the love.

'Pizza.'

The sound might have been just a burst of air, but it definitely sounded like *pizza*. 'You want pizza?' It was an absurd idea, but her lips seemed to be moving and I wasn't about to ignore even the hint of a single word. I bent down to listen.

Wine... bells... With my ear close to her lips, I could hear my mother faintly singing along with Dean Martin. No, that's not quite right; she knew the words before she heard them, and she was singing just a skip ahead of the beat. As though Dean Martin was following her. Mom, still the life of the party. Hoisting her glass and doing one last turn around the dance floor—her and Dean Martin together, singing *That's Amore*.

Mom's eyes were open, though she still didn't seem to know I was there. When the song ended her voice fell silent. Her eyes closed. For a few moments her breathing seemed a little bit easier.

'I love you,' I said, and squeezed her hand.

She didn't respond to the squeeze and returned to how she was before I put on the CD, the long exhales each followed by a sharp intake of breath. She hasn't opened her eyes since. Hasn't uttered another word.

But I'd heard the word I needed to hear. *Amore.*

Dean Martin was a drunk. Dean Martin was a social drinker who played a drunk on stage. I've heard people argue both versions and I know that for some people it's crucial to know which is the truth. For me, the only truth about Dean Martin that has ever mattered—for Claire *and* for me—is his singing. And yet for years I'd allowed myself to act as if the only truth about my mother was her drinking.

Deep down I knew that in spite of all my bungled attempts to get her to drink less, a part of me relied on Mom's drinking; it was always so much easier to be angry at her for that than to acknowledge her vulnerability. Even now, twenty-five years after she fell down her front steps, there's an image from those days that is almost unbearable for me to remember; it took place in the hospital sometime after she'd been released from the Intensive Care Ward, but before she'd been relocated to the Rehabilitation Wing. Aunt Heather and I had been with Claire all afternoon; we'd said our good-byes and were walking down the hallway when I felt an urge to go back and give my mother one more hug. I stopped at the entranceway to her room; she hadn't heard me approach.

She was standing before a stack of get-well cards on a small side table, an intense look of concentration on her face. She was wearing her own clothes, a red-and-white striped caftan. Her head had been shaved for the surgery; without hair closing in on her face, without makeup, her eyes looked big and beautiful, though the doctors had told us it was hard to tell just how much she was really able to see and how much she was relying on her other senses. I stood in the doorway and watched her pick up a card. With painstaking care she set it upright. It toppled over.

'Oh.'

Such a tiny bewildered sound.

With the same patient concentration she set the card aright; after many tries, when it remained standing, she chose a second. Each card took all her focus, all her care just to get it to remain standing. My mother was fifty-three years old; five weeks earlier she had been one of the most sought-after insurance underwriters in the city, now it was taking every molecule of her being to focus on a problem that wouldn't have challenged a five-year-old. I wanted to wrap her in my arms, protect her from anything bad ever again happening. I backed silently away from the room, fearful lest I destroy that one tiny corner of the world that my mother could still manage.

In the year leading up to her fall—the year between Buddy's suicide and her accident or aneurysm or whatever it was—my mother and my brother had been drinking heavily. Seven weeks before her accident I'd written in my journal: *Mom's and Jimmy's drinking is way out of control. If I don't find the courage to say something I'm afraid they're on a collision course to disaster. Can I find the courage?*

I hadn't found the courage. I'd seen disaster approaching and I hadn't protected her. Now, backing away from the sight of my mother labouring so intently over those little get-well cards I vowed never again to desert her. We'd both been given a second chance; I would be there to help my mother set out on a new and better path.

My first act, with Aunt Heather, was to talk to Claire's doctor about Jimmy: the drinking, the partying with his friends at the house, the unresolved charges for drinking and driving, his explosive temper.

It's so long ago now I can't remember exactly how it unfolded, only that Jimmy was asked to move. It's not as though my mother would be completely on her own; after Buddy died the basement had been converted into a suite and Mel and Cynthia, long-time friends of my mother's, were already living downstairs. Cynthia assured me she'd always be there for Claire. Even so, for the first couple of months after Mom came home from the hospital I spent at least four nights a week sleeping at her house. A neighbour asked hadn't I just recently gotten married; I told her that my husband understood.

Adapting to her reduced vision and injured brain was a long slow haul. There were a number of falls, mostly not too serious, just a small bruise or two, though one did result in a broken collarbone. I made what I thought were subtle suggestions that even a small amount of alcohol would impede the brain's recovery. Mom was not pleased. She'd come to accept that she would not be returning to work, she would talk about her 'silly old brain' not working properly anymore, but she didn't appreciate people treating her as if she had no brain at all, thank you very much. She was already volunteering two days a week at the Margaret Fulton Centre; her life it seemed had found its new normal and normal for Claire McHenry meant she'd damn well have a drink when she pleased. She didn't need me or anyone else telling her how to lead her life.

I'd vowed never to desert my mother but I hadn't bargained on her being so resistant to my help and the truth is, when my husband was accepted into a PhD program at Emory University in Atlanta a year after Mom's accident, I was eager to go.

'Well, if that's what you want to do, I guess that's what you'd better do,' said my mother, though she made it clear that she never would have moved so far away from *her* mother.

'What the fuck?' snarled Jimmy. 'You get me kicked out of my own house, then you screw off to the States?'

In the year since the accident Cynthia and Mel had moved out of the basement suite, never to return, not even for a visit. I don't remember now who moved in next or who came after that; I was in Atlanta by then. Eventually, after his wife left him with their three children, Jimmy moved home and Claire moved into the suite downstairs so that Jimmy could have the space he needed for his family. It wasn't long before a girlfriend moved in with Jimmy, and not long after that before Social Services took the children.

A succession of girlfriends moved in and moved on, while Mom remained downstairs.

There had been one more fruitless effort on my part to intervene during one of my mother's visits to Atlanta. Shocked at how much she was drinking, I'd again tried subtlety to suggest that the drinking was impeding her recovery. That time she reacted calmly, saying only, 'Thank you.' There'd been no hint of the look. When she headed back to Vancouver I was pleased that I'd found the courage to speak up, pleased that I'd persevered. I hadn't realized that she'd been hugely insulted, that she was patronizing me, and that nothing was going to change.

Except as I see it now that's when, in my own way, I came to rely on Mom's drinking. Every now and then I'd catch a glimpse of her vulnerability, or I'd remember that scene with the get-well cards and I'd feel utterly overwhelmed with love and the frantic urge to shield her from danger. But my mother didn't want that kind of protection; she wasn't looking for Christopher Robin or anyone else to fix her. When her drinking once again dominated the dynamic between us, crowding out any possibility for compassion, I could distance myself behind the armour of my anger. After that last attempt in Atlanta to talk about her drinking we never spoke about it again. At least not to each other, though ten years later she would tell Harold how I'd once accused her of being an alcoholic.

On the afternoon of New Year's Eve I was reminded of that fiasco with Harold. I was helping Mom sort through bundles of scribbled notes and scraps of paper from her desk drawers. She'd said she wanted to be proactive; she didn't want to leave loose ends, and after the mishap she'd experienced the night she slept in Nanaimo, she worried that if she left it too long she wouldn't be capable of taking care of her own business.

Neither of us could have known just how little time my mother really had. Four days later I'd call an ambulance to deliver her to hospital. But that afternoon we believed we were taking control. We'd already gone through a large stack of greeting cards that she urged me to take home and use; she'd kept a handful, enough to get through a year of birthdays and miscellaneous celebrations. Mom had a habit of picking up greetings cards in the store when they tickled her fancy. 'Always good to have something on hand.' But the "somethings she had on hand" had burgeoned into a supply that could easily last for the next ten or twenty years.

Sorting the cards had been the easy part. Next came the invoices, many of them for home repairs that had been pressed upon her by telemarketers preying upon widows. Especially older widows. Invoices for work never done, for work half-done; IOU's from Jimmy, from Tina for a loan to buy a car, from friends of Jimmy's down on their luck. People with a first name and no address. I knew my mother was generous with her money, I knew she'd become the soft touch for every sad story in the neighbourhood, but I couldn't fix that either. Not then, not now. Couldn't even talk with her about it. And then, there in the midst of that sorry pile, was the letter that Harold had written to Claire shortly after he and I divorced.

Harold had told me how over dinner my mother and Jimmy had assailed him with the endless saga of my heartlessness. He'd been so blind-sided in the moment he'd fallen speechless, but when he got home he'd written Claire to say she should be ashamed of herself as a mother. On principle Harold never visited her again, though he was sorry it had to be that way. Aside from her bad-mouthing me, he'd always liked her. 'A real character,' he said.

At the time I'd tried to talk to my mother about the dinner and

Harold's response. She said she had no idea what might have so upset poor old Harold. She denied having received a letter. Jimmy backed her up. 'Harold's weird,' he said, as if that were somehow definitive. I never doubted that Harold had sent the letter; I had the photocopy he'd given me tucked inside my journal.

On New Year's Eve, while sorting Mom's papers, the original came to the surface and slipped easily through my fingers, following the IOU's and the invoices into the wastebasket, both Mom and I pretending that we hadn't noticed what it was. By then, what did it matter?

Dean Martin sang *That's Amore* and I listened. Claire is my mother. Now the only truth that matters.

They moved Mom to Palliative Care tonight. Coincidence? The hand of Magnus? She'd been on the waiting list since last week, but suddenly at eight o'clock on a Sunday night a room comes available. It's a beautiful room. By chance—by coincidence?—a private room. It's an odd feeling though, moving into a space in which someone has so recently died. One life exited; another so tenuously present.

I love this new room. Stepping into Palliative Care you feel calm: the light salmon-coloured walls, the oak woodwork, the staff, so gentle in their welcomes.

My mother's room faces the mountains; I look outside into the dark night and see the shining lights of the ski runs. I think of my mother hiking up and down that mountain with her skiing buddies, think of them making their way home, holding their tin can lanterns before them in the night.

I'm a little girl again, my mother is holding the book open: Christopher Robin is coming down the stairs, holding onto the railing with one hand, clasping Pooh's paw in the other.

'Here we are,' says my mother. 'Are we ready?'

- 23 -
HEATHER

*A**shes to ashes, dust to dust, don't kiss a boy ...*
Oh Claire, are you haunting me already? Have you really left us?

No, the telephone hasn't rung. Nora would telephone as soon as she knew.

How can Telford sleep? Of course he should be sleeping now; he's the one who has to drive us to the hospital in the morning. And it's still snowing. I'd have stayed the night with Claire and Nora in the hospital if it weren't for Telford. He said it didn't make sense. My medications, for example. And what good would it do anyway?

Why do things have to make sense? My sister is dying. I see her walking home, pregnant with Nora. How does that make sense? Where did the years go? How can her baby girl be so much older than we were then? I miss who we were. I miss the days when everything was still possible.

Claire, you can't go, not yet. There's something I have to give you. I'm such a dithering fool, I just didn't know if I should bring the doll yesterday. I wanted to talk to Nora and then I forgot and then Annie came by on her way home from work tonight and when she heard the story she got so excited about being able to do something for you. She loves you, you know, even though she can't get into the hospital to see you. An hour from her house to our house, and then the extra hour to where you are, it's just impossible with work and her girls. Annie saw the doll and said, 'Please, let me fix her up for Auntie Claire.' She knows how to clean the hair and she wants to sew a new scarlet sash to replace the blue one I made for Cai when he was a baby.

Oh Claire, I know you wouldn't have minded the blue ribbon or even the matted hair, but I could see how much it meant to Annie to have some way to show you she cares. She's promised to bring the doll back tomorrow night so I can take it to you on Tuesday. I just couldn't bring myself to tell her I didn't expect you to still be with us by then. It's one thing for Nora and I to be so sure you're leaving tonight, but if I start talking about it with everyone ...

I feel so alone here in the kitchen, not knowing if you're already gone. Oh Claire, I wish I could be like you and Nora, both of you in your own ways finding comfort in the deep of night. Nora on her stool by the window, watching strangers pass on the street below. You, alone in your backyard at night, happiest of all when the wind is howling and thrashing through the trees, while I'd be at home laying out matches and candles in case the power went off. How many times have I phoned you after a gale to tell you how frightened I was? And you'd be over the moon. 'What a grand storm that was!' Who but you would rush out into the night like that; what could you possibly see out there with your white cane and your tunnel vision?

I've never felt such ecstasy, not even when I was young. I sit here in my kitchen and it seems so immense and dark and lonely out there. I'm still the little girl who sat in front of the radio at night listening to Walter Winchel: *Good evening, Mr. and Mrs. America from border to border and coast to coast and all the ships at sea.* I'd imagine all those men on all those ships and the sea so big and black. I'd see their boats being bombed from the air or blown up by submarines. They'd die out there alone in the dark with no one to comfort them and no one to bring them home.

Claire, where are you now? Is Nora still holding your hand? Or has Dad come to take you home? You and Dad and Mom and Bobby all together now. And Taffy. I can see Dad in his white shirt, that smile on his face, and in his arms he's cradling my little puppy.

Oh Claire, I miss our family.

- 24 -
NORA

Last night at nine o'clock the nurse told me: 'Go home. Get some rest. It could be tomorrow, or it could be next week.'

I knew by then that she was right, that the 14th of January was Magnus's time, not my mother's. I did as I was told but at midnight I phoned the hospital just in case. No change. I'd known they'd say that, but I had to phone anyway. I hung up and called my aunt.

'Thank heaven,' she said. 'Telford has promised we'll be there by ten in the morning, even if it means we have to hire a dog sled.'

Poor Aunt Heather, the day we were convinced would be Claire's last day on Earth was the one day she couldn't make it to the hospital; it had snowed Sunday afternoon and then all Sunday night, on Monday morning the roads were impossible. I could feel my aunt's helpless anxiety; when her own mother was in hospital Aunt Heather had missed visiting her on only one day, the day Agnes died. By late Monday afternoon it had stopped snowing but the roads remained treacherous. Aunt Heather had called the hospital every two hours. By early evening I'd told her, with something like confidence: 'I don't think today is the day.'

'But if you could just phone me at midnight,' she'd said.

For myself it wasn't really a day of anxiety; it wasn't even horrible, it just *was*. I'd expected my mother to die. She hadn't. Most of the day her breathing was much like the day before, the long exhales, the sharp gulping inhales. When her legs were restless, as they frequently were, I'd lay my hands gently upon them and she'd settle a little; she was calmest when the sounds of a violin drifted in waves from the music room next door. She didn't open her eyes but as the long notes rose and fell, her breathing eased and continued easier for some time after the music therapist had packed up her violin and left the ward.

I felt suspended in a sort of timeless space between "the

day before" and "the day after;" I had been so sure *this* was the day. The room seemed imbued with an almost fairy-tale quality: snow falling outside the window, violin music floating through the doorway. And because this was Palliative Care, the ward was already so much calmer than on regular floors, calmer still with so many visitors kept away due to the snow and ice. Those who had braved the weather walked in with the sting of winter on their cheeks, eyes glistening. Of those who had come to see Claire, not a one of them knew the significance of the date, yet they seemed to be playing their roles, offering their parting gifts.

There was the woman who introduced herself to me as the daughter of a Mrs. Parry, a regular at the Seniors Day Care Centre. Her mother had insisted that she visit Mrs. McHenry in the hospital and be sure to tell her that no one could ever replace her. 'They say no one could whip up a sing-along like your mother,' the woman reported. Sharon, a full-time staff member at the Centre, had accompanied Mrs. Parry's daughter. 'You have no idea how we came to rely on your mother,' she told me. 'She simply lit up the room. Everything she's been through, but her words that I'll never forget have nothing to do with troubles. She'd beam at you with that big smile and say, *Life is grand.* I tell you, you don't meet a woman like that every day.'

That's what people wanted to talk about, Claire McHenry's zest for life. Like modern-day magi they trekked through the snow to bear witness to the miracle of my mother. 'Always a smile on her face.' 'Never let life get her down.' 'Always had time for a friend.' 'The lady with the white cane, humming as she walks.' Bearing witness that my mother had been so much more than her struggles, so much more than her drinking, so much more than her pain.

This morning on my drive to the hospital the snow lay crisp and glistening white, the sky a deep bright blue, the light catching at the sharp clear edges of the morning as though the world were new again. I couldn't help but feel a trembling glimmer of hope, however irrational. Miracles do happen.

But seldom, it seems, in the way we pray for.

I felt the change the instant I entered my mother's room: her breathing, which had been so laboured over the last few days, was even worse. Long gurgling exhales followed by short gasps for air.

Her legs weren't twitching, they were thrashing against the bed covers. I laid my hands gently on her thighs, hoping to calm her. She let out a heart-wrenching moan and I jerked my hands away. It seemed impossible her body could manage even one more breath; it seemed anything I might try would only make things worse. I lowered myself into the chair next to the bed feeling helpless. When Dr. Sugar entered the room a few minutes later he found me sitting silently at my mother's bedside, hands clenched uselessly in my lap.

'Good morning, Claire,' he said gently.

Her eyes opened at the sound of his voice, opened wide, without seeing. Or possibly, seeing a reality invisible still to the rest of us. Dr. Sugar adjusted the angle of the bed a little, passed his thumb along my mother's forehead. Her eyes seemed stuck open.

I told Dr. Sugar I didn't know what to do, that I was afraid of hurting her.

'Just hold her hand. Talk to her.'

I leaned closer and reached for her hand. Our hands so similar, so different. 'Such lovely cold hands,' she'd murmured just a few days ago when I'd placed them on her fevered brow. 'Such lovely warm hands,' I used to say when I'd come in from playing in the cold, snuggling one of mine between hers while she pretended to resist. Such a very long time ago.

Now her eyes remained open as I gently stroked her hand, feeling the warmth of it, though there was no little squeeze in response, no indication she knew who I was. Dr. Sugar's tiny adjustments seemed to have calmed her and we sat there, my mother and I, while the universe dissolved and enveloped us. I can't remember how long it was since I'd arrived at the hospital, what time it was when Aunt Heather and Uncle Telford entered the room. I suppose it must have been around ten, the time Aunt Heather had promised, but I couldn't say for sure. Time had been suspended, something that existed only beyond the hospital doorway.

I felt my aunt's presence before I saw her; she was cradling a bundle wrapped in a pale yellow shawl. At Claire's bedside Uncle Telford let go of his wife's arm and she pulled back a corner of the shawl. In a voice so faint and tremulous I could barely hear it, she said: 'Annie fixed her hair.'

Tears slid down my aunt's cheeks. 'I'm so sorry, Claire,' she whispered. 'I didn't know.'

She laid the bundle on the bed and with trembling hands uncovered the doll—the blond ringlets, the scarlet sash. A fleeting image of a long ago Christmas dinner, my grandmother's sharp voice: *But Claire, the doll was never yours. You were too old ...*

Tenderly, as though she were handling a newborn baby, Aunt Heather propped the doll into a sitting position next to my mother's pillow. The doll's eyes snapped open; they were not clear and green the way that Mom had described them; they were pale and cloudy. My mother's eyes had remained wide open ever since Dr. Sugar had spoken to her. Wide open as if transfixed in place. The doll and my mother, staring into infinity.

Aunt Heather leaned down and kissed her sister's cheek, kissed the doll's forehead. She faltered as she tried to straighten and Uncle Telford was instantly at her side. I let go of my mother's hand for the first time since Dr. Sugar's visit. I moved a chair to the side of the bed where Uncle Telford was steadying my aunt; she allowed herself to be eased into the chair, but her eyes never strayed from her sister's. 'Thank you, my darling Claire,' she whispered. 'Thank you for waiting one more day.' Uncle Telford had found her a tissue and she dabbed at her eyes. 'Annie fixed her hair. You know how she loves you. She wanted to do something for you.'

Uncle Telford reached to take a hand of Claire's in his. 'We all love you Claire.' He spoke deliberately, with feeling, the way one does at these moments. My mother gave no sign, and after a time Uncle Telford released her hand and laid it gently back by her side. He stood in silence a moment longer, then acknowledged us with a solemn nod and excused himself so that my aunt and I could be alone with my mother.

We sat, one on either side of the bed, each of us holding one of my mother's hands. We didn't talk to each other. We didn't need to. From time to time Aunt Heather would reach out with her free hand, absently stroking the doll's faded ringlets; then she'd lean close to my mother's ear and whisper, 'I didn't know you cared.'

In the afternoon one of Mom's neighbours came to visit and Aunt Heather went down to the cafeteria to sit with Uncle Telford. I told myself I should get up, walk around, that I couldn't hold onto my mother's hand forever.

I couldn't will myself to move.

'Your mother's a strong woman,' the neighbour said before leaving. 'I'm going to miss her terribly.'

A strong woman. Yes, that was Claire. And I'd thought I had to look after her.

Last night *That's Amore* had brought everything into focus: Claire is my mother, that's the only truth that matters. She never needed me to be Christopher Robin. She needed me to be her daughter. Sometimes daughters have to learn to become daughters.

'Mom,' I said. 'I need your advice.'

Had I ever said those words before?

'Fred wants to get married.'

I felt myself blush, embarrassed though now there was no one else in the room, just the two of us. Three if you counted the doll. How could I not? My mother and the doll, their eyes open. Seeing what?

I'd been ashamed of my mother's drinking; in speaking now of a possible marriage I knew my mother must at times have been ashamed of me too. The daughter who'd gone forth into the world with such promise and so many expectations had become the woman with no children, the woman with four ex-husbands, the woman who didn't even have a career to offer up as justification.

When people ask about my past I'm usually vague; I'll admit to an early marriage—something most people can relate to; I'll mention another marriage that kept me living in Atlanta for so long. No, I don't have any children. Things just didn't work out.

I'm circumspect because I know that however I might say it, or whatever the person I'm meeting might actually *say* in response, at some level when they hear about four husbands they'll presume they know something significant—and not very respectable—about who I am. From then on I'll be the woman with too many divorces, the woman who obviously never tried. If I'm speaking to a parent, they'll understand me as selfish, or someone to be pitied, for not having had children of my own.

When people do piece together bits of my past, I hate the assumptions they must be making about alimony and cheating and bitterness even though there was never any of that. Still, how do I explain why nothing seems to last? Dave and I married too young; Ian and I were too similar; Dallas failed to honour his promise to have a baby: generalities that reveal nothing about me and probably just add to the speculation. After I divorced Harold I seldom spoke of our having been married; we're still friends and I'm happy if people mistakenly assume that's all there is to the story.

Why I kept marrying in the first place is even harder to explain; a common-law arrangement would surely have seemed more respectable than a third wedding. And yet I married four times. Divorced four times. It's true that all these years I've resented my mother for not taking more interest in my life, for not trying to understand why I married, for not trying harder to reach me, but how much really would I have said? I'd felt cheated that my mother hadn't trusted me, hadn't told me more about her life, about Earl, my father; about how it really felt when her own father died and she couldn't save him; what it felt like to be gang-raped; what it felt like when Buddy killed himself.

I *am* my mother's daughter: we both have things we try not to talk about.

Fred wants to talk about marriage.

I've had one foot out the door from the moment Fred and I started living together. One weekend when he was in Nanaimo

I found myself an apartment; I was going to tell him when he phoned on the Saturday night, but when he called he'd been eager to talk about his day before I could tell him about mine.

He'd been busy.

His house in Nanaimo didn't have a window in the master bedroom; it did have French doors that opened onto the patio, letting in the light, but the doors weren't screened and Fred said it wasn't practical to leave them open at night. I told him that ever since I'd been living in high-rises I'd gotten attached to sleeping with the windows opened. 'We don't need one,' Fred said. He'd tried to convince me that the continuous heat recovery ventilation system he was so proud of provided more fresh air than an open window. He hadn't shown the slightest understanding of how important the window was to me, and yet, without saying anything beforehand, on this particular weekend he'd gone home to Nanaimo to install a window. He'd gone to the hardware store, cut a hole in the outside wall, installed the window unit, replaced the outdoor siding and applied the first coat of paint to the interior trim.

How could I tell Fred about the apartment I'd found? I stopped actively looking for my own place. But marriage?

And so, belated as it was, I asked my mother's advice.

'How would it look?' I said, 'On Fred's behalf as much as mine. I mean, a woman with four husbands is bad enough, but five?'

My mother's eyes were still open, seemingly focused on nothing; her breath gurgled in and out. And yet, in that moment, I could clearly hear her voice.

Oh for Pete's sake, marry him if you want to. Fred's a big boy; he doesn't need you to protect him. And as for the number five, in the end it is only a number.

I looked at my mother and her doll, the eyes of both staring back at me.

'You're right,' I whispered. 'And he's the only one who's ever given me a window.'

A window of opportunity, perhaps.

In the other-worldly privacy of her room in Palliative Care, where my mother's body struggled for breath, our spirits were connected.

'What if I *do* leave again?'

If you do, you do. Life goes on.

Until it doesn't, I couldn't help thinking.

And I smiled, because I knew how my mother would respond. *Oh, for Pete's sake.*

In the hallway voices were approaching, Aunt Heather returning with Doreen. I moved a tiny bit closer, until my lips caressed my mother's ear and I breathed into her the words that had so often been too hard to say: 'I love you, Mom.'

I was sitting silently in my chair, still holding my mother's hand, when Doreen and Aunt Heather arrived. I wasn't about to let go.

'Can you believe it? Jimmy brought me a box of soap for my dishwasher! Claire told him to!' Doreen with her unfailing cheerfulness might have been walking into my mother's kitchen for a hot rum on a cold winter's day instead of the room where her best friend lay dying. She beamed at my mother: 'Oh Claire, you're just a marvel. You think of everything!'

Doreen wore a bright red winter coat, the cuffs and hood trimmed in white fur. Our own Mrs. Claus, elegant and comforting at the same time. Comforting like it had been when I was a little girl and I'd traipse over to Doreen's house in the morning after Mom had left for work so that Doreen could comb and braid my hair for school.

'My heavens!' Doreen blurted out, noticing the doll. 'Look at those eyes!'

Aunt Heather explained how the doll had been packed away in storage for many years, how the doll had been Claire's when she was a little girl. 'It's a Shirley Temple doll,' she added.

'Well of course she is! Oh, she's just so adorable! I had the very same doll when I was a girl!' Doreen hugged my aunt and told her that Claire was so incredibly lucky to have her for a sister. 'And isn't it wonderful,' she said. 'The three of you all together here, just like when Nora was born.'

'It was a Christmas present for Claire,' Aunt Heather said, primping the doll's dress just a little. Then she kissed my mother carefully on the cheek and said she had to leave; the roads were ugly and Telford needed to be on the highway before the rush hour.

Doreen couldn't stay either; she was off to visit her husband in the nursing home. I told them I'd be going soon as well, but when they left I didn't move. I just wanted to be alone with my mother.

I closed my eyes and took a deep long breath. My mother's breath rattled and gurgled, signaling the end would not be long, but I was no longer frightened as I had been in the morning.

When I opened my eyes again I was drawn to the snow-covered mountain visible through the room's north-facing window. *A window of opportunity.* Had those words been spoken or imagined? Last night all I'd been able to see were the lights marking the ski run; today the North Shore Mountains stood stark, white, majestic against the clear blue sky. Soon the blue would be overtaken by the early dark of winter, but not quite yet. I breathed deeply and smiled. *Life is grand.*

I looked back to the bed, to my mother and her doll.

Talk to her.

Juanita lived up the street from me when I was in grade three. I thought Juanita was perfect in every way; she was a year older than me and the only Catholic I knew, she wore a uniform and attended Catholic school, she went to something called Mass and something else called Confession. I couldn't imagine Juanita having anything to confess, but she said Confession wasn't just for things you did, thoughts were every bit as bad, or even things you didn't do, but knew you should have done. She told me the priest sat behind a screen and never judged you. Confession wasn't about getting punished for the past, it was about having a fresh start.

In the stillness of the Palliative Care room I knew there was something I still needed to say. Something that went deeper than the shame of multiple marriages, deeper than the shame of my mother's drinking. When Agnes discounted what the Shirley Temple doll meant to my mother, I'd accused Agnes of being cruel.

I could be cruel.

The night before my second wedding Ian and I were already living together in a little house we rented from his parents next door to the big house they'd moved into years before as their family expanded. The wedding would take place in the back garden, nothing fancy, a casual late spring event with family and friends, most of them from the university where Ian and I were studying. For seating there were picnic blankets; flowers would be set out in jars and buckets. My mother had offered to pay half the cost of the flowers and had come over after dinner so that she and I could go together to the flower market. Back at the house I knew I should be inviting her to come in for a drink, or at least a coffee, but Ian and I had still not written our vows and we were eager for her to be gone.

A short time after Mom left there was a knock at the door; she'd backed her car into the ditch running alongside the driveway.

Clearly I hadn't even waited to wave good-bye.

Ian and I came out to find the car halfway on its side. Ian's father and brother came over to help, but we couldn't get the car out of the ditch. The father and brother went home; a tow-truck company was telephoned. They said they wouldn't be long. The house was on a dead-end road with just the two houses and it could be a little difficult to spot; Ian said it would be best if my mother waited on the corner.

'Fine,' she said, and we went back to writing our vows. It was getting late. I don't know how late, but Mom hadn't come to our house until after dinner and I remember when next she knocked on the door it was already dusk. It turned out she'd been standing at the corner for almost an hour. She looked frightened.

I don't remember what happened later that night. Perhaps we

called and the tow-truck came right away, maybe we even stood outside with my mother. Some things I can't remember.

I do remember the day of the wedding. Mom, Jimmy and his girlfriend were there; it was the first time any of them had been around my current friends. I know I did not introduce Jimmy or Leanne. I acknowledged my mother only if someone specifically asked to be introduced. It was an afternoon backyard picnic; I don't recall any alcohol. I can't use the excuse that I was embarrassed by my family's drinking.

Harold, who in some ways knew me better than my other ex-husbands, once told me: 'You're a good person, but you're not as nice as you think you are.' He hadn't been speaking with malice; he'd simply been making an observation.

The day after the wedding where I'd mostly avoided my mother, I was already reflecting on what I'd done. In my journal I wrote: *Sad, always, about Mom. Though she says, always, that she's fine. She's so much finer than she knows. Than I know. And already in retrospect feeling bad that I didn't introduce her to more of my friends.*

It's not like I wasn't thinking about my mother. Two days later, on my honeymoon, I'd write that other journal entry, the one where I predict disaster for my mother and my brother. The one where I talk about the need for courage. In seven weeks my mother would be in the hospital in a coma; and just a few weeks after that I'd see her struggling to arrange a table of get-well cards and I'd vow never to abandon her again. I was always counting on second chances.

Harold, on another occasion, had acknowledged that side too, saying: 'What I love about you is that you're always so hopeful.'

Of course had he been in a less gracious mood that day he might also have said that when things didn't turn out as I'd counted on I would lose hope and leave by the first exit. In a way Jimmy was right when he accused me of abandoning Mom by moving to Atlanta. Sure I had to follow my husband, but after a year of Mom resisting my attempts to fix her life, it felt good to be so far away.

I didn't invite my mother to my third wedding. 'What would we do with her while we're on our honeymoon?' Dallas asked when we realized she planned to fly to Atlanta. I lied and told my mother that the wedding would be small, that we'd immediately be leaving for our honeymoon, that a visit later would be so much better value for her trouble. In fact it was the largest of all my weddings, a community event at which she might easily have been the life of the party.

I still blush remembering how I excluded my mother from important parts of my life, like the fourth wedding, which really was small, just me, Harold and a Justice of the Peace we'd never met and never saw again, but of course Mom would have liked to have been there.

It's true that Jimmy and his friends took advantage of Mom's neediness and abused her generosity, but it's also true they never excluded her. His friends all called her *Mom*, sought her advice, invited her to their weddings.

'I'm so sorry.'

I've spoken the words aloud.

I look once again toward the mountain, imagining my mother as a young girl descending the slope, holding a candle up high to light her way. I'd have been afraid, but coming home in the dark was the part Mom loved the best.

Something glitters at the edge of my vision. The room faces west as well as north; I turn my head. At my mother's side the tattered doll is bathed in sunlight, the red sash shimmering.

You Are My Sunshine: the other day I'd lamented how long it had taken me to understand that the song was a story of loss. Now suddenly it's clear to me that I hadn't heard the song *as written* because I'd been listening to the song my mother *wanted* me to hear: a joyful tune transcending lives that had fallen short of the dreamers.

Here in this room my mother will soon take her last breath and I will be left behind. A red sash shimmers in the fading light. The doll of my mother's dreams, lost to her for so many years, beside her at the end.

I thanked my mother for listening to me, for hearing what I'd needed to say. It didn't matter that most of the words hadn't been spoken aloud.

Once upon a time my mother and I sat together on our bed while I told her how Sophie had washed my mouth out with soap. My mother had rescued me from that shame. Now she lay on a hospital bed and I sat by her side. Alone with my mother in the descending twilight I felt the beginnings of release from another shame, the secret shame of my own cruelty.

'I love you.' I said. 'I've always loved you.'

And in speaking the words aloud I realized that I *had* said them over the years. In the muddle of our complicated lives, stronger than resentment, stronger than disappointments and miscommunication, stronger than alcohol could dissolve, when all of that was swept away, what remained was love. The love of a daughter for her mom.

- 25 -
HEATHER

What would Dad say about all these cars hurtling down the freeway at speeds he couldn't have imagined? Where is everyone going? Why such a rush to get there? After he put the Model T up on blocks he never drove again, and he never missed it either. What would he say about us speeding away from the hospital where Claire is dying? Oh Dad, the world isn't what you remember. Telford is old, older than you ever were; we wanted to stay longer, but it's so hard for him driving in the dark.

I felt Dad in the room with Claire today. I've said good-bye for the last time. My darling sister, I know it won't be long now. And it's right that Nora's with you; she said she'd be leaving soon, but

I know she's not going anywhere. Will Jimmy be there too? Nora said he didn't get to the hospital yesterday. Surely he will today. Should I phone him when I get home? Claire would want them both there.

What will become of Jimmy without his mother? He's nearly fifty. Almost as old as Dad was when he died, but he seems so young, too. Maybe he'll be fine. We survive. Oh Lord, we survive.

When Bobby died I was sure it would kill Mom, but it didn't. At Bobby's funeral Claire and I had to help Mom walk down the aisle of the church. At the end of the service when it was time to view the body she grasped the edge of the casket to steady herself, and just crumpled to the floor. I don't know if I was more afraid she'd pull the casket over on top of herself or try to climb inside. Thank Heaven for Telford. He was so gentle, raising her from the floor, allowing her to wail her grief as he supported her into the office. After that I remember nothing. Nothing about what happened at the graveside. Nothing about the reception. And it never occurred to me that Dad might arrive to lead Bobby to Heaven.

Poor Bobby, did we even know who he was? Dying in a hotel room in Seattle with a man none of us ever met. We didn't even know how to talk about what happened.

Just now I said to Telford that I worried about Bobby's soul. 'What if he's still out there all alone?'

'And what would Claire say about that?' my wise husband replied.

'Worrying's a waste of time!'

We'd answered in unison, because that's exactly what Claire would say. It made both of us laugh; but it didn't stop me from bursting into tears.

- 26 -
NORA

There was no need to keep talking. I turned on the radio; it was already tuned to the oldies station. I set the volume low, filling the room with soft background memories of home.

When would Jimmy get here? The only day he'd missed was yesterday, maybe because of the snow; every other day he'd shown up at some point, even if only for a few minutes.

A nurse entered the room and introduced herself as Ruth. It was 3:30 and she was just beginning her shift. I told her it seemed to be getting harder for Mom to breathe; it sounded painful. Ruth said, 'As soon as I've checked the other patients I'll see if we can't make your mother a bit more comfortable.'

She left and I sat there holding Mom's hand. Her eyes were open. She struggled to breathe. It was forever. It was no time at all.

And then something changed. All day I'd held my mother's hand while she struggled open-mouthed for air; now her lips came together, her breathing softened. Grew quieter, almost normal. I could feel her hand turning colder in mine.

I glanced at my watch: 4:35 pm.

Outside the window the sky had turned dark deep blue.

All around me felt different, the room eerily peaceful, the music on the radio, ethereal, as though it were an angel singing. The song was about the damage we all do, about our sorrow that we can't undo it. It was about healing and mercy too.

My mother's eyes remained open. Was she hearing this? Had she heard anything I'd said all day?

The song seemed to bathe the room in beauty. Oh Mom, how much damage we'd done without meaning to, out of clumsy love and good intentions. I felt myself trembling for the losses, the sorrows, the regrets. Felt myself trembling as the music flowed through me, lifting me from my sorrow, dissolving the old shame, at last, in an immense wave of gratitude. For Claire, my mother.

The song ended. In the brief space before the next song began, my mother gave one last sigh. And she was gone.

The nurse named Ruth came back into the room and stood beside me. There were tears on her cheeks too; she reached for a box of tissues and passed one to me.

'Would you like me to close your mother's eyes?'

'Do you have to?'

'No, not yet. Not if you don't want me to.'

She told me I could sit with my mother for as long as I needed.

It felt like I needed to sit there forever. To sit there all night, at the very least. Just me and my mom.

Ruth left and I reached over to turn off the radio. I hadn't stopped stroking my mother's hand. Her cold hand.

'Thank you for being my mother,' I said.

I was looking directly into her eyes, wanting to believe we weren't alone, wanting to believe that my mother's spirit, lingering close by, could see what I still could not, wanting to believe that Magnus had come to guide his daughter on her journey home.

I turned to look over my shoulder, half expecting to see the ghost of my grandfather. Magical thinking? I wasn't so sure anymore. When I turned back toward the bed I saw the doll, still propped in a sitting position near the pillow, staring back at me.

'You were right,' I whispered to my mother. 'She always wanted you to take her home.'

I lifted the doll, straightened its body and laid her gently beside my mother. Moved by the force of gravity, the doll's eyes rolled back into its head and closed.

I stood and looked around me, aware of the unaccustomed emptiness of the room, knowing Mom would have wanted someone else to be there too.

This is how it should be, she had said the day Jimmy and I stood on either side of her hospital bed, each holding one of her hands. *My children.*

Outside the sky had turned black and cold.

I kissed my mother on the lips, and with the tips of my fingers gently pulled her eyelids down to cover her eyes. What else was there to do?

I stood and walked down the long hallway to the reception desk. I took a deep breath, picked up the phone, and called Jimmy.

Jimmy. My little brother.

EPILOGUE

My funeral was lovely. Everything happened so quickly at the hospital I never had a chance to talk about it with anyone beforehand. Well I needn't have worried; of course they'd know exactly what to do. *Amazing Grace* on the bagpipes! What a send-off! Jimmy arranged that. He said it pays to have friends down at the Legion.

But really, every part of the memorial was just grand. Telford coming out of retirement to lead the service, cracking jokes just like we were all gathered together for one of our Christmas dinners. Well, a funeral does that, doesn't it? And it was so good to see Jimmy's girls. Come all the way up from Mexico. A pity Jake wasn't ready to see his dad yet, but I'll hold onto the word *yet*. Hope that one day he comes round to understanding that Jimmy did the best he could.

And Nora! Getting all those people to stand and sing *That's Amore*. Dean Martin was on the CD player to help, but it still took guts for my little girl to get up there with a microphone and lead everyone in song. I hope she could feel me beside her; I hope she knew I was there helping her along. And then Nora asking everyone to cup their hands and shield their eyes so that they could see only what was directly in front of them. She said they should turn to their neighbours on either side and the little bit they could see was all that I could see after my aneurysm. Well, bless her soul, she wanted them to be amazed at how well I'd managed these last twenty-five years; my daughter doesn't realize that it was never as hard as she imagined. Even now I'm not sure she gets it. Life happens. You do what you have to. It's not that big a deal.

It was *definitely* a big deal that Harold came to my funeral after the hard words we'd exchanged about Nora a few years back. If I could, I'd tell him now that he was right; I never should have said what I did about my own daughter. But I guess maybe he knows we all say things we'd take back if we could. After all, he came to my funeral, didn't he?

What I've always loved best about funerals is the stories people tell about all the crazy things that happened along the way. Doreen told about the time she came over one summer day and found me in my bikini, ironing clothes with one hand, a gin and tonic in the other, and singing along at the top of my voice to Bing Crosby's *Merry Christmas.* I told her you can never get too much of Christmas. That's so true. You can't. Even Dave said how much he missed my Christmases.

That was pretty fine too, Dave being there, and Fred so comfortable with Nora's ex-husbands. A funny business, what makes a family. Wouldn't that be something if Nora ended up marrying Fred and they lived on Vancouver Island. Agnes had no time for Bill Baxter, it's true, but Vancouver Island is where she was born, and it's where the revered young Robert Baxter was buried. Life is so full of surprises.

Like Wendy! Showing up like that. Telling everyone about the time I walked off the roof in Mexico. I'd forgotten all about that trip; honestly, I'd forgotten all about Wendy. Good Lord, I hadn't seen her since we worked together way back when, and we only travelled together that one time. She really wanted someone to go to Mexico with her and Buddy said sure, go ahead if I wanted to, as long as he didn't have to go too. Anyway, there we were at the hotel, I'd already changed into my nightie and had stepped out onto the rooftop patio with my gin and tonic. They don't always have railings around rooftops in Mexico and I wasn't paying attention. I just walked off the edge into the night, bounced off the awning below and slid to the ground. It took me a minute or two to get my bearings and then I had to make my way back to my room. Wendy arrived downstairs in time to find me sashaying across the lobby in my see-through nightie, as nonchalant as could be, waving my drink aloft so that the reception staff could see I hadn't spilled all of it on the way down. Well, what else would a lady do?

The whole service was like that, just a big celebration of my life. I was so tickled. And then there was the reception in the hall below the chapel with food baked by the ladies auxiliary and more stories than I can remember. Fred's sister came up to Nora placing a hand on Nora's arm. 'I'm *so* sorry I never met your mother,' she grinned. 'Hearing all these stories today, anyone could see she was a little bit of trouble.'

A little bit of trouble ... Well, well, well. Aren't we all?

Acknowledgements

Above all I want to thank my mother: Shirley Jean McNary (née Sinclair). In reading to me from *Winnie-the-Pooh,* she baptized me in the truth of stories. Silly Old Bear's trusting innocence, Piglet's anxieties, Eeyore's mournfulness, the gentle wisdom of Christopher Robin. I wouldn't have used such words back then, but my mother read with such feeling that I experienced those emotions, and I knew they were real.

It feels right that in telling my mother's story I would have turned, not to memoir, but to the emotional truths of fiction. Many of the details of *Before It Was Easy* are based on facts from my mother's life. I really do (or did) have a sister I've never met, my mother really did fall down the front stairs of her home, she really did suffer a brain injury. But if I'd limited myself to facts and details, I don't know how I could have reached the deep truths, the intertwining textures of pain and tenderness that make a life real.

For sharing her experience of life as younger sister to my mother, I want to thank my aunt, Marilyn Packham. Marilyn: we've shared so much, picking up the pieces in more ways than either of us ever would have anticipated.

I want to thank so many people. The gentle grandfather I never knew. The father who abandoned me. The men I loved and had to leave to find myself. *(Namaste.)* You are all a part of what let me finally write this story of damage done and tenderness found.

Thanks to Sandy Shreve and Deb McVittie for telling me that an early draft of this book wasn't ready. Thanks to Trudy Parsons, Michèle Mazzarotto, Greg Brown, Ellen Lyons and Barbara Davidson for reading later versions and "getting it." (Sorry Barbara, I just couldn't give up the name "Fred.")

A huge thank you to Crystal Stranaghan of Crystal Clear Solutions for taking me in hand and leading me through the maze of the digital world. Without your brilliance and inexhaustible patience this book would surely still be lingering in a Word document on my computer. Thank you too for the exquisite cover design: you got it just right.

Writing itself has given me so much. People sometimes speak of writing as a lonely enterprise, but when the writing is true, I'm with Rilke's angels who, it is said, 'often can't tell whether they move among the living or the dead.' In those moments absence disappears and I feel deeply connected: with everyone, with everything, with myself.

Other days can be dismal: the writing turns in on itself, the threads lead nowhere. Then self-doubt and the loneliness of despair move in—or might do if I wasn't blessed with a community of friends to laugh with. And so I thank my community, *The Laughing Ladies of Nanaimo*: Jan Carter, Deb Collingwood, Anna Edgar, Anne Grant, Gail Horley, Janet Jenkinson, Michèle Mazzarotto, Marlene McIntosh, Céline Nadeau, Martina Nash, Michele Ney, Trudy Parsons and Margaret Schmidt. Who ever knew that both tennis and bridge could be a source of such hilarity and love?

And love brings me back to family. To my new family, Greg, Derek, Stacey, Alex and Kaitlyn: thank you for accepting me into your lives. To my beautiful and ever curious granddaughters, Cadence and Makayla, thank you for keeping your Grandpa and me attuned to the regenerative miracle of life.

Tom Brown—my husband, my friend, my courageous editor—it took me a long time to appreciate your not always gentle, but always incisive, critiques of the many drafts of this book. We've traveled far together. Now I am enormously grateful that you gave me the courage to follow the truth to the end, wherever that might lead.

ABOUT THE AUTHOR

KATH CURRAN came of age in the sixties, when everything seemed possible and her goal was nothing less than achieving justice for the world. Now in *her* 60's, Kath still sees justice as a worthy objective, but puts more faith in the healing power of compassion. Born in Vancouver, BC, Kath lives on Vancouver Island with her *final* husband and is an occasional contributor to her website at *www.kathcurran.com*.

photo credit: Marilyn Packham

A Note From the Author

If this book spoke to you in a meaningful way or moved you somehow, I'd love for you to share it with a friend, review it on Goodreads or Amazon, or send me a message via the contact page on my website: www.kathcurran.com. There you'll also find a few questions to kick-start a discussion in your book club or stimulate your own reflections about life *Before It Was Easy*.

Made in the USA
Charleston, SC
30 August 2015